A few months Honolulu homicide detective Kimo Kanapa aka and begins a temporary assignment to the FBI's Joint Terrorism Task Force. Kimo and his HPD partner Ray Donne are quickly thrown into an investigation into threatening letters sent to a U.S. Senator. Are these screeds about racial purity related to an escalating series of attacks against mixed-race couples and families on Oahu?

When arson at a day care center on the Windward Coast brings Kimo's partner, fire investigator Mike Riccardi, into the case, Kimo worries about the future of his and Mike's newborn twins on an island falling prey to hate and a cult leader bent on death and destruction.

MLR Press Authors

Featuring a roll call of some of the best writers of gay erotica and mysteries today!

Derek Adams	Kyle Adams	Vicktor Alexander
Simone Anderson	Victor J. Banis	Laura Baumbach
Ally Blue	J.P. Bowie	Barry Brennessel
James Buchanan	TA Chase	Charlie Cochrane
Karenna Colcroft	Ethan Day	Diana DeRicci
Taylor V. Donovan	S.J. Frost	Kimberly Gardner
Kaje Harper	Stephani Hecht	Alex Ironrod
Jambrea Jo Jones	DC Juris	AC Katt
Kiernan Kelly	K-lee Klein	Geoffrey Knight
J.L. Langley	Vincent Lardo	Cameron Lawton
Anna Lee	Elizabeth Lister	William Maltese
Timothy McGivney	Kendall McKenna	AKM Miles
Robert Moore	Jet Mykles	Jackie Nacht
N.J. Nielsen	Cherie Noel	Gregory L. Norris
Erica Pike	Neil S. Plakcy	Rob Rosen
George Seaton	Riley Shane	Richard Stevenson
Christopher Stone	Liz Strange	Lex Valentine
Haley Walsh	Lynley Wayne	Missy Welsh
Ryal Woods	Stevie Woods	Sara York
Lance Zarimba	Mark Zubro	

Check out titles, both available and forthcoming, at
www.mlrpress.com

CHILDREN

OF NOAH

A Mahu Investigation

NEIL S. PLAKCY

mlrpress

www.mlrpress.com

Copyright 2015 by Neil S. Plakcy

Published by
MLR Press, LLC
3052 Gaines Waterport Rd.
Albion, NY 14411

Visit ManLoveRomance Press, LLC on the Internet:
www.mlrpress.com

Editing by Kris Jacen

Print format: ISBN# 978-1-60820-991-0
ebook format also available

Issued 2015

DEDICATION

Though my father, David Plakcy, was the son of immigrants, he spoke perfect English and drilled into me the need to speak and write clearly in order to succeed. Both he and my mother, Shirley Globus Plakcy, were avid readers and I grew up in a house full of books, reading everything from my father's H. Rider Haggard, Isaac Asimov and Walt Kelley to my mother's Erle Stanley Gardner and Harlequin romances – along with newspapers, cereal boxes, and those inserts that come with the electric bill. I am the writer I am today because of their influence.

Acknowledgments

This book bears the stamp of my terrific critique partners, who are all wonderful writers themselves: Miriam Auerbach, Christine Jackson, Chris Kling, Kris Montee, and most especially Sharon Potts, who was always willing to read drafts and provide advice above and beyond the call of duty.

This book grew out of the hours I spent at the FBI's Citizens Academy, and I thank the Bureau, and the Miami office, for the opportunity to attend.

The support of my writer-colleagues on the South Campus of Broward College, as well as the college's Staff and Program Development department, is greatly appreciated.

Thanks to all the Starbucks baristas for their welcoming greetings each morning and the caffeine-fueled drinks that keep me writing.

Most of all, I am grateful for the love and support of my partner, Marc Jacobskind, and our two golden retrievers, Brody and Griffin.

1 – With a Bang

My first day on assignment to the FBI's Joint Terrorism Task Force started with a bang on a sunny Wednesday morning in March. I had just turned onto Enterprise Avenue in Kapolei, a few blocks from my new office, when a pavement-striping machine slammed into the side of the minivan in front of me.

To my right was a strip mall under construction, of the kind that my father once built all over O'ahu. The machine, a bright red contraption with a paint brush attached to the side, had slid down the gently sloped driveway, leaving a broad yellow stripe in its wake.

The minivan came to an abrupt halt, and I hit my brakes and veered off onto the shoulder. A workman came running from the center's parking lot, yelling and waving his arms. As he rushed to the stopped minivan, I used the police radio mounted on the dashboard of my Jeep to report the accident.

Traffic moved slowly in both directions as people leaned out of their windows to gawk. The minivan's sliding passenger door had been smashed in, so the family inside had to climb out through the front door like clowns from a Volkswagen Bug.

The workman, a skinny Filipino in T-shirt, board shorts and rubber slippers, what mainlanders call flip-flops, apologized profusely to the people as they spilled out. I counted eight of them, from a wizened old Chinese woman the size of a hobbit to a bunch of keikis—little kids.

I waited for a break in traffic and then hurried across to the minivan. "I'm Detective Kanapa'aka, HPD," I said, holding up my police badge. "Is anyone hurt?"

The driver, a thirty-something gangly haole, or white guy, with sandy blond hair said, "Looks like the only one injured was the van." I told him to put his flashers on, then I led the family over to the sidewalk and out of danger from careless drivers.

"I so sorry! So sorry!" the Filipino man kept repeating.

While we waited for a police cruiser to arrive, the driver introduced himself, as well as his Chinese wife, his mother-in-law, and his sister-in-law, who was Thai. Some of the kids were his, some his nieces and nephews. His family reminded me of my own, a mix of cultures and skin tones. My parents had passed down haole, Japanese and Hawaiian strains to my brothers and me; my partner Mike was half-Italian and half Korean; and our foster son, Dakota, was one hundred percent Italian-American. Mike and I had donated sperm to a lesbian couple who were our close friends, and our keikis were a beautiful mix.

I wanted to get to work, but I didn't want to leave the accident scene until I was relieved. It gave me a couple of minutes to think about my new assignment to the Bureau, and what it might mean to me and those around me.

When I graduated from college, I wanted to be a professional surfer, and I gave it my best shot. When I finally realized I couldn't hack it, I shifted gears and went to the police academy. I began as a foot patrolman in Waikiki, worked my butt off, passed the sergeant's exam, and earned the coveted assignment of homicide detective.

I had worked for HPD my whole adult life, and though I'd still be on their payroll, I'd be taking marching orders from the Feds. Mike and my boss at HPD thought the assignment to the JTTF would help control my impulsiveness. My family had mixed emotions, from deriding government bureaucracy to wondering if I could still fix speeding tickets.

My own emotions were mixed as well, but my gut had told me that it was the right move. It was time to shake things up, put myself in an unfamiliar environment and meet new challenges. It was scary, but in a good way.

From where I stood, I could see the four-story office building that housed the Bureau, sheathed in glass and marble. Ray and I had come out to Kapolei occasionally when we had to liaise with agents, but I'd never been beyond the lobby, a conference room, and a couple of offices. It was strange to think that I'd be working there, instead of at police headquarters in downtown Honolulu.

A cruiser arrived, with a patrol officer I didn't know, and once I explained to her what I'd witnessed and gave her my contact information, I continued down Enterprise Avenue to my new job.

The building's lobby was impressive, with a somber display of FBI agents killed in the line of duty. The receptionist checked my name on a list then called a woman from HR, who met me in the lobby and escorted me back to her office. I signed a ream of paperwork, and she said, "Welcome to the FBI. Detective Donne arrived a few minutes ago so he should be in your new office. Room 313."

I took the elevator to the third floor and wandered past a warren of offices, searching for room 313. *Some detective you are. Can't even find your own office.* Eventually I did though, and Ray was sitting behind one desk, trying to log in on his new computer. "Howzit, brah," I said. I slung my backpack of personal items onto the other desk.

"We have new passwords for this system," he said. "But no one has bothered to tell us what they are."

Ray is a couple of inches shorter than my six-one, his hair is wavy brown and mine straight black, and he's stockier than I am. But he's my brother from another mother; we'd worked together since his arrival in the islands and we had developed that ability to read each other's thoughts and finish each other's sentences. He had a year-old son, and he thought we'd both be serving our keikis best in the relative safety of riding a desk instead of chasing down killers.

I looked around the plain, white-walled office, with two desks, a plush chair for each of us and a pair of metal chairs for visitors. Ray had put up a picture of his wife and their baby son and hung a big photograph of his hometown of Philadelphia on the wall. "Making yourself at home already," I said. It reminded me of my first day at the University of California in Santa Cruz, when my roommate had gotten there first, staked out the best bed, and spread his crap over half the room.

As Ray tried rebooting his computer, I turned on the desktop machine that had been provided for me. While I waited for it to boot up, I sorted through a box on the desk. Among other things, I found business cards with the address, phone number and fax number of the FBI office, a bulletproof vest and a windbreaker with FBI on the back.

The phone on Ray's desk rang. "How are we supposed to answer here?" he asked. Downtown, protocol called for title, last name, division – Detective Kanapa'aka, Homicide.

I shrugged, and he picked up the phone. "Detective Donne." He listened for a moment, then hung up. "Salinas wants to see us in his office ASAP."

Ray and I had liaised several times with Special Agent Francisco Salinas in the course of homicide investigations, and he had chosen Ray and me for his team when the previous pair of detectives rotated back to HPD. When his request first came through to us, via our boss, I was skeptical. Why would Salinas want us? We'd clashed with him every time we worked together. Eventually, in conversations with him and others, Ray and I realized that those clashes had led Salinas to respect our intelligence and our dedication. That was a pretty big ego boost.

I stood up. "Did Salinas say what it's about?" I asked. "Just a welcome to the Bureau?"

Ray shrugged. "You know him. He's a Fed. He never tells you more than you need to know. But he sounded pretty intense."

In our dealings with Salinas, he'd treated us as worker ants, who only needed to know our specific tasks. I wondered if things would change now that we were on his team.

"At least we know where his office is," I said. Though as we walked there, I realized we'd only come in previously through the guest entrance, and had limited access to the building. We passed a lot of men and women in serious dark suits and a bunch of more casually dressed staffers in cubicles as we threaded our way through halls and past meeting rooms.

I'd been willing to give up my khakis for dress slacks and my aloha shirts for button-downs—but I had drawn the line at wearing ties on assignment to the FBI. Ray was happy to follow my lead.

Francisco Salinas was on the phone, his back to the floor-to-ceiling window that faced out toward the Pacific, but he waved us in. He was a Cuban-American from Miami, with skin the color of light coffee and black hair cut military-short. He wore conservatively tailored dark suits, starched white shirts and ties with the FBI seal. Today his suit jacket rested over the back of his chair as he spoke into the phone. "I can assure you, Senator, that we'll take these threats very seriously. I'm going to put two of my best agents on it."

Ray and I sat in the plush armchairs across from Salinas's desk and I looked around. The walls were hung with citations and awards, interspersed with photographs of him with the director of the Bureau, the governor of Hawai'i, and other hotshots. A silver-framed photo of a very pretty dark-haired woman and two cute kids was the only personal touch.

That, and a bright purple stress ball Salinas was squeezing in his fist as he tried to end the conversation.

The process of vetting us for the JTTF had taken nearly a year. Even though Ray and I already had security clearance, agents had spoken to our family and friends about us. We'd been subjected to a battery of examinations like the Minnesota Multiphasic Personality Inventory Test, and had to take extensive physicals. We'd passed every one of them. I wondered how high Salinas had scored on stress.

When he hung up, he said, "That was Senator Haberman. You know him?"

"Not personally," I said. I quickly ran through what I knew of Ronald Haberman in my head. He had been elected the previous year to his first term in Washington. Prior to that he'd been a lawyer in Honolulu. Though I'd dealt with his firm a few times, I'd never run into him.

"I know his wife," Ray said, which surprised me.

"Really?" Salinas asked. "How?"

"When my wife was in the Island Studies program at UH, she got involved with a group that taught kids about the multicultural heritage of the islands. Susantee was one of the other volunteers, and I've run into her at a couple of events."

"I believe she's using the name Susan now," Salinas said. "At least that's what the campaign literature says."

Ray nodded. "She's half haole, half Indonesian," he said. "She was born there, but raised here. Beautiful woman."

"What's this about?" I asked Salinas.

"Yesterday evening, the Habermans' teenage daughter Jessica was walking home from a friend's house a few blocks away when someone in a rusty pickup truck threw a water balloon at her. In addition to the water inside, there was some white latex paint. She ended up spattered with paint, but she wasn't hurt."

"Did she see who was in the truck?" Ray asked.

"The truck slowed as it passed her and she said she got a good look at a teenage boy in the passenger seat. He's the one who threw the balloon. She thought a girl was driving the truck but she couldn't be sure. She didn't recognize either of them, and she wasn't able to get a license plate number."

"That's miserable," I said. "Poor girl."

"Then this morning, a threatening letter arrived at the Haberman home in Wailupe," Salinas continued. "Slipped under the security gate. The family received another letter about a week ago, but Mrs. Haberman threw it away in disgust. This second one is more threatening, and both the Senator and his wife are understandably upset."

"Threatening in what way?" I asked.

"From what he told me, it sounds like a pretty generic rant against mixed-race couples and families, with some warning of divine retribution thrown in. They're afraid that it's tied to the attack on their daughter."

"Anything sent to the Senator's office, either here in Hawai'i or in DC?" Ray asked.

Salinas shook his head. "The envelope had no postage, but it did list each family member's full name typed above the address. Their phone is unlisted, and they don't advertise their address anywhere, but you know as well as I do that not much is secret these days. It seems clear that whoever sent them this letter was saying 'we know who you are and where you live,' which is enough to get Mrs. Haberman upset."

He pushed a piece of paper toward us with an address and a phone number. "Here's their information. I want you to meet with Mrs. Haberman and see what you can find out. Take a print kit with you so you can get prints from her and anyone else who might have touched the envelope or the letter so we can rule them out."

"This kind of thing falls under the JTTF?" Ray asked. "Doesn't sound much like terrorism."

"If it's a hate crime, then we investigate," Salinas said. "I handle whatever the Special Agent in Charge passes on to me, and as the saying goes, the shit runs downhill. You're my newest staffers and you don't have anything on your plate yet, so the honor goes to you."

So much for being the "best agents" he'd mentioned to the Senator.

He handed us a pair of badge cases. I flipped mine open to see the distinctive FBI shield, surmounted by an eagle. The Lady Justice was in the center, between the letters U and S, holding her scales and a sword. I think that's when it became real to me, that I was no longer just an HPD detective; I was running with the big dogs.

"Welcome to the FBI gentlemen," Salinas said. We all stood, and he shook our hands. "You'll be on your own with this case, though as necessary you can bring in other members of the team to help. You work for the Bureau now, not HPD, and you should keep that in mind as you look for information and interview witnesses."

When Ray and I got back to our office, we found that someone had left post-it notes on each of our computers with temporary logins and passwords.

"This is creepy," I said, as I sat down. "You think someone is monitoring our conversations? They heard that we needed the passwords and provided them?"

"Let's not get too paranoid on our first day," Ray said. "Probably just a secretary who realized we didn't have them."

"Just because I'm paranoid doesn't mean I don't have reason to be," I said.

Ray and I did some quick online searching to familiarize ourselves with the Habermans. According to the Senator's official site, after receiving his JD he had clerked for a justice on the California Supreme Court for a year, then joined the prestigious firm of Fields and Yamato in Honolulu, where he had risen to partner.

He had a long history of civic involvement, serving on the boards of several non-profit organizations. He had worked his way up in the Democratic Party of Hawai'i, then spent two terms in the state legislature before winning his seat in Congress. He and his wife had two children, fourteen-year-old Jessica and twelve-year-old Michael. Jessica was a very pretty young woman, with rounded cheeks, dark flowing hair, and deeply tanned skin. I could see that other girls might be jealous of her looks. But why throw white paint on her?

Ray called Mrs. Haberman and made sure she would be home, and we took off in my Jeep with the flaps up. It was one of those gorgeous days in Hawai'i that reminds us that we live in a tropical paradise. The sun was bright, the trade winds cooling, brilliantly colored hibiscus and plumeria blossoming along the roads.

The Habermans' neighborhood was a small, oblong peninsula off the Kalaniana'ole Highway, between Diamond Head and Hawai'i Kai. It was a long hike there, almost thirty miles, but fortunately it was almost all highway on the H-1, and it only took us about forty-five minutes. The house was low-slung in a style I associated with Frank Lloyd Wright, with lots of square angles and terracotta designs. The property was only about a half-acre, its neighbors close by because of the value of waterfront property.

My rudimentary knowledge of property values told me it had to be worth four or five million bucks. Could these letters be a preliminary to some kind of extortion threat?

The house was surrounded by a green iron fence decorated with palm fronds, and we had to stop at a speaker box to announce ourselves. I noticed a small camera mounted on one of the fence posts and wondered if it recorded surveillance video, or just showed who was at the gate.

Ray hadn't exaggerated when he said Mrs. Haberman was a beautiful woman. She was about forty-five, perfectly dressed and made up, with a kind of China-doll beauty that made her seem like she belonged in a fashion magazine. She wore a pale pink sundress and matching sandals, and her dark hair was in an elaborate French braid.

"How nice to see you, Ray," she said. "Please come in." She had a very musical voice with just the hint of an accent. She had a slim leather folder under one arm.

Ray introduced me, and we followed her into the foyer. A wide corridor led directly to the backyard, affording a vista of water and greenery ahead of us. "Thank you both for coming," she said. "I've been very worried ever since this letter arrived."

We followed her past some museum-quality koa wood outrigger paddles mounted on the wall of the corridor. The hallway opened up to a comfortable wood-paneled living room with a cluster of couches and chairs and Indonesian batik tapestries on the walls. It had to be the most magnificent house I had ever been inside, and I'd been in a few real mansions. We passed a kitchen with a wooden ceiling and teak ceiling fans, and then stepped out on to the lanai. Several umbrellas stood sentinel over lounge chairs, and marble rimmed a lap pool, an oval pool, and a Jacuzzi.

But the real draw was the view. The Pacific stretched out ahead of us for miles. Off to one side we could see the looming shape of Diamond Head.

"We're very sorry about what happened to Jessica," Ray said, as we sat down at a round table. "But I'd like to go back to where this harassment started. You got a threatening letter?"

She nodded. "The first one came in a plain letter-sized

envelope," she said. "No name or address on the outside. Our housekeeper found it slipped under the gate and brought it into the house. Honestly, at first I thought it was going to be one of those real-estate solicitations. 'Other houses in your neighborhood are selling at record prices. Let us know if you want to sell.' We get that kind of thing quite often."

"Do you remember what it said?" I asked.

"A couple of phrases from the Bible," she said. "Something about Jews marrying non-Jews, I think. I showed it to Ron and asked if he recognized any of it. He said it was the Old Testament, but not a part of the Bible he was familiar with."

"Is your husband Jewish?" I asked.

She nodded. "He was raised that way, at least. I was brought up as Hindu, and we call our children Hin-Jews." She smiled, but then worry creased her brow again. "We've tried to provide them with an exposure to both religions as well as the cultural aspects of their heritage."

"Do you think this could have come from some kind of Jewish group?" I asked. "I know some of the ultra-Orthodox sects are very opposed to intermarriage. I believe there's at least one of those groups here in Hawai'i, because I've seen some of those men in their black coats and hats."

"We wondered about that," she said. "But Ronald says those groups are more interested in bringing lost souls back to their flock than in hurting those who disagree with them." She nervously rubbed her gold and diamond wedding band. "At the time, we both dismissed it as a crank letter, and I threw it away because I didn't want the children to see it. Now I wish I had held on to it."

"The water balloon yesterday had white paint in it," Ray said. "You think this attack on Jessica is connected to that first letter?"

"We didn't make the connection last night," she said. "Jessica says that no one at her school has ever harassed her, and she was completely surprised by the balloon."

"I don't suppose she was able to retrieve any shreds of the

balloon, was she?" I asked.

Mrs. Haberman shook her head. "She was very upset. She and I called several of her friends and their parents, and they were all as surprised as we were."

"But you didn't call the police?"

"There wasn't anything to report," she said. "I focused on making Jessica feel better. Her father asked her several times if she remembered anything, but she didn't."

She opened the leather folder and removed two plastic sheet protectors. "When we got another letter this morning, we got worried that the letters and this attack might be connected." She slid one of the protectors to Ray, and I moved to read it with him. "This is the letter that came in today. I think that some of the phrases here might be the same as in the first one, but I can't be sure."

A single sheet of paper was inside the plastic protector. From the justified margins, it looked like the words had been typed on a computer.

> The Prophet Ezra said, in Ezra 10:10-11, "Ye have transgressed, and have taken strange wives, to increase the trespass of Israel."

> The LORD declares, in Genesis 6:9: "These are the generations of Noah: Noah was a just man and perfect in his generations, and Noah walked with God." The phrase "perfect in his generations" means that all of Noah's ancestors were the same race, making him a "perfect" human being and worthy of being saved, and chosen to build the Ark and repeople the earth after the Flood.

> The righteous are white and delightsome. Our prophets tell us that people should marry those of the same racial, social, economic and educational background. To do otherwise is to defy the will of the LORD. You, your wife and your children are doomed to death and eternal damnation by your blasphemy. Beware, your fate approaches.

Below that, the letter writer had added,

Your children are mongrels, and your family are far from perfect and do not deserve to represent the people of Hawai'i.

She slid the second plastic sheet protector to us. The names on the envelope were:

Senator Ronald Jeremiah Haberman

Mrs. Susantee Verawati Haberman

Jessica Ruth Annisa Haberman

Michael Amos Abhay Haberman

"Agent Salinas believes that by including your full names and address here, the letter writer was letting you know that he knows who you are and where you live," I said. "I assume that information isn't easily available?"

"My husband has always been careful," she said. "He has known for a long time that he wanted to enter public service. But it's not like we have hidden our address. Our children's schools, for example, have records."

"Punahou?" I asked. Punahou was the elite private school I had been fortunate enough to attend, and most of the children of the island's movers and shakers went there.

She nodded. "And there are organizations that both my husband and I belong to. The parents of our children's friends. Our neighbors."

"What do you think is the most sensitive piece of information here?" I asked. "The one that is least likely to be part of the public record? That might give us some indication of where this information came from."

She thought for a moment. "When Jessica was born, we decided to give her an American first and middle name, but we wanted her to have some sense of my heritage as well. So we gave her, and then her brother Michael, Hindu names as well. Annisa was my mother's name, and Abhay my father's. We didn't put them on their birth certificates, but we've often used them informally."

"Are they written down anywhere?" I asked.

"I really don't know."

I looked back at the envelope and noticed something. "You don't have a middle name?" I asked her.

"I do. It's Jovita."

"But it's not on this envelope," I said. "So maybe whoever sent this doesn't know quite as much about your family as he'd like you to believe."

"Could you prepare a list for us?" Ray asked. "Of any groups that might have all the information here?"

"I can try," she said. "But as I said, I don't know who might know my children's Hindu names. I can't recall ever writing them down, though I might have mentioned them in conversation to someone close to us. But could someone we know well stoop to this?"

"You never really know what someone else is capable of," Ray said gently.

"The security camera out front," I said. "Does that take video?"

She shook her head. "It's just so that we can see who's at the gate. Ron has been talking about enhancing our security based on these letters, and so we may be adding video in the future."

"We'll take the letter and the envelope back to the FBI office and have them checked for fingerprints," I said. "Can you tell us who might have handled the letter and the envelope, so we can eliminate them?"

"I found the letter myself and brought it inside," Mrs. Haberman said. "And I've had it in my possession since then. My prints should be on file because of the security clearances I had to undergo."

"No other threats so far?" I asked. "No phone calls, hang ups?"

She shook her head.

"How about your kids? Has anyone said anything to them, either at school or anywhere else?"

"No. After the first letter arrived, Ron and I talked to both of them and asked if anyone had approached or threatened them, and they both said no."

"We should talk with Jessica anyway," I said. "When would be a good time?"

"I'll have to speak with my husband. She's already said she doesn't know anything, and I'm afraid it would make her more frightened to speak with the police."

"Is your husband working on any particular legislation?" Ray asked. "Anything about immigration, for example?"

She shook her head. "His focus is on economic issues, trade compacts with the Far East and so on. Nothing religious, nothing ethnic."

"We'll need to speak to him, too," I said. "Is he in Washington?"

"Yes. I'll call him for you now." She picked up a cell phone from the table beside her and pressed a couple of buttons. She looked away from us and spoke softly, then turned back and handed the phone to Ray. "This is the Senator."

Interesting, I thought. Not "this is my husband."

As Ray began to speak, I slid my iPad over to him so he could take notes, and then watched over his shoulder. *No threats in DC,* he wrote. *Doesn't want us to speak to daughter without him present; won't be back in HNL for 2 wks. Talk to law firm.*

"We'll follow up with Fields and Yamato this afternoon, Senator. You'll call first and smooth the way for us?"

Great, I thought. My ex-girlfriend, Peggy Kaneahe, was an attorney at Fields and Yamato and it was always awkward when we ran into each other.

Peggy and I sat beside each other whenever we were alphabetized as kids, and we had dated in high school, when I was confused about my attraction to other boys. She had been my prom date, but we'd broken up when we went to college. When she returned to the islands, after college, law school and a few years with a mainland firm, we had dated again briefly. That was my last-ditch effort to live a straight life, and I'd been dragged out of the closet then, which had made for icy relations with Peggy for a while.

"Sarah Byrne?" Ray asked into the phone. "Yes, sir, we know her. She's been helpful to us in the past."

We'd worked with Sarah, a paralegal at Fields and Yamato, on several cases. She was a sharp Aussie with a pink streak in her hair and an awesome singing voice. And even better, she was not Peggy Kaneahe.

Ray ended the call and handed the phone back to Mrs. Haberman. We thanked her and told her we'd call as soon as we learned anything, and reminded her that she had both our cell numbers. "Call either of us, any time," I said.

She led us back to the front door and we walked outside. "The senator wasn't very helpful, was he?" I asked Ray as we got back into the Jeep. "You think maybe he's hiding something?"

"He's a typical bureaucrat. But I got the sense that he was genuinely confused, and worried for his family. I'd be worried, too, if someone was threatening Julie and Vinnie."

Billowing cumulous clouds with gray bellies had massed over Diamond Head, so Ray and I rolled the flaps down on the Jeep and prepared for a downpour.

Before we backed out of the Haberman driveway, I called Sarah Byrne. After we exchanged our greetings, she asked, "How can I help you?"

I explained that we were looking into the threats against the senator. "He suggested you could help us look into his case history for suspects."

"I did some work for the senator, before he left for Washington," she said. "I'll check with Mr. Yamato, and get back to you, but if Senator Haberman has already given his okay it should be fine for you to come over."

I thanked her. Ray and I had met with Yamato on a previous case, and I was sure that Sarah would remind him of that, and knowing her, also remind him of the need to cooperate with any investigation into threats against the senator and his family.

We were only a few blocks from Magoo's Burgers, a hole in the wall in a strip shopping center. I used to stop there for a calorie boost back when I was surfing Diamond Head, and I'd been missing those days, so I drove us over there. I ordered the MaGooGoo, a quarter-pound burger on a freshly toasted bun, with a side of spicy fries. Ray, who is much more of a healthy eater than I am, got the grilled chicken Magoo sliced over a salad. I ordered a chocolate shake with mine.

"You are a bad influence on me," Ray said, giving in and getting a strawberry shake for himself.

We were finishing up our lunch when Sarah called back. "Can you come over this afternoon?" she asked.

"We can be there in about half an hour," I said.

Fields and Yamato occupied the whole twentieth floor of a glass-encased high-rise in downtown Honolulu. Every time I passed it I wondered what would happen if a hurricane devastated O'ahu like Iniki had done with Kauai. Would there be shattered glass everywhere, legal files whirling through the air and ending up in sodden masses amidst the debris of a thousand computers?

We stopped at the receptionist, who stamped our parking ticket and called for Sarah. Sarah came out a few moments later.

"It's always a pleasure to see you," she said. It seemed like her Australian accent was just as sharp as ever, even though she'd been in Honolulu for years. The pink stripe in her dark hair had gone to a pale lavender but otherwise she looked the same, round-faced and smiling.

"It's always work for us," I said, but I smiled.

Ray sang, "Hello again, hello," and I recognized the opening lines of the Neil Diamond song. He and Sarah enjoyed singing back and forth to each other, because they shared a love of music.

"Hello darkness, my old friend," she sang back to him. "Come on back with me. Mr. Yamato wants to speak with you first."

She led us down a corridor of plush carpet and framed photographs of old Hawai'i. "I'm singing on Saturday night with the Beachcombers," she said to Ray. "You guys should come."

"If Julie and I can get a babysitter, we'll be there," Ray said. We stopped in front of the managing partner's office, at a corner of the building with a commanding view of downtown Honolulu and the Aloha Tower, with the Pacific sparkling in the sunshine beyond.

Winston Yamato had to be in his sixties, with a mane of white hair and a tanned face. He was still a competitive sailor, and often participated in races on his own boat. "Good afternoon, gentlemen," he said, rising to shake our hands. "Ron says he's been getting threatening letters?"

Ray, Sarah and I sat down, and Ray and I alternated telling Yamato about the letters the Habermans had received and about the attack on the senator's daughter.

"That's very low," Yamato said, when we had finished. "To throw paint on an innocent girl." He shook his head. "I hoped we'd put all that race nonsense behind us."

"Has anyone else here at the firm gotten similar threats?" I asked.

"Not that I've heard of," Yamato said. "Sarah? Anything going on sub rosa?"

"I asked around after I spoke with Detective Kanapa'aka," she said. "No one I spoke with has received any letters."

"Any personnel issues?" I asked. "Disgruntled ex-staff who might hold a grudge against the senator?"

"Ron's a politician through and through," Yamato said. "I doubt he'd have antagonized anyone to that degree. And in any case we haven't let anyone go under unpleasant circumstances for quite some time."

"Was the senator involved in any cases that might have triggered this?" Ray asked.

"I'll let Sarah handle that." Yamato turned to Sarah. "Use your judgment in what to release. But if there's anything of a sensitive nature, check with me first."

"Of course," Sarah said, and after we thanked Yamato for his cooperation Sarah led us to a conference room with a sweeping view of Honolulu Harbor. A jet was taking off from the reef runway at Honolulu International, and the scene could have been an ad for the Tourism Board. Hard to believe sometimes that there's crime in a place as beautiful as the one where we were privileged to live.

"What was Senator Haberman's specialty when he was an attorney?" Ray asked as we sat down.

"Primarily land use," Sarah said. "He represented clients on both ends of the spectrum, from a non-profit that wanted to prevent development near a wetland bird preserve in Kailua to a developer who wanted to purchase air rights from a church in Waikiki. He often represented large landowners, and in those cases there were often many complaints, sometimes very aggressive ones."

She turned to a pile of documents on the conference room

table and handed one sheet to each of us. "I went over the cases Senator Haberman worked on for the last year he was associated with the firm," Sarah said, as we sat down. "There weren't many, because he had stepped back in order to focus on his campaign. We don't have our case files categorized by race, so it was hard to look for any incidents involving mixed-race clients or cases. But I did find one case that sounded relevant, a Mr. Warren Kahananui who owns property in Waimanalo. He was a referral from Ms. Kaneahe, who I believe had a family connection to him."

Since Peggy came from a big native Hawaiian family that wasn't surprising. "What was the case?" I asked.

"He hired us to handle a Request for Non-Homesteading Land Use Purposes with the DHH. He wanted to build a mini-mart on land that was zoned residential," she said. The Department of Hawaiian Homelands was a division of the Hawaiian Homes Commission, founded long ago by Prince Kuhio to manage land for the Hawaiian people.

"Mr. Haberman shepherded the application, and when the request was denied, Mr. Kahananui got very angry and blamed Mr. Haberman. I copied this letter for you."

She pushed another pair of pages toward us. "You'll see it includes some racial aspersions."

The letter had been written by hand, on plain white paper, and addressed to Mr. Ronald Haberman at his office address. It was full of grammatical errors and spelling mistakes, but the intent was clear. Haberman wasn't Hawaiian and neither was his wife, and they didn't belong in the state. He and his poi dog family should clear out. It was signed in a scribble, but I recognized the capital letters W and K.

I didn't want to have to talk to Peggy, but I sucked it up and asked Sarah if Peggy was available. "If these people are related to her she might have some insight."

"She's in a meeting now but she'll join us when she's finished."

"Any other cases?" Ray asked.

"The only other case I could find was one that involved the

blood quantum requirement as part of a real estate deal," she said.

The blood quantum was a relic of the 1920s and governed consideration for state benefits like homestead land and attendance at the Kamehameha Schools, among other things. To be considered a native Hawaiian, you had to submit documentation tracing your genealogy to your full Hawaiian ancestors. My parents had registered me and my brothers, tracing our heritage back to my father's father and my mother's mother, both of whom were documented full Hawaiians.

For a while, my mother had been involved with a group of native activists who wanted to change the laws; she wanted to make sure that all her grandchildren, even those with less than fifty percent, were treated equally. Once my father's health began to fail she'd had to give it up.

"How did that blood quantum case turn out?" I asked.

"Positively for the petitioners. They were able to provide the required documentation and got the permission they wanted."

I was beginning to think that it had been a waste of time to come to Fields and Yamato. But it was one of those threads that had to be followed to their conclusion.

We were just finishing when the door to the conference room opened and my ex-girlfriend walked in.

Every time I saw Peggy I was reminded of the girl she was in high school, though she was twenty years older and there were gray threads in her close-cropped dark hair. She was just as slim as she was then, and she dressed as if she was about to pose for a formal portrait, in a high-necked ivory silk blouse with a single strand of pearls, and a navy blazer and matching skirt.

She kissed my cheek and said hello to Ray. "I understand you wanted to talk to me about Warren Kahananui?"

She sat at the table with us, and I explained about the threats to Senator Haberman and his family. "How well do you know him?"

"Not well," she said. "He's a distant cousin of my mother's, and I ran into him at a luau a couple of years ago and mentioned that I was an attorney. When he needed someone to represent him in this filing, he called and I recommended Ron to him."

"Do you think Warren could be harassing the senator because he lost this case?"

"I really can't say. You'll have to talk to him yourself. But I can tell you, there seems to be an epidemic of harassment going on. I had one myself a few weeks ago."

"Really? What happened?"

Ray, Sarah and I all listened intently as she described going up to Laie with a haole male associate to take a deposition. Peggy had classic Hawaiian looks—a heart-shaped face, dark eyes, and skin the color of light coffee.

"Steve and I parked in the Foodland lot because we were taking a deposition from one of the clerks. After we finished in the back, I picked up a couple of things and checked out, and I carried my own bag."

Of course she would, I thought. Peggy was still single, as far as I knew, and I thought part of the reason was because she was so fiercely independent. Though I suppose there was always the possibility that I had hurt her so much that she'd sworn off men. I hoped that wasn't the case.

"Steve and I were walking out when this haole woman with a couple of kids looked at me and sneered. She said something like 'Leave the white men for us white women,' and then pushed passed."

"What did you say?"

"I was so surprised that I didn't say anything. I just looked at Steve, and both of us laughed. I didn't even think about it until now."

Sarah nodded. "Something similar happened to me and Wing a few weeks ago," she said. "We were at Makapu'u Point, holding hands and looking at the sunset, and a beat-up ute with a big set of boots slowed down as they were passing us. The Seppo in the front seat leaned out and called Wing a Chink, and told him to lay off the white women."

Sarah must have seen our confusion, because she laughed and said, "Sorry, I was thinking like an Aussie. A beat up pickup truck with those huge tires."

"And a Seppo?" Ray asked.

Sarah seemed to blush. "Derogative slang for a Yank," she said. "You know, the people who empty the septic tanks? Tank rhymes with Yank."

"Okay," I said. "You get the make or model?"

Sarah shook her head. "But we did see the first couple of numbers of the plate, and Wing insisted I take a note on my phone."

"Good for Wing," I said.

She scrolled through her notes and said, "The first three letters were KTF, but that's all we could catch."

"It's another piece of the puzzle," I said. I made a note in the case file about what we had learned from both Sarah and Peggy, and then we thanked them and left.

"You want to head up to Waimanalo, try to find Peggy's cousins?" Ray asked as we rode down in the elevator.

"I suppose we ought to," I said. "No stone unturned and all that. But it's hell to get there from here, and then back to Kapolei. Why don't I call first?"

We stopped at the Kope Bean coffee shop in the building's lobby. "You want something?" Ray asked.

"Boogie board decaf mocha, please," I said. The Kope Bean reinforced their island vibe by naming all their drink sizes after surfboards, from the twelve-ounce boogie board to the eighteen-ounce longboard.

I stood in the building's lobby and dialed the number on the sheet Sarah had given me. "Howzit, brah," I said, when a man answered. "I'm looking for Warren Kahananui."

"Who wants him?"

"Detective Kanapa'aka, HPD. I'm calling about the lawsuit over the minimart."

"That's me, brah. What you looking at?"

I thought if I phrased my questions with a bias against Haberman, I might get Warren to be more open. "We're investigating your attorney," I said. "You were pretty upset with Ronald Haberman, weren't you?"

"Big mistake hiring dat guy, brah," he said. "Gotta have a Hawaiian for da kine homestead paperwork. Haberman, he haole, do things haole way. Once I got me a Hawaiian guy, he push the papers through just fine."

"Did you hold a grudge against Haberman?"

"Nah, life too short for dat, brah. We islanders got to stick together. Mistake to go for the big downtown boys. I don't boddah wid dem anymore."

We talked for a couple of minutes, until I believed that he had no beef against Haberman, nor any prejudice against mixed-race people. By the time I finished Ray was there with my decaf.

"Dead end," I said, and told him what I'd learned.

"Isn't our first, won't be our last," Ray said, as we walked back to the Jeep. Before I put it in gear, I slid in a Springsteen CD.

As the distinctive cadence of "Born in the USA" began to play, Ray asked, "Boss today? No Hawaiian music?"

I skipped ahead to "Dancing in the Dark." Once it began, I said, "This song says it all. It's what we're doing with this case."

On our way to the H-1 highway for the trip back out to Kapolei, we got stuck behind a tourist couple driving a rented convertible with the top down. The woman kept snapping photos with her phone, as if she'd never seen a palm tree before. That's one of the downsides to life in paradise; rental cars full of sight-seeing visitors clog our streets, consulting maps every mile, slowing to ogle bikini-clad surfers and snap pictures of sights we take for granted.

"According to Haberman, he hasn't gotten any threats at his Washington office," Ray said. "And it looks like none of his cases at Fields and Yamato are relevant. So what else do we have?"

"The paint balloon attack on Jessica Haberman," I said. "I wish her father would let us talk to her, see if maybe another kid at school has a grudge against her."

"A kid wouldn't have written those letters," Ray said. "And we should look for any similar incidents. Look at what Sarah and Peggy said. Maybe someone is organizing a harassment campaign."

We finally made it onto the highway. Ray leaned back in his seat. "You or Mike ever experience anything like what happened to Jessica? Anybody bother you because you're mixed race?"

I shrugged. "A couple of times when I was a kid, but nothing that scarred me. For a couple of days after my mom came to our elementary school once, this one kid started saying 'sayonara' to me and pulling his eyes up at the corners."

"What did you do?"

"I was taking karate back then," I said. "Not in a serious way, just something to keep me from bouncing off the walls and bothering my brothers. I wanted to be able to do one of those high-jumping kicks, and I practiced on him."

Ray laughed so hard he snorted. "I can just see you. What

happened?"

"He fell backwards, and I landed on my butt. We both had to stay after school and clean the blackboards."

When we got back to Kapolei, we unpacked the boxes that had been left for us and filled out more paperwork. We had to watch an online video about sexual harassment in the workplace, and another on the history of the FBI. Ray took the folders down to the fingerprint lab and then I emailed myself copies of the letter and the envelope, which I added to the case file I was developing on my iPad.

While Ray looked for churches who used the kind of rhetoric in the letters, I did a search through the police database for pickup trucks with KTF as the first three letters of the plate, and got about three dozen matches. None of them on the Windward Shore, though, so I put that information aside in case it matched something in the future.

When I got home, our golden retriever Roby tackled me as soon as I walked in. I scratched behind his ears and then followed him to the kitchen, where Mike was foraging through the freezer.

Until you get up close to him, Mike looks completely haole and distinctly Italian, from his dark curly hair to his swarthy skin. His Korean heritage is only visible in the slight epicanthic fold of his eyes—though it was distinctive enough to make him uncomfortable when he was a kid growing up in Long Island, around his dad's Italian-American family.

Mike looked up from the freezer. "When was the last time we went grocery shopping? There's nothing in here but ice packs, half a bag of meatballs and two boxes of creamed spinach."

"Can't be," I said. "Dakota and I filled a grocery cart last weekend. Could he have eaten everything?" I looked over Mike's shoulder and saw he was telling the truth.

"The kid must have a tapeworm," Mike grumbled. "Oh, crap."

"What?"

"I'm starting to talk like my father. When you hear me do that, slap me, all right?"

"Can I spank you?" I asked, with a smile.

"TMI!" Dakota said. I looked around to see him standing in the kitchen doorway. "What's for dinner?"

"I guess we'll order a pizza," I said.

"Two?" Dakota asked. "One for you guys and one for me?"

Mike and I groaned in unison. I called the pizza place at the bottom of the hill and put in our order, and Dakota went into the living room to play with Roby.

Mike sat at the kitchen table with a bottle of Fire Rock Pale Ale. "How was your first day as a special agent?" he asked.

"Ray and I have our first case. Our newest senator has gotten some hate mail." I got a bottle for myself and told Mike about Senator Haberman's wife and the threats her family had received. "Peggy Kaneahe and Sarah Byrne told me that they've both gotten similar harassment." I looked at him. "You had problems on Long Island when you were a kid, being mixed race," I said. "Anything once you moved here?"

"Not specifically that. But I remember we were studying the Korean war in middle school and I said that's how my parents had met, when my dad was a soldier and my mom was a nurse. One of the kids got confused between South and North Korea and accused my mom of being a Communist."

"What did you do?"

"I stuffed him in a locker."

I laughed and told him about my own experience. "I'd better get a move on," I said. "There's a grocery by the pizza parlor. I'll get Dakota to go with me and buy some food."

When I parked in the grocery lot, Dakota took a picture of my Jeep, and then another of the storefront. He kept taking photos of aisles and products and our cart as we grabbed enough food to carry us through the next day. When we were in the checkout line, I finally had to ask. "What is so fascinating about this store?"

I asked.

"I'm posting to my Instagram account," he said. "Dylan and I are competing to see who can take the most different pictures."

"Who's Dylan?"

"Just a guy. He's in my English class." Dakota slouched against the rack of tabloid magazines, his head down.

Hmm, I wondered. Just a guy. Back home, Dakota took photos of his pizza as he ate each slice, but I resisted the urge to say anything. After dinner, he retreated to his room, and Mike and I lounged on the sofa, reading.

The next morning Mike's cell went off at six. I used the bathroom while he spoke, and by the time I came out he was almost dressed. "Fire up in Kahuku that looks like arson," he said. "Gotta run."

I fed and walked Roby and made sure that Dakota got off to school. I was about to leave for Kapolei when my cell phone began to sing, "When the moon hits your eye like a big pizza pie, that's amore." Dakota had picked ring tones for all of us, and that was mine for Mike.

"Howzit, sweetheart?" I said.

"I'm up here in Kahuku, and I spotted some racist slogans sprayed on the remaining walls, which makes this look like a hate crime. Since you were talking about that kind of thing last night I thought maybe you ought to come up and check it out."

"I'll have to see what Salinas says. I'll call you back."

I dialed Francisco Salinas's personal cell and explained the situation. "Probably not related," he said when I finished. "But hate crimes come under our purview, so you might as well pick this one up, too. But remember, even though you and Donne are still on the HPD payroll, you're not the primary investigators. Focus on the hate crime angle."

"Got it," I said. "We'll keep you in the loop."

I called Ray. He was getting on the highway toward Kapolei, but he'd circle back and meet me at the Kope Bean in Aiea, so we could drive up to Kahuku together. When he climbed into the Jeep, he was holding two longboard sized coffees. "Fill me in," he said.

"I'll let Mike do it." I put my phone on speaker and called Mike. "I've got Ray with me, and we're on our way," I said. "Give us some background, will you?"

"The site is a day care center a couple of blocks from Kahuku Medical Center. Wood frame building that went up quickly, though a couple of walls and part of the roof are remaining."

"A day care center?" Ray asked. "Were there kids there?"

"Fire started at about five a.m., before any kids were there," Mike said. "Otherwise it would have been a real tragedy."

Mike gave us directions and Ray wrote them down, and I made a quick turn onto the H-1 highway, which would take us around the looming mass of Diamond Head. "Who would set a day care center on fire?" Ray asked as we sped along, the palm trees along the highway swaying restlessly in a chilly wind.

"Somebody seriously whacked," I said. For as long as I'd been a cop, I'd had a special anger for crimes committed against kids. After I came out of the closet, I volunteered with a gay teen group, and I'd focused on the ways those kids were victimized— verbal, emotional, economic and sexual abuse. That was how I'd first met Dakota, and taking him in as our foster son was one of the ways Mike and I tried to make things better.

When our friends Sandra and Cathy had asked Mike and me to donate sperm, my first response had been no—I didn't want to bring kids into the world I saw every day as a cop. But eventually I'd come around to the idea, and now I loved the twins fiercely and I was determined to protect them from anything the world wanted to throw at them. The fact that there were kids involved in this case, even only peripherally, made it matter that much more to me.

I had grown up with a sense that ohana meant more than your blood relatives. My family was a big and diverse one, and I had lots of mixed-race friends. What would I do if someone came after me, or my family?

I hoped I'd have a few better moves in my arsenal than that failed roundhouse kick.

The wind picked up as we drove along the tree-lined Likelike Highway, which went through the center of the island. The mountains were shrouded in mist and I was glad we had the hot coffee to counter the chilly damp.

The divided highway followed the contours of the Ko'olau mountains, and verdant slopes and craggy cliffs loomed beside us. It was a wilder part of O'ahu, and it was almost like going back in time. People lived up there in the mountains, off the grid, but they had modern conveniences like solar panels and water purifiers. And some of them were growing pakalolo and manufacturing ice, which were distinctly modern problems.

As we approached the Wilson Tunnel through the mountains, I noticed some graffiti scrawled on rocks beside the road, and recognized one tag, the letters FTP, with an X over the stem of the T, a reference to an LA-based gang call the Fruit Town Pirus. Beside it was a scrawl of the Nazi swastika.

I'd heard that some of the mainland gangs were trying to make inroads in Hawai'i, but that was the first physical evidence I'd seen. And the fact that someone had painted a swastika nearby wasn't a good indicator of racial harmony.

When we came out of the tunnel we drove right into a downpour, and I had to slow down and turn my wipers on high because of the slick roadway and the slow-moving tourists. We rounded a bend and ahead of us was the town of Kaneohe nestled against a cove along the Pacific shore. No gleaming glass high-rises like downtown Honolulu; just a spread of houses and low buildings, with only occasional buildings of more than four or five stories.

We passed a standard suburban sprawl of houses and fast-food chains as well as the Honolulu Church of Light, the *Iglesia Ni Cristo*, the St. Anthony Retreat, and the Central Samoan Assembly of God, a testimony to the religious diversity of the island.

On the route to Laie, we passed a couple of big family farms with chain link fencing around them, and signs for several different churches that sounded fundamentalist, but as we approached the center of town, I was disappointed to see that the area was as mixed as the rest of the island, though I did notice a higher proportion of the kind of white, clean-cut people I associated with those Mormon missionaries on bicycles.

Further evidence of the religious character of the area was that local supermarkets wouldn't sell alcohol on Sunday in deference to Mormon beliefs. Like Kaneohe, the streets were lined with single-story bungalows and small stores. I kept an eye out for graffiti but didn't see much more than the occasional scrawl.

Kahuku was at the very tip of the island, in an area that tourists don't generally frequent; the big waves of the North Shore crash around the other side of Kahuku Point, and usually the farthest that visitors get on the Windward Shore was the Islands of History theme park in Laie, where I'd gone many times as a kid.

You could drive for miles up the twisting Kamehameha Highway, paralleling the coast, and see spectacular cliffs and water views, and not much else. It was near the northernmost point on the island, Kahuku Point; in Hawaiian, *ka huku* means 'the projection.'

It was nearly ten o'clock by the time we approached the day care center. There was only one fire engine remaining, though the police still had the street blocked and were directing traffic away.

I parked behind Mike's truck with its distinctive flames painted down the side, and Ray and I flashed our IDs to the uniform keeping people away from the site.

From the charred foundation that remained, we could see that the day care center was a free-standing building, probably once a single-family house. There wasn't much around it—no immediate neighbors, and a screen of trees around the back and sides.

The scene reminded me of damage I'd seen after Hurricane

Iniki devastated Kauai just before I left for college, the way you could look right into someone's home or office and witness the devastation first-hand. In this case, I could see a cluster of half-burned tables and chairs piled in the center of the main room. The front wall of a bathroom was gone, but the toilet and sink looked untouched.

We stopped in the parking lot, a few feet from the front wall, and looked around. Two of the four walls remained intact—the rear and the right side—and part of the roof. An interior wall that looked like it separated an office from the main area had been reduced to a tangle of half-melted studs; behind it was a desk and a file cabinet and the rear wall of the building. Children's drawings had been posted there, brown edges curling around colorful scrawls of houses and flowers.

The front door was long gone, but just inside was a misshapen coat rack with a single sweater hanging on it, miraculously untouched. Below it were a pair of pink rubber Crocs in an impossibly tiny size—one of them intact down to the tiny charms in the holes, the other a melted lump. We'd bought shoes just like that for the twins.

Mike's large metal toolbox stood just outside the charred foundation. It contained a wide range of equipment that he used to investigate, from activated charcoal to tweezers. He kept a supply of common tools like hammers, screwdriver, pliers and wrenches, along with dust masks, evidence bags, brushes, cotton swaps, dental tools and baby wipes. Everything he could possibly need to examine or collect evidence that would tell him the story of the fire.

The acrid smell of burnt wood and plastic filled the air. What looked like a heap of charred furniture was mounded in the middle of the room. Charred teddy bears, melted rubber ducks, and other kids' toys were scattered around the room.

Mike was inside what was left of the building, talking to one of the firefighters, and I called to him. "Okay for us to come in?"

The firefighter walked away, and Mike approached. "Just be careful where you step."

A tool belt hung at his waist, with a carpet knife, tin snips, a flashlight, a chisel and a roll of duct tape attached. He had a brand-new wooden broom in his hand, the price tag still wrapped around the shaft. He had a bunch of them in our garage, since he had to use a new one each time so as not to cross-contaminate. Once I'd used one to clean up a spill in our living room, and gotten my head bitten off.

Ray said, "What a disaster. You're sure no kids were hurt?"

"No one was here when it happened," Mike said. "The owner of the center, Haley Walsh, opens every morning at six-thirty, so that staffers on their way to the medical center down the street can drop off their keikis. This morning she arrived about six and she saw fire coming out of the back window. I'm calculating the fire was set around four-thirty or five. She called it in and the first engine was here in about ten minutes, but by then most of the building was gone."

"I assume the local cops were there before we were," I said.

"Yup. Guy named Rizaldo Amador. You know him?"

I nodded. "Met him at a couple of those continuing ed classes we have to take."

"He had a couple of crime scene techs out here as soon as I was finished with my investigation. He went back to his office about an hour ago to start calling the parents who had kids here, see if any of them knew someone with a grudge."

"You know how the fire started yet?" I asked.

Mike motioned to the haphazard pile in the middle of the room. "I'm calling this second degree, since the building was in use but unoccupied. Looks like the arsonist gathered all the chairs and tables together, then collected a lot of paper for kindling beneath it. Mrs. Walsh told me there was a snack cabinet in the back. He—and I know you get picky about grammar so let's just assume it's a he for the present—grabbed a bunch of bags of potato chips and cookies, too."

"Potato chips are a good accelerant, right?" I asked. I remembered the first case Mike and I had investigated together, years before, where an arsonist had laid a trail of potato chips in order to draw the fire along the back of a building.

"Very good," Mike said. He looked at Ray. "You know what the fire triangle is?"

Ray nodded. "Fuel, heat and oxygen. I thought they were calling it a fire tetrahedron now, but I forgot what the fourth thing is."

Mike licked his finger and made a mark in the air. "Points to the boy from Philly for remembering all that. The fourth element is chemical reaction. In this case, the fuel is the furniture and the paper." He pointed to the pile. At the bottom I saw a few circles of red and green construction paper folded into a chain, and I remembered making those as a keiki.

"I found the remains of a cigarette lighter in the back. To increase the oxygen flow, he knocked out the window in the wall over there."

Mike pointed to one of the two remaining walls. "The first firefighters on the scene reported yellow and red flame and brown smoke, which is consistent with the wood and particle board furniture. I haven't found any evidence of accelerants other than the potato chip bags, but our arsonist had a pretty good idea of what he was doing."

"Forced entry?" Ray asked.

"Spotted some pry marks on the back door. There's a playground back there with a low fence, not visible from the road. Would have been easy to hop that fence and jimmy the lock on the back door."

I looked around. The lack of neighbors meant there was little chance that any intruders would be spotted, especially if they'd entered around the back of the building.

"What about that racist graffiti?" Ray asked.

"Over there," Mike said, and he led us around to the right-hand wall, where we saw what had been written. "Only the pure white are righteous," was scrawled in blood-red spray paint at about eye level. Below it, in the same color but a different style of writing, was "Mongrel children are a sin in the eyes of the LORD."

Something about that phrase rang a bell. Mongrel was such an odd word, but one that I'd heard somewhere recently. I turned to Ray. "That second letter Mrs. Haberman got," I said. "Didn't it say something about mongrels?" I opened my iPad and found the photocopy of the letter I'd emailed to myself. Sure enough, there was a reference there to mongrel children. I showed the letter to Mike.

"You think whoever sent this letter was responsible for the arson here?" he asked.

I remembered the gang-related graffiti we'd seen on our way up to Kahuku. "Not necessarily the same person, but maybe a member of the same group."

"There are some charred pieces of drywall over there," Mike said, pointing to where the other side wall had once been. "Some bits and pieces of graffiti on them, too. Whoever did this took their time inside, scrawling on every available surface."

We looked at the fragments but couldn't piece together anything reasonable from them. It looked like there had been at least two graffiti painters, because there were minor differences in the handwriting. The writer with the can of red paint was careful to cross every T and dot every I, while the one using the blue paint was more free-form.

"Why spend all that time painting the graffiti, and then burn the building down before anyone could see what was written?" I asked.

"Maybe one of the graffiti writers had a change of heart," Ray suggested. "Or got scared they'd get caught. So he or she set the fire to cover up what they'd done." He looked at Mike. "That fit your scenario?"

Mike shrugged. "Hey, I just examine the fire. Means, motive and opportunity are your department."

Mike found me out in the yard behind the building, taking photos of the low fence. "I need some hydration," he said. "There's a country store about a mile away and I'm going to get some water. You want anything?"

"Yeah, I could use some water myself. I'll come with you."

"What about your other boyfriend?" he asked, nodding back toward the building, where Ray was taking notes on his laptop.

"We use the term partner," I said drily. "I'll see if he wants to come, too."

Ray said he had a couple of calls to make, and asked me to bring a bottle of water back for him. I hopped into Mike's truck and we headed for the store. Puffy white cumulous clouds massed out over the ocean to our right, and the tree-shrouded peaks of the Ko'olau loomed to our left. When there was no traffic on the road and no development around us, I could imagine this was what the island had been like when my Hawaiian ancestors first arrived in outrigger canoes.

"Can you tell if there was more than one arsonist?" I asked Mike as we drove.

"Hard to say. It took some work to move all the furniture into the center of the room, and that would have been a lot easier with somebody to help. As far as I can tell the fire was only set in one place, under the pile of furniture. So there's nothing to specifically point to more than one person present, but there's also nothing to rule that out."

As we pulled up at the store, my cell rang. I told Mike to go on inside, and answered Ray. "I spoke to Amador," he said. "He's at his office, and has Haley Walsh there with him. I said we'd go over there as soon as you get back."

"Will do."

When I walked inside the store, Mike was standing by the

refrigerated case talking to a teenaged boy. He looked a few years older than Dakota, and he was skinny, with stringy hair and bangs that kept flopping in front of his eyes. "They charge a lot of money for water," the boy said.

"Yeah, but water means life," Mike said. "You gotta stay hydrated, right?" He opened the case and pulled out three bottles of Hawaiian Isles water. He looked at the boy. "You want one?"

The boy shook his head. "My father says that we're not allowed to buy anything we could produce ourselves. Our rain barrels give us all the water we need."

Mike shrugged. He turned to me and called, "Catch!" and tossed one bottle to me. I grabbed it in mid-flight. The boy turned and saw me, then looked back at Mike. His face was so open that it was as if I could read his thoughts, comparing me and Mike.

"You're impure," the boy said to Mike. "I'm not allowed to talk to you."

"Donnie!"

Mike and I turned to see a teenage girl standing at the ladies room door. She was as skinny as the boy, with the same dirty blonde hair. But there was something much harder about her. "You know what father said about talking to strangers," she said to the boy.

"I'm sorry, Marie. I didn't mean anything," he said to her. He hung his head. "I didn't realize he was impure until I looked at his eyes." He began speaking rapidly to her in a kind of gibberish as Mike and I stood there and stared.

She grabbed his arm and tugged him out of the store. Mike and I watched them go.

When we walked up to the register, the clerk said, "No let dem twins bodda you," he said. "He's a lolo buggah but she keep him okay."

"They're twins?" I asked, as Mike paid for the water.

"Yeah. Dey fadda has a big place up the hill, lots of keikis."

He leaned forward. "I tink dey had some problem wen dey born, maybe he not get no oxygen or sumting."

"Shame," I said. We thanked the guy and walked outside.

As we drove back to the day care center, I said, "I'm glad Alpha and Omega were born healthy. I'd hate them to end up like those two." Once Sandra discovered she was carrying twins, she had called them Alpha and Omega, because they were the first and last children she was ever going to carry.

Once they were born, we had chosen the names Addie and Owen for them, but I was still accustomed to calling them by their nicknames.

"You don't know what the problem with those two is," Mike said. "So don't go imagining problems for ours. They'll be fine. They've got great genes."

"I hope you're right," I said. "What do you think he meant about us being impure? You think he figured out we were gay?"

Mike shook his head. "I had my cap pulled down over my forehead so he couldn't see my eyes at first. I think he thought I was haole."

"What is it with these people? It's like there are racists everywhere we look."

"Maybe it's just because you're looking for them," Mike said.

After Mike and I returned to the day care center, Ray and I drove to the Kahuku substation, a non-descript low-slung building next to a tall electrical tower with a siren on top, surrounded by scrub and scraggly palms. We checked in with the aide at the front desk, and she sent us back to Rizaldo Amador's office, a small square with just enough room for a cheap metal desk and three chairs.

Some guys just look like cops, even in plain clothes, and he was one of them. Despite his relatively small size—he was a slim five-eight—he had a toughness about him that said law enforcement. His weathered face and dark skin, along with the rigidity of his posture, reminded me of photos I'd seen of Philippine guerrillas during World War II.

We shook hands and sat down. "What's the Bureau's interest in this?" he asked.

"When Mike Riccardi saw those slogans on the wall he called the Bureau because of the possible civil rights violations. We have another case involving mixed-race harassment so we got the nod."

I decided not to tell him about the similar wording in the letters and on the day care center wall. Crap. I was becoming an FBI agent, holding out on local cops.

"What can you tell us?" Ray asked.

"I have Mrs. Walsh in the other room. You can talk to her yourselves. She's hapa haole, and that might be why those things were written on the walls."

Hapa meant "half" in the Hawaiian language, and the term hapa haole had been used for decades, to describe everything from people to a type of music that added English lyrics to Hawaiian melodies. It was the kind of thing we said so casually that it was hard to believe anyone still found that kind of mix offensive.

"Any indication that her background was the cause of the arson?" Ray asked.

"Just the things scrawled on the wall. But it could have been directed at keikis she took care of, too. From what I understand she has a variety there—white, Asian, native Hawaiian, and some mixed-race as well."

"What did you think of the graffiti?" I asked. "You ever see similar religious scrawls around here?"

Amador sat back. "This is the first time I've seen the graffiti, but I've heard bits and pieces about racial harassment over the last couple of months. Nothing reported officially, just hearsay."

"Such as?"

"My sister-in-law is haole, and her husband's black. Her kids are kind of coffee-colored, with curly hair, and when she was at the Foodland one day some haole woman made some nasty comments. She ignored it at the time, but she told me later. I've heard a couple of similar things from people I've talked to, but nothing actionable."

"I was wondering about the word mongrel," I said. "That was odd, wasn't it? A Hawaiian person wouldn't use that. We'd say poi dog."

Amador nodded. Poi dog was the Hawaiian term for a dog of mixed breeding, and if you wanted to say something really derogatory about someone's background, you'd be more likely to use that than the Anglo word mongrel.

"That makes me think that whoever did this isn't from here," Amador said.

"There's a big Mormon community up here," I said. "Any of them come from off-island? Maybe have mainland prejudices."

"I'll have to look into it," he said. "It's not politically correct to categorize offenders by race so our records aren't organized that way, but I know a lot of these people personally."

"It's a small island," I said. "I know a lot of perps myself."

"You got it. I doubt that there's a moke or a tita on this island who doesn't have a cop somewhere on his or her family tree."

Moke was our island slang for a male troublemaker, tita his female equivalent. But I had the feeling that our arsonist wasn't a local, though I couldn't quite say why other than that discordant word mongrel, especially since it had now come up twice.

Amador led us down the hall to where Haley Walsh was sitting with a female officer. He introduced us, and he and the uniform left.

Haley was a plump, cheerful woman with shoulder-length dark hair. Her Hawaiian heritage was written in her round face and brown eyes. "We're sorry for what happened this morning," I began.

"At least none of the keikis were there," she said. "And I have insurance. It's going to take time for the money to come in, but I'm opening up again. Nobody's knocking me down."

"Have you experienced any harassment prior to today?" I asked.

She was about to shake her head, then stopped. "There was one thing. Maybe it's connected," she said. "My father is haole, and he and I were walking in Laie a few weeks ago, just talking and laughing, and he leaned over and kissed my cheek. A haole woman in a long dress was coming toward us with a little girl. When she saw my dad kiss me, she spit on the ground and said something mean."

"You don't remember what?"

"No. At the time my dad and I thought maybe she didn't realize he was my father, and thought I was a gold-digger with an older man. We laughed about it. But maybe it was because of the difference in our races."

"How about the word mongrel?" I asked. "Anybody you know use that? Hawaiians would use poi dog instead."

"No, it seemed strange." She looked at both of us. "Did you know that in the Hawaiian religion the poi dog is the spiritual protector of children? That was why we had so many pictures of dogs up on the walls." She stifled a tear. "Guess they didn't protect these keikis enough."

"Sure they did," I said. "Nobody was there when the building burned, right? That's got to be some pretty strong *mana*." Mana was a Hawaiian term for spiritual energy, and it seemed that something had protected all those kids from the fire.

"I guess so," Haley said.

"Detective Amador said that the kids you take care of are pretty mixed," Ray said. "Ever have any tensions between parents?"

She shook her head. "Most of the parents work at the hospital," she said. "Doctors and nurses and administrators. Nobody has ever complained."

"We're not far from Laie," I said. "And we passed a Mormon temple near the police substation. Is there a big Mormon community here?"

"Yes, it's very active here," she said.

"Are they mostly haole?" I asked.

She shook her head. "Our community is open to anyone. We have converts from different backgrounds and cultures. I can't imagine a Mormon doing something like this."

I stood up. "Thank you very much. This has been helpful." I handed her my card. "If you think of anything else, please call."

"I will."

As we got into the Jeep, Ray looked at his watch. "Vinnie has a routine checkup at the pediatrician's late this afternoon, and I told Julie I'd make it if I could. What do you say we find ourselves a Kope Bean and do some research online rather than going all the way back to Kapolei? Then you can drop me downtown."

"Sounds good to me," I said. "It'll give us a chance to use that new private VPN software so we can access the department's database securely."

We drove down the Kam along the Windward Shore, stopping at a Kope Bean in Kaneohe. Ray and I split up our research; I would look for incident reports in the HPD database, and he'd search for individuals who'd been accused or convicted of similar crimes. It was clunky, cumbersome work, pulling up incident reports and reviewing them for key words, especially because I was using the web interface for the database, not accessing it directly. I was looking for "mongrel" in particular, and not having much luck.

An African-American soldier from Schofield Barracks was out at Hanauma Bay with his haole wife, and a man parked in a neighboring space began saying derogatory terms about the soldier and his wife, telling them that racial mixing was a sin against God. A bystander called park security, and the unidentified male who had made the comments drove away.

Someone had set off a stink bomb at a Unitarian church in Kaaawa during the wedding of a Hawaiian man and a haole woman. A guy who identified himself as half Samoan and half haole, with brown skin but Caucasian features, had complained that he had been taunted at a grocery store. Someone had scrawled racist slogans on the walls of a church in Kaneohe the day before a program on mixed marriages.

There were a lot more. Each one was small and more meaningful to the individuals involved, but we began to see a pattern. Most of the incidents had taken place on the Windward Shore, from Kahuku down, with a few additional ones sprinkled around Honolulu. Because none of the incidents were very serious, the police investigations had been cursory, and there were no suspects connected to more than one incident.

I was reading about vandalism at a psychologist's office off the Pali Highway when I stumbled on the word "mongrel." Dr. Alan Feldberg focused on counseling mixed-race couples, and he had received several threatening letters which included some of the terms we had seen at Haley Walsh's day care center. Once I finished reading through the report, I spoke to the doctor's receptionist, who said she could get us in the next day at ten.

When I finished my call with the doctor's office, Ray said, "Come look at this case."

I scooted my chair over. It was a temporary restraining order issued by the District Court in Honolulu, which handled such orders when the parties were not related, dating partners or roommates. The petitioner was a thirty-eight-year-old man named Jasper Kita, who resided in Sunset Beach on the North Shore. The respondent, or accused, was Brian Hartman, a few years younger, with a Kahuku address.

In the section of the form indicating the relationship between the parties, Kita indicated that he had been hired as catering manager at the Turtle Bay Resort a year before, where he became Hartman's supervisor. Hartman was resentful and indicated on numerous occasions that he should have received the position. Over time, the resentment escalated into threatening comments.

On several occasions Hartman had physically assaulted Kita, including pushing and shoving. Kita believed that Hartman was responsible for slashing the tires on Kita's vehicle, and for the theft of various personal items at work. Kita regularly wrote up corporate complaints against Hartman, and after six months of the behavior Hartman was fired.

Subsequent to his termination, Hartman had visited Kita's residence and made additional threats, calling him, among other things, a mixed-race bastard. At that point Kita had requested the Temporary Restraining Order, which had been granted.

"You think this guy could have widened his net?" I asked Ray. "Started to go after other people like Kita?"

"Certainly worth looking into. And what do you know? Our buddy Rizaldo Amador took the initial complaint."

Ray called Amador and got his voice mail. He left a message asking Amador to look into Brian Hartman.

When he finished, I said, "I think we ought to consider any religious groups that are preaching this kind of racial separation."

"That's going to be tough," Ray said. "Most churches I know of are pretty welcoming. At ours we've got a big Korean population, which you know, as well as a few Chinese Catholics, some African-Americans—all kinds of people."

"The Mormons are out there recruiting," I said. "Like Haley Walsh said, they have converts from all different cultures. The only group I know who don't like to let outsiders in are the Jews. My friend Karen Gold—you know, the one from Social Security? She married a guy who wasn't Jewish and he decided to convert. They made him go through a whole long process, including that ritual circumcision."

"Muslims?" Ray asked. "They can be pretty insular."

"The rhetoric we've been reading comes from the Bible, not the Koran," I said. "Maybe one of those Apostolic churches?" I turned back to my laptop and did a quick search. "There are nearly two dozen of them in the state. Some don't have websites, though."

We split them up. One of the ones I got was jesusisonhisway. org, and I got a kick out of the creativity of the name. But that church was clearly welcoming to people of different races, as were all the others we found sites for.

By the time we'd gone through them all, Ray said, "The whole world is getting less tolerant. Must be one of those cycles. Look at what's happening in the Middle East, Muslims killing other Muslims because they disagree about some point of liturgy. Parents are still kicking out gay kids. And people still use ethnic slurs without even thinking about it."

Because Hawai'i is so multicultural, I took for granted that everyone felt the way I did, that the more cultures you could be part of, the better. Most of my friends had a mix of different backgrounds, and it was common to go to a luau when I was a kid and be able to choose between everything from poke, a salad of greens and raw fish, to Jell-O molds in pink or bright green.

But clearly there were still people on the island who resented that kind of blending, and were willing to take action against it. "We'll have to raise our kids differently," I said.

"You think we can make a difference that way, when there's so much hatred all around us?"

"I think we have to try," I said. "And locking up the lunatics who burned down that day care center will be a good start."

We left Kaneohe and drove to Honolulu, where I dropped Ray on North King Street near the Queen's Medical Center. As long as I was close to Waikiki, I thought I'd see my parents. It was late in the afternoon by then, and I knew they'd be home.

I knew by the roads between downtown and Waikiki by heart—I had begun my career as a patrol officer in Waikiki, lived there for years and surfed breaks from Ala Moana to Makapu'u Point, even spent a year as a detective based in the Waikiki substation in an ill-fated experiment in community policing.

The building where my parents had bought a condo was a few blocks from the beach, in a quiet part of the neighborhood overlooking Diamond Head. I checked in at the front desk and verified that I was on the approved visitors' list, then rode up to the thirtieth floor. The elevator seemed to sway in the wind, which was not very reassuring.

I had a key to my parents' condo but because I hadn't been planning on this visit I hadn't brought it with me. It was weird having to knock on their door; even after I moved out, I'd always walked into our old house as if I still lived there.

My mother answered and looked me up and down as if she didn't know who I was. "May I help you?"

I flashed my new badge. "FBI, ma'am. I need to ask you and your husband a few questions."

I leaned down and kissed her cheek and she laughed. My mom was about five-eight, but compared to my brothers, my father and me, she seemed tiny. At seventy, her once flawless skin had begun to wrinkle and her black hair was streaked with gray, but I could still see the beautiful young woman she had been.

"Your father's napping," she said. "Come inside and I'll wake him."

"Let him sleep," I said, following her to the living room. The view of Diamond Head and the ocean through the sliding glass doors was magnificent, and I recognized the furniture and family photos from my parents' house. "I was passing by and thought I'd drop in and see my favorite parents."

"Your only parents," she said, with a snort. "And how are my grandchildren? Do you have any new pictures?"

"Nothing I haven't already emailed to you," I said.

"We haven't had a new keiki in this family in years. I want as many pictures as you can take. Owen looks just like you when you were a baby."

I thought both kids looked more like Winston Churchill than Mike or me, but I'd already said that to my mother, who had pooh-poohed the idea. The four of us had decided we were going to take our co-parenting as far as we could. Several of Cathy's eggs had been fertilized with sperm donated by both Mike and me, and then Sandra had carried the babies to term. We didn't know whose sperm had fertilized which egg, and we didn't want to know.

"Aren't you working out in Kapolei?" my mother asked. "What are you doing way over here?"

I sat on the floral-print sofa and resisted the urge to rest my feet on the glass-topped coffee table. I explained how we'd been up on the Windward Shore, then how I'd dropped Ray downtown. "We're working two cases—an arson in Kahuku, and some nasty letters sent to a senator and somebody threw white paint on his daughter."

"That's terrible," my mother said. "I thought we put all that hatred behind us years ago. When you were at Punahou we all got along, didn't we?"

"I remember you were always up there volunteering with Terri's mother," I said. Terri Clark, Harry Ho and I had been inseparable friends at Punahou, and we were still close years later. "You two certainly got along."

"I remember those days," she said. "Virginia Clark is still one of the nicest women I know." She thought for a moment. "What was that club you belonged to where you celebrated all those holidays?" my mother asked. "I was always baking something for those parties."

"That was the Pan-Asian Society." We were a mixed bag of kids from Asian and Pacific Islander backgrounds. We'd protested against tuna fishing and North Korean autocracy, and celebrated everything from the Vietnamese New Year to *keiro no hi*, a Japanese ritual of longevity and respect for the elderly when we visited nursing homes.

One of the quirks of membership in the Pan-Asian Society was that each of us had to choose a name related to our ethnicity, and I'd used my grandfather's first name, Daisuke.

An idea about ethnic names began ticking at the corner of my brain and I struggled to make the connection. Then I remembered that the letter to the Habermans had included the Hindi middle names for both kids. What if Jessica and her brother had joined the club, and used those names? That might have been how the letter writer discovered it.

While my mother talked about those old days with Terri's mother, I pulled out my phone. I was going to search for that club, but instead I simply Googled "Jessica Haberman Punahou."

One of the links on the first page of results led to a Facebook page for the Pan-Asian Society, and I discovered it was no longer an official club at Punahou, replaced by groups specifically for Japanese, Polynesian and other specific ethnicities.

But the group still lingered unofficially, with a public page. I was able to see all their messages and a database file that listed all members, who included Jessica Annisa Haberman and Michael Abhay Haberman. So all the letter writer needed was a web browser, and the idea that knowing such a personal piece of information would be threatening.

"How is Dakota doing at Punahou?" my mother asked as she returned the conversation to the present. "Is he able to keep up?"

"He's a smart kid," I said. "We've been more worried about the social aspect, but it seems like he's making friends." I looked at my watch and realized that Dakota would still be at Punahou, and texted him that I'd pick him up when his last club meeting was over. It would be rush hour, and with him in the car I'd be able to take the HOV lane—not that it moved all that much faster than the regular lanes.

"I should get moving," I said to my mother. "Let me go in and see Dad."

The carpeting was plush and muffled my footsteps as I walked into the master bedroom. My father was asleep, and I was startled at how old he looked. His cheeks were sunken and his sparse dark hair showed pink scalp beneath it. His hands and arms were mottled with black and blue marks.

"What's all this?" I asked quietly to my mother, motioning to the bruises.

"I'm not torturing him, if that's what you're thinking. It's the blood thinner he takes for his heart. All I have to do is press down on his skin and it leaves a mark."

In his sleep, my dad gasped for breath a couple of times and I looked at my mom. "He does that a lot," she said. "I give him oxygen treatments twice a day."

My father had been such a vibrant presence in my life. He was tall and strong, and in his youth he was a talented surfer. He had a big personality, a good heart and a bad temper. I owed so much of who I was to him. And I was depending on him to be a doting grandfather to my kids, the way he'd done to my nieces and nephews.

My mother walked back out to the living room and I stood there for a while, watching my father breathe, as if just by being with him I could transfer some of my strength to him.

I left a few minutes later and drove up to the Punahou campus. As I got close, I saw Dakota slumped against a tree, his earbuds in his ears, intent on his phone. I pulled up beside him and he didn't notice me, so I honked the horn.

He jumped, and one of his earbuds fell out. I snickered.

"Your tutu says hello," I said, when he climbed into the Jeep.

"My who-who?"

"You know what I mean. I went to see my parents this afternoon and my mom asked about you."

"Your parents aren't my grandparents," Dakota said. "My Nonna and Poppa are back in New Jersey."

"Nobody says you can't have multiple grandparents." I resisted the impulse to say that his Nonna and Poppa hadn't stepped up when their daughter, Dakota's mother, had been sent to prison. They hadn't come to Honolulu to see her, or to look after Dakota, or even offered a plane ticket back to Jersey and a home with them.

"Whatever," he said, and he slouched against the car door.

By the time we got home, Mike had returned from Kahuku and was heating up a huge pan of frozen lasagna for dinner. After we finished eating, Dakota retreated to his room once again, and Mike and I lounged on the sofa together. "You find anything interesting after Ray and I left the day care center?" I asked.

"Nothing worth mentioning. I went back to the office and looked through the database to make sure I wasn't dealing with a serial arsonist."

"Remind me what you look for," I said. I stretched out and rested my feet in his lap. It was his turn to give me a foot rub.

"There are four main reasons why people set fires," Mike said. He held up his hand to tick them off. "Revenge, financial gain, covering up another crime, or pyromania. Amador is talking to all the parents who use the day care center, including the ones who don't take their kids there anymore. He's also got somebody looking into Haley Walsh's finances to make sure she wasn't trying to collect on her insurance."

He began massaging the ball of my foot, and I groaned with pleasure. "There was no evidence of any other crime, right?" I asked. "No dead bodies, no stolen goods?"

"Nothing we could find. Which leaves us with a pyromaniac—

somebody who has a compulsive need to see something burn." He sighed. "That's the scariest one, because there doesn't have to be a motive, or a connection between the location and the firebug. You never know where the next fire is going to be and all you can do is look for clues in a signature."

I already had a good idea what that meant, but maybe the brainstorming between us would lead to something. "Such as?"

"A serial arsonist or a pyromaniac will follow the same steps, use the same materials, in each fire. You find something that works, you stick with it."

He shifted to my other foot. "Here, it looks like the arsonist used the materials that were on site, which implies a lack of planning. So either it was his first big fire, or it was more of an impulse."

"I'm still thinking about the slogans that were scrawled on the walls," I said, as Mike massaged my toes. "Amador said he's been hearing occasional complaints about racial harassment, but nothing actionable."

That reminded me of the harassment both Peggy and Sarah had experienced. "I almost forgot. When Ray and I spoke to Sarah Byrne at Fields and Yamato, she mentioned that she's going to be singing with a group on Saturday night. You want to go hear her?"

"That's the woman who sang at our housewarming luau, right?" he asked.

I nodded.

"Sure. She has a beautiful voice. Where and when?"

I found the details online. The Beachcombers were going to perform at eight at the Waikiki Bandshell half a block from the Honolulu Zoo in Queen Kapiolani park. It was a concrete semi-circle with rows of seats, and when I lived in Waikiki, I'd often gone there for smaller, informal concerts. People could also bring blankets and chill out on the grass. I asked Dakota if he wanted to go with us, but he had plans with some friends from Punahou.

I was glad he was settling in at school. I had worried that because of his academic deficiencies and his time on the street, including a stint as a teen prostitute, he might have trouble fitting in. But he had knuckled down to school work and seemed to be thriving.

When I finished ordering the tickets, I rejoined Mike on the couch. "I had to drop Ray off downtown after we left Kahuku, so I stopped by to see my parents."

"How are they?"

"My mom's fine. I'm worried about my dad, though. He's on some medication that makes him bruise easily, and he has black and blue marks all over his hands and arms."

"Coumadin," Mike said. "I wouldn't worry about that. It's pretty standard for heart patients, and some have worse bruising than others."

Mike had been a firefighter for years before becoming an investigator, and still kept up his EMT certification, so he sometimes surprised me with his medical knowledge. I was sure that growing up with a doctor and nurse for parents helped.

I turned to the side to look at him. "Do you think we'll be good parents?" I asked.

"Why wouldn't we?"

"Whenever I see Ray with kids, he's so good with them, so natural. He says it was because he grew up around lots of younger brothers and sisters and cousins. But I'm the youngest, and you're an only child. Neither of us ever babysat. And both of us have seen plenty of rotten parents, who don't give a shit about their kids. Look at Dakota's mom."

"She's a selfish bitch," Mike said. "So of course she'd make a lousy mom. But your parents are good people, and so are mine. Because of that, because they cared and worked at it, they were good parents."

"So you think that good people make good parents?"

"I think it's a start," he said. "And you know what? I wouldn't have chosen to spend my life with you if I didn't think you had a good heart."

I reached out, and our hands met halfway between us. "Back at you," I said. "And whatever happens to us, we're a team."

Mike squeezed my hand. "Team Kanapa-Ricca," he said. That was the name we'd coined for our partnership, that incorporated the first parts of both our last names.

"Team Kanapa-Ricca," I said, and squeezed his hand, too.

Ray and I arranged to meet at the Kope Bean in Aiea on Friday morning instead of driving all the way out to the FBI offices in Kapolei and then backtracking. When I walked in, I found him seated at a corner table with two super-sized coffee cups in front of him. "I'm hoping one of these is for me," I said as I slid into the seat across from him.

"A raspberry mocha with whipped cream and mocha drizzle," he said, and tapped one cup with his finger.

"I could get accustomed to this kind of service," I said, as I picked up the cup.

"It's a partnership," Ray said. "You fly, I buy."

It reminded me of my conversation with Mike the night before, and our nickname. Ray was my partner, too, in a different but no less important way. "I was talking about the case last night with Mike and he's looking through his database for arson suspects whose MO matches, but he's hasn't come up with anything yet."

I opened my iPad and hooked up to the VPN. I did a quick search for information on Alan Feldberg, the psychologist we were to meet. He had a PhD in clinical psychology and was vice president of a Tibetan Buddhist meditation center called Kagyu Thegchen Ling, located off the Pali Highway not far from his office.

When I clicked through to the meditation center's site, I saw several pictures of Feldberg with his wife, Tashi, and the resident teachers. Feldberg was a haole in his late fifties, with dark curly hair and a wide, open face. His wife looked typically Tibetan, with oblique eyes and droopy lids, and her upper lip curled to reveal square teeth. I could see where Feldberg's interest in multiculturalism came from, with a Tibetan wife. Many of those in the other pictures were a mix of white, Tibetan, and other races.

We finished our coffees and drove to Feldberg's office, a one-story building with a peaked roof that reminded me of Haley Walsh's day care center. I hoped Feldberg had kept up his insurance.

I recognized Feldberg's wife at the reception desk, where she sat behind a glass window. I showed her my badge and she said the doctor was with a patient, but could see us shortly. "Do you know anything about the harassment the doctor reported?" I asked her.

"I saw the graffiti." She had a heavy accent, made even more difficult to understand by the glass between us. "Very bad. I tell my husband to call police but he didn't want to. He say they will not do anything. And they don't."

Her phone rang, and I retreated to sit beside Ray. Several panoramic photos of Tibet had been hung on the walls, and on the table beside me was a square wooden tray filled with sand and a few small rocks. A tiny rake lay beside it so patients could relax by grooming the sand while waiting for the doctor.

After a few minutes the interior door opened and a diminutive woman who looked Thai came out. A moment later, Feldberg was there to usher us into his office.

"I'm glad that someone in law enforcement is still pursuing this," he said, as we sat down. "Though we haven't had any incidents lately, my wife and I were very upset by what happened."

"We've read the report filed by the investigating officer," I said. "But we'd like you to tell us in your own words what happened." I pulled out my iPad so I could take notes.

"It started with some nasty letters pushed under our front door," he said. "Lots of gibberish about races mixing, how it was against the Bible and so on."

"Did you save any of them?" I asked.

He shook his head. "I tossed them as soon as I could. That kind of negative energy can be very infectious and I didn't want it around."

"Do you remember how many letters you received? How much time passed between receiving them?"

"There were three," he said. "The first one came about a month ago, then there was perhaps a week between each, though I don't think there was any kind of pattern."

"You mentioned in the report that you found some of the wording unusual. Do you remember that?"

He nodded. "Bastards, mongrels, that kind of thing. Forbidden unions, iniquities, profanation."

Interesting, I thought. I flipped over to the photos I had taken of those scorched fragments at the day care center. The fragments "iniqu" and "forb" could match those phrases. "Excuse us for a moment," I said to Feldberg, and I showed the pictures to Ray, who nodded.

"When did you receive the last letter?" Ray asked.

"About a week ago. But then when we came to work on Monday morning someone had thrown a rock through the front door and scrawled graffiti on the outer wall."

All that was consistent with what had happened to Haley Walsh. But at least Dr. Feldberg's office hadn't been burned. "You reported that incident, too," I said.

He nodded. "And the detective promised to alert the officers who patrol the area to keep an eye out. But will that be enough?"

"I'll be honest with you, sir," I said. "I don't know. But we are investigating two cases that are very similar to yours, and so I promise you your incidents won't be ignored."

I was about to get up, but I stopped. "You're a psychologist, Doctor. Can you give us some insight into why somebody would commit this kind of harassment?"

"That's a big question, Detective. Most people who commit hate crimes aren't psychotic, but they display high levels of aggression and anti-social behavior. They often have a history of parental or caretaker abuse and use of violence to solve family problems."

He sighed. "But I think the bottom line is the human desire to find a scapegoat to blame problems on. Look what happened after 9/11—people lashed out at anyone of Muslim or Arabic ancestry."

"But most perpetrators of hate crimes are white males without previous criminal records," Ray said. "Why does that group need to find scapegoats so much?"

"White males historically have occupied a place of privilege in our society, so perhaps they're most likely to lash out when privilege is denied," he said. "But that's speculation."

"What about in this specific situation?" I asked. "These incidents have all targeted mixed-race people and families. What would make someone choose that particular target?"

"You're getting well beyond my range of expertise, Detective. I can't even speculate."

"Fair enough," I said. We gave Feldberg our cards, and asked him to notify us immediately if anything else happened.

Ray called the District 5 station to make sure that Detective Ito, who had investigated the Feldberg case, was in the office. "He's there," he said to me when he hung up. "Let's roll."

As we drove, I asked, "Feldberg wouldn't speculate on what motivates violence against mixed-race people. Will you?"

Ray had an undergraduate degree in sociology and his ability to get into the heads of suspects often balanced out my desire to bull forward with a case.

"I think the scapegoat thing Feldberg mentioned is a big part of it," he said. "And the abuse thing, too. Suppose that you got beaten up by some mixed-race bully when you were a kid. Or sexually abused. Maybe you had a bad teacher or a stepmother or something who fit that profile."

"What about the Biblical references?"

"There's so much in the Bible, you can support any opinion you have. You hate lobster? There's a Bible verse that tells you not to eat it. But so far we haven't turned up any evidence that there's a preacher or a church that's advocating this."

At the District 5 station, Ray slid his badge into the tray below the receptionist's window and asked if we could speak to Detective Ito. She made a phone call, then slid the badge back. "He'll be with you in a moment."

We waited. Philip Ito was a slim Japanese guy in his early thirties with a highly evolved fashion sense. He wore a smartly cut navy blazer, black jeans, and polished loafers. His open-necked shirt was in a blue and black plaid. We shook hands and he led us back to his desk. "What can I do for you?" he asked.

I sat back and let Ray take the lead. He explained about our visit to Dr. Feldberg, and the connections we were starting to make. "Do you have a lot of that kind of incident around here?" he asked.

Ito sat back and toyed with a class ring on his finger. "We get these complaints all the time, you know," he said. "Most of them are just teenagers with time on their hands."

"Let me throw some words out," I said. "You tell me if you've seen them around. Iniquity." He shook his head. "Forbidden unions?"

"Nope."

"How about mongrel?"

He was about to say no again, but then stopped. "We had an incident a couple of weeks ago," he said. "Two people in a pickup truck were cruising past Moanalua Middle School. They threw some water balloons at kids out by the fence at lunchtime. Balloons had some white paint inside, and one of the girls said she heard a boy from the truck call her a mongrel."

"A boy?" I asked. "Any idea how old?"

"I asked her. She said he sounded like a teenager but she couldn't be sure. Nobody got a plate number or recognized the truck. I've had an officer stationed nearby every day since but no repeat performance yet."

"I don't suppose you were able to retrieve any of the

balloons?" I asked. "Process for fingerprints?"

He shook his head. "It was a big mess, and by the time officers arrived on the scene the kids were already in the washroom getting cleaned up. I did send a crime scene team out but they couldn't retrieve any fragments of the balloons."

When we left Ito's office, we got caught in the school zone around the sprawling campus of Dole Intermediate School. "Thank God for pineapples," Ray said as we crept along. "Where would we be without them?"

"If not for a job picking pineapples, my grandfather might never have come over from Japan," I said. "Lots of immigrant groups came here for work. That's why we have such a mixed culture."

"Which someone clearly doesn't appreciate," Ray said.

On the way back to Kapolei, Ray got a call from Rizaldo Amador. He talked for a couple of minutes, then hung up. "Brian Hartman moved back to Massachusetts two months ago," he said.

"If he's out of the running, then we're back to square one," I said. "We have that cork board in our office. Why don't we print a big map of the island and lay out the locations of all the incidents and see if there's a pattern."

Once we were back in the office, I dug up a box of push pins and Ray printed a map. He called out the locations and I stuck pins where they had occurred. We had the Haberman home in Wailupe, the psychologist's office in Honolulu, and the day care arson in Kahuku. "And don't forget that Haley Walsh told us somebody bitched at her when she was with her father," Ray said. "Where was that?"

I looked up my notes. "She just said Laie." As he put a pin there, I added, "And we have the black soldier and his white wife at Hanauma Bay."

Maybe it was thinking about water, but I needed to use the bathroom, so I threaded my way through the labyrinthine hallways to the rest rooms. A tall redheaded woman in a dark green business suit stood beside the door with the skirt-lady on it. She had Chanel sunglasses on her head and what looked like a very expensive watch on her wrist.

"Both occupied right now," she said as I approached. "You new here?"

"Kimo Kanapa'aka, HPD," I said, as we shook hands. "Assigned to the JTTF."

"Katherine Carson, but you can call me Kit. I'm on the High-Intensity Drug Trafficking Task Force."

"You've got your hands full, I'm sure. I can't tell you how many people I've busted who were high on ice."

"Marijuana is on the rebound," she said. "There are pakalolo plantations popping up as fast as we can shut them down, particularly on the Windward Shore."

I thought it would be interesting to see Kit Carson and her high heels tromping through fields of marijuana. "I'm working on a case on the Windward Shore right now," I said. "Racially motivated arson. Have you seen any evidence of that kind of animosity?"

"Most of the people I investigate are scum," she said. "So they have all kinds of problems and prejudices. I can't think of anything right now but if I do I'll let you know."

I thanked her, and after I was finished in the men's room I went back to the list of more minor incidents we had dug up from police complaints and the *Star-Advertiser*. The occasional graffiti, a fight that broke out at a bar in Waimanalo, a few others. I spoke with a woman in Laie who said two haole men in a pickup had yelled epithets at her as she walked along the road between her home and the store where she worked. "That's two similar incidents," I said to Ray, after I hung up with her. "Could be the same guys in the pickup who harassed Sarah Byrne and her boyfriend."

"And it happened in Laie, where Peggy Kaneahe and her associate were bothered," Ray said.

I looked at the clusters of pins. All but a few were on the Windward Shore, from Laie down to Honolulu. "This reinforces the pattern we've already seen," I said. "But we've already checked for anyone with hate crime violations in that area."

"Must be someone who hasn't been caught yet," Ray said. "What if we consider the timing of the incidents?"

The earliest one we found was in early spring, the most recent just a couple of days before. "Is there any pattern to the time of day or day of the week?" Ray asked. "Or are these opportunistic?"

We went back to our data and established that several incidents had occurred on Saturday nights, often involving alcohol—someone got drunk and started making trouble. Not an unusual pattern. All the alcohol-fueled problems had been around Laie.

Most of the witnesses to the incidents had been under the influence, too, so descriptions of the perpetrators were vague. Sometimes there were two men, sometimes three. They were tall, short and of average height. Sometimes they had a woman with them, sometimes not. Many of those described were haole, but there were also a number of Hawaiians and Japanese and mixed-race men mentioned.

No one had been arrested for any of the incidents, probably because none of them was that serious, and because there was little evidence to point to anyone in particular.

"There has been some kind of problem every Saturday night for the last month," I said. "I'm sure there will be something else this weekend."

"But we don't know that the same individuals are responsible for all the incidents," Ray said. "Most of the descriptions are different."

"I know, but I get a bad feeling." I called Rizaldo Amador and asked him to have the local officers keep an eye out for any mixed-race harassment. "Particularly two haole guys in a pickup truck, first three letters of the license plate KTF."

I explained what Sarah Byrne had told me. "I know it's a long shot, but I wanted to let you know."

Amador agreed to add that information to the regular briefings over the weekend, and to let me know if anyone who matched the description was brought in on charges.

Ray looked at the clock. "I don't know about you, but my brain is tapped out for the day. I say we call it quits and start Monday morning with fresh eyes."

"And hope that whatever happens over the weekend isn't too serious," I said.

Roby tackled me as soon as I walked inside the house, putting his big paws up on my chest and trying to lick my face. I hooked up his leash and took him for a walk, and we got home just in time for the arrival of the twins. They lived with their moms, but they came to us for short play dates, and that night, we'd agreed to babysit so that Sandra and Cathy could attend a fancy charity dinner.

Dakota was no fool. He'd already arranged to go home with a friend, then to the movies with a group of kids from Punahou. Cathy delivered the keikis to us around six. She handed Addie to me, then gave Owen to Mike. "Say, Mike, do you think your mom could make some more of that Korean barbecue for us? Sandy's been talking about it non-stop."

"She'd love to. But it wouldn't be ready by the time you come back for the kids."

"Tomorrow, maybe?"

Mike looked at me. "What time are the concert tickets?"

We agreed that if we went over to their house at five, we'd be able to make it to the concert by eight. "That would be awesome," she said, and she kissed each of the babies in turn, then made a quick exit.

As soon as she was gone, Addie started to cry, followed immediately by Owen. I held her up and sniffed. "She's good," I said.

Mike held up Owen. "He's not. I'll change him."

I tried to stick a pacifier in Addie's mouth but she wasn't taking it. I carried her out to the backyard and walked around, bouncing her in my arms and cooing, but nothing worked.

Mike's mother, Soon-O, stepped out the back door and into our common yard. "She's not a ball you can juggle, Kimo. Give her to me."

I handed her over and immediately the little brat shut up. "You rock her gently in your arms," she said. "Not up and down."

She handed the baby back to me, and I was sure Addie was going to start screaming again, but I mimicked Soon-O's movements and my little darling cooed in my arms. "You're a miracle worker," I said.

"It's always easier with grandchildren," she said.

I carried Addie back inside, where we found Dominic Riccardi demonstrating the fine art of baby changing to his son. I noticed a big wet spot on Mike's T-shirt. "The little so and so squirted me," he said. "I called next door but Dad said Mom was out back with you."

Roby sat at attention between his father and his grandfather, as if he was learning about changing diapers, too.

"Pay attention, Michael," Dom said. "Tell Kimo what I told you."

Uh-oh, I thought. I knew Mike hated that tone of voice from his father.

"Baby boys pee as soon as their genitals hit the air," Mike said. "And because of their position, the pee squirts up. So we should hold the old diaper over him until he finishes."

"Exactly," Dom said. "Smart boys like you. I can't imagine why you haven't figured that out yet."

"Neither of us went to medical school, Dad," Mike said.

Soon-O laughed, but Dom said, "You don't need a medical degree. Just common sense." He finished putting the new diaper in place and handed Owen to Mike.

"Come on, Dominic," Soon-O said, taking his arm. "Let's leave the boys alone."

"Don't go!" I said. "Stay. We'll make dinner. You'll get to know your grandchildren."

"Sorry, we have plans," Dom said. "Dinner at Le Pavilion, and then that new James Bond movie."

"You're leaving us?" Mike said plaintively.

"You'll be fine," Soon-O said. "When you were born, I had your Nonna looking over my shoulder giving me that *malocchio* every time you cried."

The malocchio was Italian for evil eye, and I'd heard many stories of the clash between Soon-O and her mother-in-law. "Before you go, Mom," Mike said. "Do you think you could make some bulgogi tomorrow for Sandra?"

"For the mother of my grandchildren? Of course."

She and Dom walked out the front door, and I said to Mike in a low voice, "You watch. These kids are going to start crying as soon as they're gone."

But they didn't. With Roby dancing around us, each of us carried a baby to the living room, where we sat beside each other on the sofa. Roby sprawled protectively in front of us, and we cuddled the babies until they fell asleep. "Now what?" Mike murmured, over their gentle gurgles. "We haven't had dinner."

"We starve," I said. "For as long as these kids sleep."

I looked down at the two of them and wondered how we could keep them both safe from all the terrible dangers around us.

My brothers and I, and Mike, had grown up safely. The only times I had been physically threatened had come because of my job. But sometimes those threats had bled over to my family. Haoa had nearly been shot protecting me once, and after I had introduced my mother to a young woman who desperately needed parenting advice, the baby's daddy had held a gun to my mother as she tried to help.

Should I quit my job in order to keep the babies out of harm's way? That wouldn't matter; I'd seen plenty of innocent people and their children end up in mortal danger. Then Addie started to cry and I couldn't worry about abstract threats any more. I had a real baby to deal with.

For the rest of the evening, Mike and I were constantly on the run, looking after one baby or the other. Addie and Owen had spent nine months together in the womb, which apparently had resulted in a desire to do everything they could to be different. When she wanted to sleep, he wanted to play. When he wanted to eat, she needed her diaper changed. It was enough to make both Mike and me crazy.

Roby insisted on being underfoot, following one or the other of us between kitchen and living room and bathroom. "On the bright side, we could have had triplets or quintuplets," I said. "Golden retrievers have litters of eight to ten puppies."

"If Sandra hears you comparing her to a dog, you're dead."

By the time Sandra and Cathy returned, we had finally gotten the babies to sleep, but we were exhausted. "I don't know how you manage," I said, as I opened the door. Sandra had always been a stocky gal, but her charcoal-gray business suit had begun to hang loose on her. Her dirty blonde hair, always perfectly coiffed in a no-nonsense pageboy, was longer than I'd ever seen it, and needed a good trim.

Cathy wore a very chic little black dress with rhinestone spangles, and black high heels that brought her up a couple of inches. Roby tried to jump up on her but Mike called the dog to him.

Sandra and Cathy headed straight for the crib in the center of the living room, where both babies dozed like little angels. Within a few minutes after they'd all left, Dakota returned, as if he'd been hiding somewhere in the neighborhood waiting for the coast to be clear.

Mike and I stumbled up to our bedroom, but before we went to sleep we compared notes on our cases. "I went by the hospital this afternoon and put up flyers," he said. "I figured that since the day care center is just down the street, and a lot of staff take their kids there, somebody might have seen something. I put down Amador's information as well as mine."

"Good idea," I said. "There are probably too many people going in and out for Amador to do an effective canvas. I spoke to him this afternoon and asked him to keep an eye out this weekend for any incidents."

Saturday morning, I took Roby for a long walk around the neighborhood, then made breakfast for myself and Dakota. "I need some exercise," I said to Dakota, as we ate. "You want to go surfing with me?"

"I'm going over to Dylan's to hang," he said.

"The one you've been Instagramming with? Do you like him?" I asked.

He shrugged.

"You know you can be honest with us, right, Dakota? Mike and I already know everything you've done and we still love you. Nothing's going to change that."

"I hate it when you get mushy," he said, looking down at the remains of his omelet.

"Haters gotta hate," I said, and he snorted. "You probably know more about sex than I do, so I'm not going to lecture you. Just be careful."

"We aren't having sex," Dakota said, still looking down. "Dylan's a nice guy."

"Nice guys have sex, too. Let me guess. You haven't told him about…you know."

After Dakota's mother went to prison, he had been on the street for a while, and he had survived by turning tricks. Fortunately, he'd been careful, and his last two HIV tests had been negative, putting him in the clear as long as he refrained from risky behaviors.

"And I'm not going to," Dakota said. "So leave it, all right?"

He stood up and started out of the kitchen. "Dakota," I called, but he ignored me.

Had my brothers and I been so dramatic when we were teenagers? I didn't think so. I watched Dakota leave, then cleaned up the kitchen. Roby was sleeping by the sofa, Mike was still in bed, and Dakota was in his room. I left a note for Mike, then tossed my short board into the back of the Jeep and took off.

I'd never surfed the Leeward Coast much before moving in with Mike in Aiea, but when I had the chance I had begun exploring the breaks there. The one called Power Plant was a rocky reef, and at Turtles Reef the waves were hollow, fast and powerful—and my skills were too rusty to attempt it. The crowd at Nanakuli Blackrocks wasn't friendly, so that left me with Nanakuli Tracks. It was a fun break with large waves, and it was easy enough to avoid the sea urchins and the rocks.

A half hour later, I parked and saw swells of four to six feet, and only a half-dozen surfers out on the water. It felt good to be on my own. I loved Mike, Dakota and Roby, and I enjoyed working with Ray. But I needed time by myself.

My short board was six feet long—my height—and I had customized it over the years, working with a board shaper I knew to sharpen the nose and rails and balance it with a good amount of rocker. I changed into my rash guard, a protective spandex shirt, then carried my board down the beach and waded into the surf. The water was a toasty eighty degrees or so and the sun was glinting off the wave tops.

I duck-dived through the incoming tide and paddled out beyond the break. There wasn't much competition, and I took my time, waiting for the right wave. One of the many things I love about surfing is the way it clears my head, pushing aside all my uncertainties and fears, about the case, about my new job at the FBI, about Dakota and the twins.

It was glorious catching that first wave, scrambling to my feet and gaining my balance, riding the crest toward the shore. I managed a couple of shaky turns, then splashed down, turned around, and paddled right back out. Because my board slowed when heading straight, I had to pump it from rail to rail, putting pressure on the board's flex pattern and fins. Then I'd release that pressure by straightening out into my next maneuver.

I surfed for close to an hour then collapsed on the beach to relax and enjoy the sun. Down at the water's edge, a dad was teaching his son to boogie board. How soon would it be before I could start teaching Addie and Owen to surf?

I couldn't remember how old I'd been when my dad first planted my feet on a board and guided me through the last gasp of waves as they hit the shore. But I had a feeling I could surf almost as soon as I could walk or run. I'd spent most of my childhood pestering first my dad, then my older brothers, to take me down to Waikiki or out to Makapu'u Point. As a teen, I'd skipped school with Harry Ho, hitchhiking to the North Shore with our boards.

Those days were gone. I was a responsible adult with a job and a family. But I had to squeeze in some surfing time because it was part of what made me who I was.

I majored in English in college because I loved reading, and because most of the classes were held in the afternoon, so I could surf in the mornings. Without realizing it at the time, I'd gained skills in research, writing and analysis, which had been very helpful to me in my career. Lying there on the beach with my eyes closed, I realized I hadn't been as analytical in this case as I could have been.

I saw a tickertape of words passing in front of me. Iniquity. Profanation. Forbidden unions. Mongrel. Where in the Bible did those words come from? And would that shine any more light on our investigation?

Once my brain was racing forward I had to leave the beach and hurry home, where I pulled up a Bible concordance online and began to search for those words. Iniquity was a general-use synonym for sin, so that didn't help. Nothing useful for profanation or forbidden unions. But after some digging, I came up with some interesting uses of mongrel, in both the Old and the New Testament.

The book of Zechariah contained the following passage: "A mongrel people will occupy Ashdod, and I will put an end to the pride of the Philistines." Bible experts said the book was apocalyptic and prophetic—it seemed to me to be a call to return to worship, banishing outsiders and those whose blood wasn't pure.

Several places, including the Second Book of Kings, referred to "mongrel worship," a mixing of different traditions. In Matthew 10:5, the Samaritans were a "mongrel sort of people, partly Jews, partly Gentiles, a mixture of both." And elsewhere in the Bible, Satan sent demons to earth "Seeking to produce a mongrel, half-human half-demon and thus unredeemable race of men."

"We need to go soon. You'd better get in the shower."

I turned around to see Mike in the doorway. "Sorry, I got caught up in some research."

I saved my results and emailed them to myself so I could add them to the case file. I showered and dressed for dinner and the concert, and then Mike and I drove up to Cathy and Sandra's. They had bought a house a mile away from us, up higher in Aiea Heights, so they could have a yard for the keikis and be close to us, and Mike's parents, for babysitting help.

"I smell something delicious," Cathy said, when she opened the door. She was a tiny little thing, five feet tall and a hundred pounds. She was half haole and half Japanese, the daughter of a military marriage, with sleek black hair that flowed down over her shoulders.

"My mom's bulgogi is the best," Mike said, leaning way down to kiss her cheek.

I walked into the living room, which was lined with bookcases on two sides, with big glass windows looking out to a lush back yard. It was the kind of room I wanted to have someday, such a great combination of literature and nature.

Sandra was sitting on the sofa holding Addie on her left and Owen on her right. "How do you get them to behave so well?" I asked her.

"It's all a sham," she said. "As soon as you walk out the door they'll start screaming."

"Good to know it's not just us."

Sandra had never been what you'd call petite. Though she wasn't tall, about five-six or so, she was built like a linebacker, and it was funny to see the two tiny babies in her lap. "Take one of these little creatures so I can get up," she said, and she handed me Owen. I was worried he'd start crying immediately, but instead he nestled against my shoulder. I leaned down and kissed the top of his head. Mike had been right; all I had to do was see Addie and Owen and I was in love.

Sandra and I put the keikis down for a nap in a crib in the living room, then we joined Mike and Cathy at the table.

"Now this is Korean barbecue," Sandra said, after she'd tasted the first ribs. "Mike, have I mentioned that I love your mother?"

We talked and laughed as we ate. I had known Sandra and Cathy for years, back to the time when I'd begun mentoring a youth group at the GLBT center in Waikiki, where Cathy worked. She had left that job to take care of Sandra and prepare for the arrival of the babies, and also, she said, to work on a chapbook, a short collection of poems.

Our conversation turned to Cathy's work. "Her poems are perfect," Sandra said. "You should hear her read the one about her mother being Japanese and living in Oregon, like it was some kind of exile from her family and her country. It makes me cry."

"Everything makes you cry," Cathy said. "It's the hormones."

In my opinion Cathy's poems were terrific, but she didn't have enough confidence in her work, and hadn't pushed enough to get published. "You need to get your work out there more," I said.

"I know," Cathy said. "Sandy keeps telling me that. I've been pulling together the poems I've had published in literary magazines and journals, and I read a couple at an open-mic night at a bookstore a few weeks before the babies came, and people liked them."

"Except for that one woman you told me about," Sandra said.

"She was a crank," Cathy said. "And the bookstore owner went over to her and made her leave right after she spoke up."

"Somebody criticized you?" Mike asked.

"I have one poem about my parents, how they were different races and different backgrounds and how they had to adapt. She didn't like it. She even called me a mongrel."

That word again. "Tell me more," I said. "Was she haole?"

"What, you're going arrest her for being an asshole?" Sandra asked.

I shook my head. "It's this case Ray and I are working on. I'm collecting data for it." I explained about the threat to Senator Haberman's family and the day care center arson. "Do you remember exactly what she said? Any Bible verses involved?"

"Honestly, I was nervous," Cathy said. "Everyone else in the audience was very nice, and I tried to forget about it as soon as I could."

"Where was this bookstore?"

"Kaneohe," she said.

"Windward Shore," I said. "There have been a lot of similar incidents in that area. Can you call the bookstore? See if maybe that woman is a regular there? If they know her name or anything about her?"

"It was too long ago, Kimo. I'm probably the only one who remembers her."

We talked for a while longer, and then it was time to go. "Thanks for the barbecue," Sandra said. "You're leaving the leftovers, right?"

"I'm smart enough not to take food from a new mother," I said.

The seats up front were sold out by the time I'd gone online to buy tickets for Sarah Byrne's concert at the Waikiki Bandshell, so Mike and I brought a couple of old blankets and a picnic basket of drinks and snacks. We met Ray and Julie just outside the entrance a few minutes before eight.

Julie was a dark-haired beauty an inch or two shorter than Ray, with a shapely figure and manicured nails. Her Philadelphia accent was more pronounced than Ray's, with a few mumbled consonants, but she was smart and deeply compassionate, as he was.

While Mike and Julie were talking, I pulled Ray aside. "I did some research this afternoon on some of the words that have been coming up. They all show up in the Bible, and always in a negative way. I think we need to focus more on religious groups. And I heard another story at dinner." I told him about the woman who had harassed Cathy at the poetry reading.

We followed Julie and Mike to an open space on a slight incline where we could spread out our blankets. The sky was clear and once the lights went down, a star-spangled sky was spread above us.

A spotlight came up on a drum set and a grand piano, and a woman in a long flowing dress walked out to sit behind the keyboard. A skinny hipster guy with a goatee carried a double bass, followed by a young woman with bright blue hair who took her place behind the drums. The last of the group were an older guy with a clarinet and Sarah Byrne in a long sleeveless dress.

The music was lovely and Sarah's voice was pure and clear. The audience applauded after each number, and as an encore the group launched into Israel Kamakawiwo'ole's mashup of "Somewhere Over the Rainbow" and "What a Wonderful World." The lyrics seemed to take on a special meaning to me as Sarah sang, "The colors of the rainbow so pretty in the sky, are also on the faces of people passing by," and I knew that when Bruddah Iz had sung them he was talking about the cultural mix in Hawai'i. If only everyone felt that way.

We stood up for a final ovation, and then after the crowd had filed out we walked down to see if we could catch Sarah and tell her how much we had enjoyed the concert. We spotted the quartet at one edge of the stage, talking to fans, and Sarah waved us over.

"I'm so glad you came," she said, hugging each of us. She stopped with Ray. "I need to get you up there sometime to sing with us."

Ray shook his head. "No way."

"You have a beautiful voice," Sarah said. "Doesn't he?"

Julie threaded her arm through Ray's. "You should hear him sing lullabies to Vinny." She pulled out her phone and pressed a couple of buttons. "I recorded one."

"No, Julie," Ray said, but she wasn't paying him any attention. She held up the phone and Ray's gentle tenor floated out.

"*Stella stellina, la notte si avvicina.*" He continued in Italian for a moment or two.

"My Nonna used to sing that to me!" Mike said. "What does it mean?"

"Star, little star," Ray said. "Something about all the farm animals, and they're all sleeping in their mother's heart."

"It's beautiful," I said. "Can we have a copy of that? We can play it to the twins."

"Absolutely," Julie said. "I'll email it to you."

We said goodbye to Sarah, and walked with Ray and Julie to the parking lot. "See you Monday, partner," I said to Ray, and we all hugged goodbye.

Dakota was home from his date by the time we got there, playing with Roby on the living room floor, and the four of us sat together for a while before going to our rooms. I used the bathroom and when I was finished I found Mike sprawled on the bed, buck naked, his stiff dick waving hello.

"That's a sight I'm never going to get tired of," I said. I shucked my shorts and pulled off my T-shirt and joined him in bed. We rubbed our bodies against each other, and I tangled my hands in his wavy hair and pulled him close for a deep kiss.

Both of us were on fire. Precome leaked from his dick and mine, sweat pooled on our chests, and I was so hard I was afraid my dick would break. I turned on my side and pushed my ass against his dick, and he took the hint. He reached into the bedside table for lube, and quickly I felt the cool burst of liquid at my hole, and then the hot, heavy warmth of him pressing into me.

He wrapped his arms around my chest, moving only his hips in and out, and I matched his rhythm, both of us in perfect sync, the way you can only make love if you know your partner inside and out, know what makes him tick, know the way he moves.

He muttered endearments into my ear, then reached down to fist my dick as his pressure inside me increased. I came before he did; just the touch of his hand against my erection was enough to get me off. He kept rubbing me, though, and I was in exquisite agony front and back, my senses on overload, until he shot off inside me and then slumped against me.

"We've still got it," Mike mumbled. "Even as we're closing in on forty."

Mike was a few months younger than I was, and we were facing that same milestone in a couple of years. "Don't say the F word," I said. "Not until 10:17 p.m. on my fortieth birthday."

"You know the exact time you were born?" he asked.

"Don't you? My mom made a baby album for each of us with all the details. I used to look at them when I was a kid and wonder why there were so many more pictures of Lui and Haoa as babies than me. It wasn't until I was older that my brothers told me I was a mistake, and who wanted pictures of a mistake?"

"You weren't really, were you?"

I shrugged. "My parents always said no. Lui was ten and Haoa was eight when I was born, so it's possible. But my mom told me a few years ago that once my brothers were in elementary school she was lonely and she wanted to have one more baby."

"Here's to loneliness," Mike said. "Let's hope neither of us ever feel it."

The next morning we slept in and woke around ten to the smell of bacon frying. "Where's Roby?" I asked after I yawned.

"I doubt he's the one making bacon. He doesn't have thumbs," Mike said. "Did he wake you to go out?"

"Nope." Roby was on a schedule, regardless of the day of the week. He expected at least one of us up around seven to take him out for a quick pee, then feed him breakfast, then go for a longer walk around the neighborhood.

"Dakota?" Mike asked.

"Roby couldn't wake Dakota if he jumped on the kid's head and peed."

"Gross." Mike pushed me. "Go see what's up."

I pulled on a pair of shorts and walked downstairs. Dakota was standing by the stove with two frying pans on the burners. One had scrambled eggs on a low flame, the other several rashers of bacon. Roby sat on his haunches looking up expectantly.

"Are you feverish?" I asked, only half joking. I couldn't recall Dakota ever getting up before us, and certainly not making us breakfast.

"Roby woke me this morning and I decided to stay up," he said. "Let you guys sleep late." He handed a piece of bacon to Roby, who wolfed it down.

Mike stumbled into the kitchen bleary-eyed, and he and I sat at the table. "Your *petit dejeuner, messieurs*," Dakota said, as he presented us with our food. He was taking French at Punahou and though his accent was terrible his enthusiasm made up for it.

Dakota made a plate for himself and we all ate together. "These eggs are great," Mike said. "Where'd you learn to cook, and why have you been hiding that from us?"

"I can just make breakfast and microwave stuff," Dakota said, between bites. "My mom used to sleep in after her benders, so I learned to make my own breakfast."

It was that kind of occasional comment that broke my heart, thinking of Dakota living with his mom, having to be the grownup when he was still a kid.

"I just kind of wanted to say thanks," Dakota said, looking down at the table. "For taking me in and everything."

I looked at Mike, and my heart skipped a beat. Dakota wasn't very emotional; I guessed that growing up the way he did had convinced him he had to hide what he was feeling. It felt great that he was able to open up to us but I couldn't think of the right words to say to acknowledge that.

"We're the ones who ought to thank you," Mike said. "Bringing you into our ohana was the best decision we ever made. Right K-Man?" He looked over at me and smiled.

I nodded. "I don't think we'd have agreed to be dads with Cathy and Sandra if we hadn't seen how great it was to have you around." Dakota looked down at his plate but I could see he was smiling. "How was your date last night?" I asked.

"It was fun," Dakota said.

"What did you do? Go to the movies?"

He shook his head. "We just hung out and talked. He had turned me on to this book by Carlos Castaneda, which totally blew my mind when I read it. It was awesome to be able to talk to him about it."

"*The Teachings of Don Juan?*" I asked, and he nodded. "I read that when I was in high school. You're not going to take peyote, are you?"

"Get a grip," Dakota said. "It's about an alternate view of reality, you know? All these famous people got into it, like John

Lennon and Federico Fellini. Dylan's parents have all Fellini's films on DVD and we watched *Amarcord* together, about growing up in Italy. It was totally weird but very cool."

A year ago, I thought, Dakota didn't know Fellini from linguine, and here he was watching foreign films and reading Yaqui Indian philosophy. But I always knew he had those abilities inside him.

We finished eating, and Mike and I cleaned up the kitchen while Dakota took Roby out for a long walk around the neighborhood. "How do you go through what he did and come out such a good kid?" Mike asked as he scrubbed the frying pan. "He's a star."

"If we could figure that out and bottle it, the world would be a much better place."

It was a sunny day with a nice trade wind coming off the ocean and sweeping up the hill, so we relaxed in the backyard. Dakota was on the grass reading George Orwell's *1984*, with Roby sleeping beside him. Mike was in one lounge chair with his reading glasses on, catching up on fire journals, and I had my iPad open, playing solitaire, when my phone rang.

I didn't recognize the number but I answered anyway.

"Kimo? It's Rizaldo Amador. We've got a situation up here in the hills outside Laie. Two victims, a man and a woman." His voice cracked and I knew it had to be bad. "They were tied up on wooden crosses."

"Holy shit," I said. "That's awful."

"I thought about you and your investigation because the woman's haole and the man's a dark-skinned Latin, and we're not far from that day care center fire. I've already got a team at the site, but I thought it might be good for you to see the scene yourself."

"I'll call Ray and we'll get up there as soon as we can. Any ID on the victims?"

"Nope. But we're taking prints, and I hope like hell they'll be in the system. This is not a case I want to spend a lot of time on."

I thanked him and hung up, and the horror of what he had told me sunk in. Mike looked at me and must have seen something in my face. "What's wrong?" he asked.

I told him what Amador had said. "There's no ID on the victims, but there's a chance they could be people who've been threatened before." I took a deep breath. "Which means that maybe if Ray and I had worked fast enough they might still be alive."

I called Ray, then picked him up. On the way up to the Windward Shore, he and I talked about how the crucifixion might relate to our case, and I told him that I was worried the victims might be someone we had already talked to.

He shook his head. "None of the people we talked to match those details," he said. "And there aren't that many Latinos around here, so we'd have noticed if one of them was mentioned."

The sun was a fiery gold disc in a clear blue sky, and with the flaps up on the Jeep and the warm breeze blowing past us, we could almost pretend we were on a fun Sunday outing. Except I kept remembering what waited for us, thinking back to how upset Rizaldo Amador had been on the phone. He was a seasoned cop, so the scene had to be pretty bad to affect him.

We drove through Laie, which was very quiet, as many businesses closed on Sunday in deference to Mormon beliefs. We passed Hukilau Beach on the right, and then turned left onto Cackle Fresh Egg Farm Road, following the directions that Amador had texted me. "You'd really have to know this area to find your way up here," I said.

"Anybody live up here?"

"I wouldn't be surprised," I said. "There are lots of people squirreled away into these ridges, living off the grid."

"Raising marijuana?" he asked.

"Could be that, too." I remembered my conversation with Kit Carson and repeated it to Ray as I followed the deep ruts in the ground up a long dirt trail that wound around hills. It was very bumpy and I had to hold on tight to the Jeep's steering wheel. We finally rounded a curve and saw a cluster of police vehicles ahead of us.

"Whoever did this sure picked the back of beyond," Ray said. "Their bad luck the Boy Scouts chose today for their hike."

"I'm sure the Boy Scouts weren't too thrilled, either," I said.

I pulled up on a flat stretch at the bottom of the hill and grabbed my iPad as we got out of the Jeep. Though there were some skinny trees and low scrub on the hillside, the two crosses were very silhouetted against a blue sky dotted with puffy white clouds. From that angle, the sun was behind them, illuminating them with eerie halos.

"Holy Mother of God," Ray said. "Why haven't they taken those bodies down yet? That's not just blasphemous, it's inhuman." He crossed himself and whispered something that sounded like Latin.

Ray and Julie were practicing Catholics, so the sight had to be even more disturbing to him than it was to me. From that distance all we could tell was that the body on the right was female, from the long dark hair, the low-cut dress and the tiny bare feet. The one on the left was male, in a short-sleeved T-shirt, faded jeans and metal-studded boots.

Both the man and the woman had their arms outstretched, tied to the horizontal bar of the cross. Ropes had also been tied around their midsections, and stones had been piled up around the base of each cross to keep it upright. Both of their heads slumped sideways.

It was a gruesome scene, made even worse by the buzz of activity around the site, as evidence techs combed the dirt and took photos. We showed our IDs to a cop at the base of the hill and began to climb. As we got closer, more details became evident. The man's right hand hung awkwardly; it looked like it had been broken. Both the man and the woman had bruises on their faces and arms.

The dirt beneath the crosses was soft and looked fresh. It rained frequently up in the hills, so that meant the crosses had been erected since the last rain, perhaps even just before the bodies were raised. I looked around for deep ruts that would indicate how the lumber had been brought there, but the ground was too disturbed for an amateur like me to tell anything. I hoped that the crime scene techs would find more.

I turned on my iPad and began taking pictures of the area as Ray and I talked through the process of putting up the crosses and mounting the bodies. "How long do you think it would take to build those?" he asked.

I'd spent a lot of time working on my dad's construction projects, so I had a fair idea. "It would be pretty quick to nail a couple of two-by-fours together in the shape of a cross," I said. "If they tied the bodies to the wood on the ground, then they had to dig a pair of holes deep enough to keep the crosses upright. You'd need at least two, maybe three people to do it all." I toed the ground. "The Ko'olau were formed from volcanic eruptions, so the soil here is tough to dig into. You'd need a place where there was a lot of wind-blown soil—hence the top of the mountain."

"So our killers must have a lot of local knowledge," Ray said.

"And a pickaxe for digging, a tool kit and a bunch of two-by-fours."

We spotted Rizaldo Amador on his cell phone. While we waited for him to hang up we looked around. Neither of us wanted to face the two bodies on the crosses.

We walked around the perimeter of the area where the crosses had been built. The wood looked pressure-treated to me, which was interesting, because that kind of lumber was more expensive, used for decks and other areas exposed to the elements. Did whoever put those poor people up there really expect the crosses to stay there for a long time?

Amador joined us. "Scouts left Kahuku at seven this morning for a nature hike through the mountains," he said. "They turned off the Kam around eight, and the first hikers had made it up here by eleven."

I forced myself to look at the two bodies, and take pictures of them. Up close I could see that both of them had suffered knife wounds to the abdomen, though there wasn't a lot of blood in the area, which meant that they had probably been killed elsewhere.

"How come you haven't taken them down yet?" I asked.

"The ME's backed up this morning, and one of their wagons is out of service. Should be here soon, though. In the meantime I had one of the crime scene techs take prints from both of them, and I sent a guy down to the office to see if he can pull up a match from IAFIS." That was the fingerprint database maintained by the FBI, which contained the records of anyone who'd ever been printed. Since the state of Hawai'i had begun requiring fingerprints for drivers' licenses, it was likely we'd get a match.

"You have a cause of death?" I asked. "I hope they weren't still alive when they were hung up there." The thought made me shiver.

"Have to wait for the ME to give us the definite word, but my money's on those knife wounds to the abdomen."

"How do you know that he's Latino?" Ray asked. "Just from skin color?"

"He has a tattoo on his neck in Spanish," Amador said. "Says *Soy Mexicano*. Don't need a genetic test to read that."

Behind us, I heard the rumble of the ME's van climbing slowly over the rough ground. Ray and I turned around to watch their progress as Amador's cell rang. By the time he'd hung up, the ME's techs had parked and begun to unload their equipment.

Amador said, "We got hits on both of them from IAFIS. His name is Rigoberto Flores, born in Mexico but raised in LA. Forty-seven years old, with a long rap sheet. Mostly small time stuff—public intoxication, drug possession, breaking and entering, that kind of thing."

I asked Amador to spell the name and then added it to my case notes. "And the woman?"

"Lina Casco. Forty-two. Born and raised here. Same kind of minor crap on her rap sheet—possession with intent to sell, prostitution. Never served time, though."

The ME's techs set up two ladders and began the process of taking down Lina Casco's body from the cross. Once they had her on a gurney, Ray and I joined Amador to look at her. She was a pretty woman, with delicate features, though I could see that hard living had taken its toll on her. Her hands were marked with what looked like defensive wounds.

The ME's techs bundled her into their van, then returned to take down Rigoberto Flores. As they lifted him off, one of them called to Amador. "Detective, you want to see this." He pointed to the cross, where writing had been hidden by Flores's body.

While Amador climbed the ladder, I zoomed the camera on my iPad to see if I could read what had been written there. "Ezra 10:10," I said to Ray. "Why does that sound familiar?"

I flipped to the file of my case notes and searched. "Holy crap," I said. "It's the same phrase that was in the letter to the Habermans." Amador got down from the ladder and I showed him and Ray.

The Prophet Ezra said, in Ezra 10:10-11, "Ye have transgressed, and have taken strange wives, to increase the trespass of Israel."

I explained the connection to Amador, and he whistled. "A senator? What would these two have in common with a United States senator?"

"That's what we've got to figure out," I said.

"So this connection to the Haberman case means the FBI is going to take over?" Amador asked.

"We'll work together," I said. "You know this area and the people. Ray and I will work on the larger connections. And I know what it's like when the Bureau steps in on a case. I promise we'll try to keep you in the loop on our end."

"Best we can hope for," Amador said.

Ray and I followed the ME's van down the hill. "I say we head back to that Kope Bean in Kaneohe," Ray said. "We can do some research there instead of driving all the way to headquarters downtown or to the FBI office in Kapolei."

I agreed with him, and a half-hour later we had reached the coffee shop. Ray got us Longboard-sized coffees—mocha with raspberry for me—while I set up Ray's laptop and my iPad, initiated the secure VPN software, and connected to the Wi-Fi. I had us both logged in to the police database by the time he joined me.

"I'll take the woman," I said. "Since she's an islander. Maybe I know someone who knows her." I started with Lina Casco's earliest arrest, at age twenty-five, on a misdemeanor drug charge. She'd been released into the custody of her brother, Martin.

Her brother kept popping up. He had posted bond for her. Had vouched for her, enrolled her in a drug rehab program. My brain itched with the idea that I knew him, but I couldn't place him until one of the later cases referred to him as Lieutenant Martin Casco. Then I remembered—he headed up the traffic homicide division at headquarters. I had worked with him a couple of times in the past, but only in the most casual way.

"Take a look at this," I said, shifting my iPad so Ray could see what was on the screen. "You know him?"

"The guy from traffic homicide?"

"Yup. Now we can see how come Lina skipped serving time so often."

"You think Amador knows that already?"

I shrugged and pulled out my phone to send him a quick text. "At least he can notify the lieutenant as next of kin," I said.

Lina's most recent arrest for drug possession had been four years before, and the address she had given matched her brother's home. Rigoberto's last arrest had been around the same time, and he listed a halfway house near the airport. I had a feeling that both of those addresses were out of date. "I wonder if they lived around here," I said.

"I'll check the DMV database, see what they've got."

While Ray logged into that database, I did some more searching on Martin and Lina Casco. "Get this," I said to Ray. "They're twins."

"He's a cop and she's a con," Ray said. "Sounds like the plot for a TV show. Driver's licenses still have those old addresses, but I've got a Kawasaki EL250B 88-95 motorcycle registered to Flores at 55-510 Kamehameha Hwy, number 488. There's a bike registered to Casco at the same address."

I Googled the address, and it came up as the Laie Post Office. "Clever," I said. "You get around the restriction against using a PO box to register by just putting the post office address in."

"So Rigoberto and Lina are doing their best to hide where they live," Ray said. "Which raises a red flag. Were they involved somehow with whoever attacked them?"

"Could be drugs, out there in the hills. Or maybe weapons—makes sense that if whoever's behind this is accelerating they'd need guns."

"There are a lot of loose ends here," Ray said. "Where were they killed? Where are the bikes registered to Rigoberto and Lina?"

"Where did they live?" I added. "Was this a premeditated crime? Having the lumber and the tools handy makes that possible."

Ray shook his head. "Out there in the country people drive pickups," he said. "My brother has one back in the Philly burbs, and he's always got crap loaded in the back."

We kept looking for information for another hour, checking drug busts and known arms dealers, and coming up with nothing. I sat back in my chair and stretched, my coffee long since finished. "I say we quit now, let Amador gather all the information from the crime scene, get the ME's report, and tackle all this tomorrow."

Ray agreed, and we packed up and went back to the Jeep. I plugged my iPhone into the dashboard jack and the soothing slack-key guitar and the soaring vocals of Hapa, one of my favorite groups, filled the Jeep. The group, long-since disbanded, was a mix of natives and transplants and they brought that blend to their music. Probably not that popular with the kind of people who were targeting mixed-race couples and families.

After I dropped Ray at his house, I picked up a bucket of fried chicken for dinner. I told Mike the bare details of the case and then pushed it away, to enjoy the evening with him, Dakota and Roby, and let my questions percolate in the back of my brain.

I caught the late news on KVOL, the station my brother Lui managed. They were the scrappy station in the market, without a network affiliation, and they could be counted on for the most scandalous news. I wondered if they had gotten word of the crucifixions and sure enough, it was the lead story.

"Disturbing news from the Windward Shore leads our report this evening," the anchor began. "Ralph Kim was in Laie this afternoon and he has the story for us. Ralph?"

Ralph was an investigative reporter with the station. When I first came out as a gay cop, he pushed the story on the news, and that made things a lot harder for me. When I'd had to deal with him on subsequent cases, our relationship had been rocky. I didn't like him and didn't trust him, but the nature of our jobs forced us to work together occasionally. Sometimes I had to stonewall him, pushing him off on the police information officers, and other times I used him to leak details that might help in investigations.

The screen switched to Ralph, looking snazzy in pressed khakis and a dark green polo shirt. Behind him, we could see the two crosses still standing, surrounded by yellow crime scene tape.

"Earlier today, a group of Boy Scouts on a hike through the Ko'olau made a horrific discovery." He turned sideways so that the cameraman could zoom in on the crosses. "A man and woman were brutally murdered late last night, their bodies tied to these crosses." The camera backed up and turned. "As they rounded the hill below me, these impressionable young men were shocked with the violence ahead of them. The scout master quickly moved them out of sight and called HPD."

The focus went back onto Ralph. "Police sources refused to comment today, citing the ongoing nature of the investigation."

"Seems like they always say that," the anchor said. "But you'll keep on top of them, won't you, Ralph?"

"You bet I will. There are vicious killers on the loose, and the people of O'ahu deserve to know. KVOL is the place to watch."

"I'm surprised your brother hasn't called you," Mike said when I turned the TV off.

"I'm hoping he doesn't know the Bureau is involved," I said. "But I'm sure Ralph Kim will figure it out eventually and put two and two together."

"See," Mike said to Dakota. "This is why you need to study math. So you can always put two and two together."

"As if," Dakota said.

The next morning Ray and I sat down with Salinas to bring him up to speed on what we had. "The same language was used in the letters to the Habermans, the graffiti scrawled on the wall at the day care center in Kahuku that was burned, and the crucifixions of Rigoberto Flores and Lina Casco," I said.

"What do you mean, same language?" Salinas asked.

Ray explained about the Bible verses.

"Have you been investigating the religious angle?" Salinas asked. "Any groups out there preaching this kind of nonsense?"

"We did some preliminary searching," Ray said. "Couldn't come up with any viable suspects, though we didn't dig that deeply."

"Sounds like a good direction for you to take," Salinas said. "Tell me more about the two crucifixion victims."

I told him what we knew, which wasn't much. "We need to liaise with Detective Amador this morning and see what his crime scene techs came up with, and then get the ME's report."

"Let's try and keep the connection to the Habermans hushed up for now," Salinas said. "I don't need the pressure of a U.S. Senator breathing down my neck."

We agreed and went back to our office, where I called Amador and put him on speaker so Ray could hear, too. "The ME did an inventory of their stomach contents, and two things jumped out at me," he said. "Fiddlehead ferns and tempura batter. My wife is a vegetarian, so I know that a couple of restaurants up here prepare tempura-fried fiddleheads. I sent out guys to canvass everywhere I knew sold them, and we got a hit at a rundown place, more like a shack than a real bar, in Hauula. They don't cook much, but they serve the fiddleheads as snack plates."

He took a breath. "Bartender ID'd them both, said they were there on Saturday night and got into an argument with three haoles."

"Some kind of religious beef?" I asked.

"Bartender wasn't sure how it got started, but the haoles were talking stink about what a pretty haole woman was doing with a wetback. Apparently a couple of punches got thrown, and the bartender kicked them all out."

"He know the haoles?"

"Nope. Says he never saw them before. Gave us the names of some of the regulars, and none of them recognized the haoles either. One guy said that he noticed a pickup in the parking lot with some two-by-fours sticking out the back, little red flag hanging from them like they'd just come from the lumberyard. Didn't get a plate, though."

"Both Flores and Casco had motorcycles registered. You find either of them?"

"Nope. And the registration address was the Laie post office. I have an evidence team going out to the bar's parking lot to look for traces of blood. That might turn out to be our crime scene."

Ray leaned toward the phone. "Has the ME determined cause of death?"

"He says the knife wounds killed them. I'll email you the report."

"Martin Casco give you anything?" I asked.

"Nah. Didn't know his sister was dating Flores, didn't know where she was living."

"Ray and I have worked with him in the past. You want me to give him a call, see if I can get anything more from him?"

"Be my guest."

Amador said he had guys canvassing businesses in Laie with photos of Flores and Casco, to see if anyone recognized them and knew where they lived.

By the time we hung up, Ray had Martin Casco's extension at headquarters on his screen, and I dialed it. I told him that I was sorry for his loss, and explained about the case Ray and I were working, and how we'd heard about his sister's death. "I was hoping we could talk to you, see if you can add anything. I can relay what you say back to Rizaldo Amador, and keep you in the loop as much as I can."

"I'd appreciate that. You're not here at headquarters anymore?"

"Nope, we're on assignment to the FBI's JTTF in Kapolei. But we can come in and meet with you."

"Not here, though," he said. "I'd rather keep my family business off premises. How about lunch in Chinatown? Little Village, twelve-thirty?"

I agreed and hung up, and then Ray and I read the autopsy reports on Lina Casco and Martin Flores. Doc Takayama had conducted the autopsies on Sunday afternoon, a very quick turnaround, probably due to the high-profile nature of the crucifixion. He was a smart guy, very politically astute, and I was sure he'd seen the need to do the job personally.

Flores had died from a deep abdominal cut that transected the descending aorta. There was a downward angle to the cut, which implied that the assailant was slightly taller than Flores. And the angle indicated a right-handed person.

Lina Casco had also died from a knife wound, this one to her right inner thigh, which transected the femoral artery and vein. She was fairly petite and the wound was in her leg, so the downward angle of the cut was more pronounced, but in her case the twist was in the opposite direction, which meant she'd been cut by a leftie.

Two different knives had been used. Both had a stainless steel blade of approximately three inches, with a drop point and a serrated edge. The one wielded by the right-hander had been used much more than the other, which accounted for the difference in the cuts. Doc Takayama speculated that both were relatively inexpensive automatic knives, or what others could call switchblades.

Such knives were common all over the island, often carried in a pocket for a multitude of uses. The precision of these cuts implied someone who was very familiar with handling knives.

I called the ME's office and spoke to his cheerful receptionist, Alice Kanamura. "Howzit, detective?" she asked. "We don't have a case on the docket with your name on it. What can I do for you?"

"I'd like to speak to Doc about the crucifixions," I said. "He available?"

"He's in his office doing paperwork, though I'm sure he'd rather be cutting up bodies. Please hold."

I put the call on speaker, and Doc came on the line a moment later. "I knew this was going to be a hot one," he said. "Already spoke to the chief of detectives, and the woman's brother, a lieutenant from Traffic Homicide."

"What can you tell us that didn't go into the report?" I asked.

"You know me, Kimo. My middle name is thorough."

"Sure. Paul Thorough Takayama, MD," I said. "Any idea as to who was killed first?"

"Because of the nature of the wounds, I'd postulate that the man was killed first, perhaps impulsively, with a sharp force injury to the stomach. It's hard to pinpoint the artery there, so that means either the killer was lucky, or very knowledgeable about anatomy, with excellent reflexes that allowed him to pinpoint that artery without having to think about it. Flores had no defensive wounds, which implies that the killer took him by surprise. The woman's cut was more planned."

"What do you mean?"

"When I was in medical school, one of my anatomy instructors called hers a "butcher block cut," supposedly because it's an occupational hazard of meat-cutters. You lose control of your knife, cut yourself in the thigh, and you're done. Someone accustomed to butchering meat would know about that kind of wound and how deadly it is."

"But she was fairly short," I said. "Wouldn't that mean the assailant had to lean way down to cut her there?"

"The angle and position of the bruises on both her wrists implies that someone significantly taller than she was held her up from behind, and the second assailant leaned down and slashed her thigh."

"Any trace evidence from the killers on either of the bodies?" I asked.

"I bagged their clothing and sent it for forensic analysis," he said. "I'll let you know if anything comes up."

"There was very little blood in the area where the bodies were found," I said. "Wouldn't wounds like the ones you've described bleed a lot?"

"Absolutely. If there's no blood where the bodies were found, that's not your crime scene."

"Wouldn't the killers be drenched in blood from wounds like that?" Ray asked.

"Not necessarily. The precision of these cuts implies that the killers knew what they were doing, so they might have been able to anticipate the spurt of blood and pivot away."

That was all Doc had to offer, so I thanked him and hung up.

"I wonder what they did with the bike," Ray said. "If we assume that Lina and Rigoberto went to the bar on at least one of the motorcycles registered to them, then whoever killed them had to dispose of the bike."

"Bike like that's got to be worth some money. You could dump it somewhere but somebody who's willing to kill might have the contacts to get rid of it and make a profit."

While Ray put out an alert on the bike using its description and VIN, I called a couple of informants we had used in the past, asking them to be on the lookout for a hot bike, and then we left for lunch with Martin Casco. I hoped he'd have some clues as to where his sister was living and who she was involved with that might lead us to her killers.

"My sister was always a wild child," Martin Casco said. "My parents used to say that I must have done something in the womb to steal all the sense from her. Made me feel guilty as hell."

We were sitting at a rear table at Little Village, on the edge of Chinatown. It was a hole in the wall, with fluorescent lights and the only decoration some posters of China. It smelled like decades of soy sauce and ginger, overlaid with a chemical cleaner, and the food was only average.

The place was often favored by cops and attorneys, because the tables were far apart, the tinny Chinese music covered the sound of conversations so that no one could eavesdrop, and the waitresses all pretended to speak only enough English to take your order.

A dish of cucumber pickles sat in front of us, and I picked one up and nibbled on it. "When did she first start getting in trouble?"

"As soon as she could crawl." He was a stocky guy with a five o'clock shadow. The collar of his white shirt was worn and he looked tired. "But the first time cops were involved was when we were fifteen and she shoplifted lingerie from a store at Ala Moana."

The plump Chinese waitress, in a red uniform with a huge white fake flower on her lapel, brought us cups of steaming wonton soup.

Casco said, "My dad was a cop, so he made things go away. Now that I look back on it, that was a mistake."

We sipped our soup. It wasn't as good as my godmother's, but it was okay.

"I wonder if my dad had let her take her lumps back then, things might have turned out differently," Casco said. "But I doubt it. I know Lina inside and out, and she just doesn't care what she does, who she hurts."

"That must have been tough on your parents." I knew how much my parents had suffered each little thing my brothers and I had done wrong.

"Sent my father to an early grave, I'm sure," Casco said. "Even though on some level he knew Lina was trouble, it still destroyed him when she got caught dealing ice a couple of years ago. I don't think he'd stopped thinking of her as daddy's little girl until then. I was able to pull some strings, get her into rehab. Right before he died he told me that I had to look after my sister."

He shrugged. "Like he had to tell me. I've been looking after her all my life." He choked back a sob. "I finally failed her."

I shook my head. "You didn't fail her at all. Like you said, she was who she was, and nobody could change that but her."

I couldn't help thinking about Addie and Owen. How would they turn out? Would they be identical, or opposites like Martin and Lina? Or somewhere in between?

We finished our soup in silence. The waitress returned with platters of catfish fillets in ginger and green onions for me, clams in lemon sauce for Casco, and General Tso's chicken, extra spicy, for Ray.

"When did she get into motorcycles?" Ray asked once Casco had composed himself.

"Couple of years ago," Casco said. "After her last stint in rehab. She said she was going straight, that she'd met a new guy who was into bikes and he was teaching her how to repair them."

"Rigoberto Flores?" I asked.

"Never met him. I'll be honest, when I stopped getting calls from lockup about Lina, I was glad, and I didn't press her. I thought she was turning her life around."

"She may have been," Ray said. "She had no arrests for the past three years. Could be she was just in the wrong place at the wrong time."

"You don't know my sister," Casco said. "But that's a good

way to think."

"You know where she was living?" I asked.

He shook his head. "I had the feeling from things she said that she was up in the Ko'olau, with that guy, off the grid. We talked once or twice a year. One of us called the other on our birthday. Even if she switched phones or numbers, she let me know how to reach her."

"Your sister didn't have any personal property with her when she was found," I said. "That's why we had to identify her by her prints. Have you tried her phone? If it's still on, the phone's GPS might help us find the crime scene."

"She called me Saturday night, late, but I'd already gone to sleep so the call went to voicemail, but she didn't leave a message. Detective Amador asked me for the number. I'm assuming he tried it."

Once he'd spoken I had a feeling that Martin Casco agreed with something my father had always said, that when you assume, you make an ass of you and me. Casco pulled out his phone and pressed a couple of buttons. It rang twice, and I heard a woman say, "Is this your phone?"

Casco held the phone out so that all three of us could hear. "It's my sister's," he said. "Who's this?"

"My dog found this phone in the bushes near our house. The ground's all torn up there—looks like a bad accident, but I didn't know what to do to get the phone back. Is your sister okay?"

"May I come up and get my sister's phone, ma'am?" Casco asked.

"Sure." She gave him an address and he wrote it down. He thanked her and hung up.

"I guess you guys should do this," he said, pushing the piece of paper towards us.

"We'll call Amador and meet him there," I said. "My guess is that dog might have found the crime scene."

Martin Casco insisted on paying for lunch. Ray plugged the

address into my GPS, and we took off for the Windward Shore. As I drove, Ray called Amador and told him what we'd learned, and we agreed to meet at the home of the woman who'd found the phone.

We turned left onto a narrow two-lane road just beyond Hauula, only a half mile or so beyond the bar where Flores and Casco had been drinking. Amador's car was parked in the driveway of a white ranch-style house, and I pulled in behind him.

Amador stood beside a short Hawaiian woman with a dark ponytail, pregnant and looking the way Sandra did when she was about to deliver. Her dog was a female with a lot of black lab in her, and she was eager to sniff Roby on me.

Mary Makao had already turned the phone over to Amador. "My doctor wants me to exercise so I walk Pua a lot," she said. "Here girl, let's go for a walk."

The dog romped over to Mary, who bent down with effort to hook up her leash. We walked outside. It was bright and sunny, but there was a stiff trade wind coming in off the ocean. Mary's was the last house on the road; beyond it was scrub and the occasional cluster of trees.

The dog led the way up the street a few hundred yards. There was no swale, just dirt and clumps of molasses grass topped with wheat-like stalks and tiny pale orange flowers. Mary pointed ahead of us to a couple of rough-barked ironwood trees surrounded by weeds. "It was in there," she said. "Pua picked it up and brought it to me."

"Thank you, ma'am," Amador said. "We'll take it from here."

"If you go much farther down the road, be careful," she said. "I think there's a dead animal up there. Pua went crazy on Sunday morning and I smelled blood in the wind."

I looked at Ray. Could the blood be human? Amador must have had the same idea because he said, "I'm going to call for a crime scene team to meet us out here."

It wasn't possible to see any tracks in the pavement, but as we walked down the road, I spotted a long, deep rut in the dirt with the look of a single track of a motorcycle. Farther ahead the track veered into another patch of molasses grass, the pale flowers flattened in a circular pattern that implied the bike had spun out of control.

"That blood the dog smelled has to be here somewhere," I said. The three of us walked around with our heads down until I stopped suddenly as I spotted dark brown stains in the flattened grass.

There were no other vehicle tracks in the molasses grass but it did look like several different sets of feet had walked through it. We backtracked carefully, doing our best not to contaminate the scene.

"The bartender says he kicked Casco and Flores out of the bar around eleven o'clock," Amador said. "The techs I sent out to comb the parking lot found some shards consistent with a vehicle taillight. Looks like the damage had been done recently, because the shards were close together."

"So the fight spilled out into the parking lot, and somebody's taillight got smashed," I said. "Flores and Casco took off on the bike, most likely with the other vehicle in pursuit."

Ray picked up the thread. "Whoever was driving the bike spun out back there in the grass. Looks like they abandoned the bike and ran for the cover of these trees."

We had made our way back to the road by then, and ahead of us I spotted what looked like heavy boot prints leading back toward the trees. "Looks like whoever was chasing them continued on foot," I said, pointing at the prints.

"Confrontation over there where the blood is," Ray said. "If it was the three guys from the bar fight, then they killed Flores and Casco here."

"Why not just leave them here?" Amador asked. "Turn the pickup around and get away. Why take the bodies to that hill and mount them on the crosses?"

"These are guys who aren't scared of getting caught," I said.

"They wanted to make a statement. They wanted us to find Flores and Casco and see that Bible verse on the cross."

Amador shook his head. "Crazy shit."

"The guys had to have been driving a vehicle big enough to hold the two bodies," I said. "Didn't you say someone saw a pickup at the bar with lumber sticking out the back?"

Amador nodded.

"So if we find a pickup with a broken taillight we can check for blood in the back."

"They had to do something with the motorcycle, too," Ray said. "If it was drivable one of them could have ridden it, or they could have thrown it in the back with the bodies."

Amador was taking notes furiously as we spoke. By the time the crime scene techs had arrived, we had spun out our theory. It was full of conjectures, but that's the purpose of police work, to find the evidence that proves or disproves those ideas.

The road past Mary's house continued on up into the hills, and I wondered why Flores and Casco had turned onto this road. Did they live up in the hills? Or were they trying to get away from someone chasing them?

"You mind if Ray and I take a ride up the hill while the crime scene team works?" I asked Amador. "See what's up there?"

"Go ahead. I'm going to be tied up here until these guys finish."

We walked back to Mary Makao's house. She was sitting on the porch with the dog. "Did you hear anything late Saturday night?" I asked her.

"The other detective asked that. No, we go to bed real early. But I told him I'd ask my husband."

I pointed up the hill. "Anybody live up there?" I asked.

"I think so. I hear motorcycles going past sometimes—Pua hates them so she always barks. I couldn't tell you who's on them, though. Between the jackets and the helmets they all look like giant bugs instead of people."

We thanked her and got into the Jeep. The two-lane pavement petered out after a quarter of a mile, and we were on another one of those narrow tracks like the one that had led to what I'd started thinking of as Crucifixion Hill, which was only a couple of miles away. If I'd been more religious, maybe I'd have thought of it as Calvary, where Christ had been crucified, but then again, maybe not. Though I believed we were all God's children, I doubted Casco and Flores had been as innocent or spiritual as Jesus.

When we reached a stand of trees, the dirt road became too narrow for the Jeep, and we had to get out and hike. From the ruts in the dirt, though, it was clear that a motorcycle could make it up there, adding credibility to the idea that this was where Flores and Casco lived, or at least visited regularly.

It was cool there in the shade, almost chilly. Ray and I moved slowly and carefully through the dim light filtering through the tree canopy, and we had no idea what might be waiting for us.

From what I knew of the Ko'olau, I figured we were about two thousand feet above sea level. The trees around us were a mix of towering koa, nearly twenty feet tall, and red-flowering ohia, a tree sacred to the fire goddess Pele.

I spotted some light off to the right side, and stepped off the path a few hundred yards until I could see through it. The clearing couldn't have been more than a few hundred yards across, small enough to be undetectable from the air. It was filled with neat rows of green plants, and even without venturing closer, I recognized the distinctive seven-pronged marijuana leaf.

"Nice little operation," Ray said. "You think this belonged to Flores and Casco?"

"Either them, or somebody they were coming to for protection from whoever was in that truck."

We walked back to the path and continued to climb, as silently as we could. Ahead of us, we saw another clearing, this one with an old Airstream trailer up on concrete blocks. A motorcycle stood beside it on a kickstand. As we stepped out of the cover of the trees, two German Shepherd mixes came racing toward us, growling and barking.

Ray and I both drew our guns, though I was determined to try kindness first. "If they belonged to Casco and Flores, they're probably hungry," I said. I knelt down on the ground and extended my left palm, keeping my gun aimed with my right.

The dogs skidded to a halt in front of us. The dog on the right squatted and peed. "Good girl," I said to her in a soft voice. "It's all right. Nothing to be afraid of."

She went down on her front paws. The other dog, a male, sat up on his haunches.

I inched forward, my hand still out, palm up. The male growled at me, but the female opened her mouth and her tongue lolled out. "You're probably hungry and thirsty, aren't you, girl," I said. "You let us come in, and we'll take care of you."

She scooted forward a foot and sniffed my hand, then licked it. She was probably smelling Pua the black lab, and maybe Roby as well. I reached around and scratched her behind an ear, and she rolled on her belly.

Slowly and carefully, I holstered my gun, keeping my eye on the male dog. Then I reached my other palm out to him to sniff.

He was a harder sell. I scratched the female's belly for at least a minute or two before he went down and sniffed me.

"Just call you the dog whisperer," Ray said.

"You guys want some bowl food?" I asked. I stood up. "Water, chow?"

They jumped up and raced toward the trailer. Though we were pretty sure there was no one home, we still announced ourselves, and then I stepped in the front door gingerly.

"I'll check the bedroom," Ray said, as I turned for the kitchen. I saw a big bag of dog food on the counter, and two bowls.

I lifted the dogs' water bowl from the floor and filled it, then put it down for them. They drank eagerly, water spilling from their jowls onto the linoleum.

"Bedroom is clear," Ray called.

I poured big helpings of food into their bowls. The dogs began eating quickly. Once the dogs were occupied, I pulled out my cell to call Amador, but my display showed no lit bars.

I looked around the kitchen. An old-fashioned kerosene lantern sat on the counter, and I realized they probably didn't have power up there, either. "This is where Flores and Casco lived for sure," Ray said. "Found some photos and other ID in the bedroom."

"I tried the phone but can't get a signal," I said. "We'll have to go back down to Amador and tell him what we found."

"What are we going to do about the dogs?"

I looked around and spotted two worn leashes. "Have to take them with us," I said.

When the dogs were done eating, I hooked them up, and they led me eagerly down the trail. Ray kept checking his phone as we walked, and by the time we reached where we had left the Jeep, he was able to get a call through to Animal Control. "Hopefully somebody will be able to adopt them," I said, after he was finished.

"Maybe other dope farmers," Ray said drily.

I opened the door to the Jeep and tried to get the dogs to jump in, but they weren't going. They backed away, straining to go back up to the trailer. "You drive down, I'll walk," I said. I tossed my keys to Ray, then took the dogs back up the trail a few hundred yards and waited until he was gone and they were calm.

At least it was all downhill, though it was quite a walk. I felt bad for the two dogs, because their world was being turned upside down. Had Flores and Casco loved them? Or just used them as guard dogs? It didn't matter, in the end. The humans were gone, and unless these two shepherds could be adopted, they might be following.

The dogs seemed to enjoy themselves, stopping to sniff and pee. We finally reached the bottom of the hill and continued along the two lane road. Ahead of me I could see the cluster of police cars.

As we approached the crime scene, the dogs started barking wildly. I didn't know if it was because they smelled the blood, or because they had been trained not to like police. I stopped with them and sat on the grassy verge, one dog on either side of me, petting them and speaking in calming tones.

A female officer from Animal Control came toward us. The dogs growled and she stopped, but I said, "They're good. Just give them a couple of minutes."

She approached slowly with treats in her hands, and after introducing herself to them, she fed them the treats. Her partner drove their van up closer to us, and she and I walked the dogs down there. "They don't seem to trust cars," I said.

Her partner, a tall, tough-looking guy with prematurely gray hair, joined us, and I turned over the dogs' leashes to the two of them. "You guys be good," I said, scratching them once more.

The officers began coaxing the dogs to their van, and I joined Ray by my Jeep. "Good thing we found them," Ray said. "I hate to think of them up there all alone with no food or water."

"I'm glad, too," I said. "Any news down here?"

"They're taking samples from everywhere. I told Amador about the *pakalolo* field and he's going to check it out when he looks at the trailer. He said he's going to call Agent Carson from the Drug Trafficking Task Force."

Ray and I walked over to Amador. "Anything else we can do for you?" I asked.

"It's all donkey work from now on," he said. "The crime scene guys will do their thing, and I'll take a shitload of pictures and document everything. Probably be here until it gets too dark to see."

"We know the drill," Ray said. "Better you than us."

Amador laughed. "They need anybody else over at the Bureau?"

As we laughed with him, a big dark blue SUV pulled up, and Agent Carson stepped out, wearing another stylish business suit, this one the shade of ripe cherries. Her white tennis shoes were a funny contrast. She walked over to join us, and between me, Ray and Amador, we filled her on in what we'd found.

"Were Flores and Casco on your radar?" I asked her.

She shook her head. "You found just one field?"

Ray and I nodded.

"I'll bet there are more small fields up there. These guys like to minimize the chance that they'll be spotted from the air. I'll head up there and take a look around."

Ray and I said our goodbyes and walked to the Jeep. "And another day passes with us way up here on the Windward Shore," I said. "You want me to drop you at home and then pick you up tomorrow? I hate having to drive all the way back to Kapolei."

"Sounds like a plan."

On the way home, he texted Salinas with an update, and a promise to fill him in on everything the next morning. Then he turned to me. "I'll do some homework tonight, see if I can find any religious groups with connections to crucifixions," he said.

Something registered in my brain and it took a minute to make the connection. "Homework," I said. "Crap. It's my turn to help Dakota tonight."

"How's he doing?"

"The academics are very demanding, but so far it seems like he's keeping his head above water," I said. "All that tutoring Mike and I did over the summer to bring him up to grade level seems to be paying off. Mike focused on science and math, and the kid lapped it all up. It was harder to get him to read books and study grammar. But you know me. Once I get my teeth into something I don't let go."

"I'm well aware of that trait," Ray said. I dropped him off, and we traded shakas, the Hawaiian hand gesture sometimes called 'hang loose,' with the thumb and pinky extended and the middle three fingers curled under. Ray may have come from Philadelphia, but he'd transitioned well into island life.

I was more worried about Dakota than I was willing to let on. He'd been managing the academics well enough, but I was worried about his socialization. He had so many strikes against him when it came to fitting in—he was openly gay, a mainlander, son of a single mom who was in prison. He had lived on the streets and been a prostitute, and now he was bunking with two gay foster parents. Though my friend Terri had paid his tuition, we weren't rich and couldn't give him the kind of pocket money his classmates had, buy him designer duds or take him on exotic vacations.

But he was also resilient, and I hoped that he'd be able to fit in. With typical teenaged reticence he'd said little about the social aspects of the school, and I hoped he was making friends. My friendships with Terri Clark Gonsalves and Harry Ho had been forged at Punahou and were still important parts of my life.

After dinner, Dakota and I sat in the living room to review the major themes in John Steinbeck's *Of Mice and Men*. Mike was on Dakota's other side, with his reading glasses and a fire investigation journal.

As Dakota pulled the paperback from his backpack, a greeting card fluttered out, and though he reached for it, Mike was quicker, and he held it up so I could see. It had a cartoon of a boy's face on a giant balloon, and the inside said, "I think you're swell!" It was signed with a single initial, D.

"You have a boyfriend?" Mike asked. "Who is he?"

"Daaaaad," Dakota said, mocking him. Dakota had always called us by our first names, reserving the "dads" and "pops" for sarcasm with just an edge of truth.

"Come on, Dakota, dish," I said. "Who's D? A boy?"

He looked down at the table. "Like duh."

"Someone from Punahou?" Mike asked.

"It's no big deal."

"This isn't that guy Dylan, is it? Did you give him a card, too?"

No response.

"Dakota!" I said.

He looked up. "I didn't know he was going to do it. I didn't even know he liked me. We've just been, like, hanging out."

I looked at Mike, and he gently shook his head. "Sounds good," I said. "Now, let's get into the book. What did you think of it?"

"It was sad," he said. "How George and Lennie just want a home of their own but they can't have one."

I was sure that would be one of the themes that resonated with Dakota, because of his own homelessness in the past, and my heart ached for him. "They were difficult economic times," I said. We talked about the Dust Bowl and the Okie migration to California, and how Steinbeck's background influenced that book and others like *The Grapes of Wrath.*

We were finishing up when Dakota asked, "Do you think George and Lennie are gay?"

"I think they love each other," I said. "Steinbeck wrote a lot about manhood and male relationships, and he was influenced in that by Ernest Hemingway. But I don't think there's any evidence in the text that there's anything sexual between them."

"So you think two guys can love each other without sex?"

"Sure. I love my brothers. And Harry, and Ray." I grabbed my iPad and Googled different kinds of love. "The Greeks identified four kinds of love," I said. "*Eros* is sexual love. *Storge* is the love you have for your family and very close friends. *Phileo* is what they called affection for friends, and *agape* is a kind of unconditional love for the world."

I wanted to carry the concept further, to tell him that Mike and I loved him, but he was a teenager, after all, and you have to tread softly around deep emotions with them.

"Interesting," Dakota said. "I could maybe use that in the paper I have to write."

"You totally could," I said. "I'll email you this link."

We talked some more, and then I tuned in the ten o'clock news on KVOL. The crucifixions were still the lead story, and Ralph Kim appeared to have staked out Rizaldo Amador's office in Kahuku. "Police sources revealed the identities of the victims of Saturday night's horrific crucifixion," he said. "An unmarried couple from the Laie area, Rigoberto Flores and Lina Casco. KVOL has learned that both of them had extensive criminal records. Casco's twin brother is HPD Lieutenant Martin Casco."

The scene on the TV shifted to some stock footage of HPD headquarters downtown, where Martin Casco worked, with a voice-over from Ralph. "I attempted to speak to Lieutenant Casco today, but he refused to meet with me."

The camera went back to Ralph in Kahuku. "The investigating detective here in Kahuku released a statement this afternoon that both Flores and Casco were involved in a bar brawl in Hauula shortly before their murders. Police are still interviewing witnesses to that event and tracking the couple's movements."

He looked directly at the camera. "Is there is a police cover-up going on? You can be assured that KVOL will stay on the story. This is Ralph Kim on the Windward Shore."

"Police cover-up my sweet *okole*," I said, patting my butt. "Ralph Kim is such a bullshit artist."

"You've got to admit, he can dig for information," Mike said. "Just be glad he hasn't figured out that you're working the case, or he'll have your brother after you for the inside scoop."

"He will soon," I grumbled. "He's relentless."

"Probably make a good cop," Mike said. "I know a detective who's like that."

"Excuse me? Are you comparing me to Ralph Kim? Because those are fighting words around here."

I tackled him on the sofa, holding him down and tickling him, and he laughed and struggled half-heartedly under me.

"*Non davante bambino*!" Dakota said, and we both stopped and looked at him.

"Huh?" I asked.

"It means not in front of the child," Dakota said. "My nonna used to say it all the time."

I could only imagine the kind of things that shouldn't have been said in front of Dakota when he was growing up. I looked at Mike, and it was clear we had the same idea.

So we tackled Dakota together and tickled him until he couldn't stop laughing.

The next morning as Ray and I were passing through the commercial clutter of Pearl City on our way to Kapolei, my phone buzzed with a text from Judy Evangelista. She was a tita, a tough girl, a sometime hooker and a sometime pickpocket, and she had a good line on an awful lot of underworld activity in Honolulu. She was one of the informants I'd called the day before to ask about a hot bike, and her message was an address on the Nimitz Highway, along with "u owe me" at the end.

Ray popped the address into the GPS system, which told me to turn around on the H-1 and head back toward the airport. In that area, the Queen Lili'uokalani Freeway rises above the ground-level Nimitz Highway, leaving the car rental shops, cheap motels and fast food places in deep shadow. Those shadows also attracted some of the less savory business on the island, the ones the Tourism Bureau doesn't brag about. Asian massage parlors, cash-basis food trucks that also operate as money launderers and so on. It wouldn't be a surprise to find a chop shop there.

The GPS led us to Hana Hou Garage, a bay in a worn-out warehouse complex of roll-down metal doors and makeshift signs. Hana Hou meant "again" in Hawaiian pidgin, indicating the place was a used car operation. I drove past the row of bays slowly, as if I was looking for an address. Hana Hou had a double-wide bay, and a single grease monkey working on an old Toyota. The interior was dark, and the walls were spattered with paint.

I circled around the back of the complex and out to the Nimitz. "Lend me your sunglasses," I said to Ray. He wore mirrored aviators that he thought were tough, though privately I thought they made him look like a jerk. But I was aiming for that look. "What for?" Ray asked as he handed them to me.

"Going undercover," I said. I pulled in at a Kope Bean down the street and parked. I reached behind my seat for the T-shirt, board shorts and rubber slippers I kept back there in case I decided to go for an impromptu dip in the ocean or surfing session.

"Let's go," I said, opening the door. "I'm going to change in the men's room."

"You sure this is a good idea?" Ray asked as he got out. "We can call in and have the place raided."

"We'd need a warrant, and we won't get that without something more than Judy Evangelista's word." I strode ahead of him to a tiny cubicle in the men's room, where I pulled off my Salinas-approved khakis and white shirt, banging my elbow on the stall wall. I wasn't as limber as I used to be, and I made a mental note to do some exercise that weekend.

I folded the shirt and khakis neatly, then put on the shorts and T-shirt. I looked in the mirror, then mussed up my hair, put the sunglasses on, and sneered. I figured I could pass for an aging moke, and I'd match the surfing decals on my Jeep.

Ray was in line for coffee when I passed him. He just shook his head.

I put my clothes on the back seat and made sure my collection of surfboards were visible through the open flaps, then drove back to the garage and parked in front of it. "Howzit, brah," I said to the mechanic, a Hawaiian guy in his late twenties. The name on his grease-stained shirt was Hani. "Brah, I know from *hanabata* days told me I could maybe find a bike here."

He wiped his hands on a rag and said, "Howzit, brah."

"Looking for a Kawasaki." I tried to mimic the way Ray stood when confronting someone. He wasn't all that short, five nine, but he had a short guy's way of pushing out his arms and squaring his feet that could be intimidating.

"Got nutting now," Hani said.

"You sure, brah? 'Cause I don't mind a little *pilikia*." Pilikia, or trouble, was just what I was looking for. "I can keep my mouth shut."

He looked at me and then shrugged. "Mebbe got sumtin,"

Hani said.

"Shoots, brah," I said, using the pidgin for 'go for it.'

He dropped the rag on the car's fender. "Come to da back."

We walked through the shop, dodging the skeletons of dead motorcycles, a damaged engine block, a pile of fancy rims, and greasy spots on the floor. The smell was a mix of oil and the tang of metal shavings. A makeshift wall had been constructed toward the back of the bay, with a wooden door with a foot-sized hole in it.

He led me through the door into a back room, where a banged up Kawasaki stood on its kickstand. The exhaust pipe had been crumpled and the taillight smashed, and there was a long scrape on the right side of the fork. It was the right model and the right color, and had a bumper sticker that read "Blood, Sweat and Gears."

"Gotta haad rub," he said, acknowledging the bike's damage. "Need plenny kokua fo' I can sell it."

I stepped over to sit on the bike. Casually I looked down at the headstock, the piece that holds the forks, where the serial number ought to be, and saw that it had been filed away. That was a good enough indication for me.

Hani said he could give me a good price if I would take it as is, and I took a couple of pictures and wrote down the details of the make and model. I was pretty sure they matched the one registered to Rigoberto Flores, but it was nice to have some insurance. I told Hani I'd go to the bank and get the cash, and be back in an hour.

Then I drove back to the Kope Bean. "It's the right bike," I said to Ray. I left my phone and notes with him while I changed back into my FBI drag.

By the time I got back, he had called Amador to let him know. "The details you copied down match Flores's bike. Amador's going to do the paperwork for a search warrant," Ray said, handing my phone back to me. "He says because this is such a high-profile case, he's got a judge ready to sign it as soon as he gets it together."

"I'm starting to like working for the Bureau," I said. "Get somebody else to do our dirty work for us."

"That's what Salinas has been doing with us for years," he said.

Ray had already finished his coffee, so I got a Longboard sized raspberry mocha for myself. We walked back down the street to a bus shelter that had a sideways view of the chop shop, and settle in for some surveillance, to make sure that the bike didn't disappear before Amador and his warrant arrived.

"Flores wouldn't have scratched off the VIN number," I said. "The bike was registered to him. So was it the guys who killed him? Or the guy in the shop?"

"Either way, we'll be able to retrieve it," Ray said. "I had this case back in Philly, where the perps thought they were so smart by scraping off the VINs. But the metal underneath the number is compressed and hardened, and even after the number is ground off, you can apply an acid solution and raise the serial number."

"How long does that take?"

"Up to a few hours, depending," Ray said. "Once they have the number up they take pictures of it, then apply modeling clay to get a cast of it. But if we're lucky there will be some prints on the bike that don't match the mechanic or Flores. That will give us a head start."

As we watched Hana Hou to make sure no one took the bike away before Amador could arrive with his warrant, I drank my coffee and Ray and I recapped where we were. "We have a bunch of connections," I said. "The threatening letters to the Habermans, the graffiti at the day care center and the psychologist's office, and the Bible verse on the cross."

"And we have a lot of additional reports of two or three white males harassing mixed-race couples and families," Ray said. "Which match the three haoles at the bar who were bothering Flores and Casco."

"But we still don't have any idea who those guys are," I said. "I hope we can pick up some prints from Flores's bike." I couldn't help but think that we were still missing some crucial clue, and no matter how many different angles Ray and I talked through the case, we couldn't come up with it.

We made a bunch of phone calls while we waited, sent some texts and emails, even surfed the web for some information. I went back to the Kope Bean for a potty break and returned with sandwiches and bottled water, and early in the afternoon Amador called to say that he had the search warrant in hand and he was on his way.

He said he wanted me to come in as soon as the property was secured and show him the bike. I said I would.

From our vantage point at the bus stop, we saw two squad cars approach and pull up in front of the warehouse bay. Amador got out of the first car and walked up to the door, with a couple of uniforms behind him. I watched him speak to Hani, the mechanic, and show him the search warrant.

When a uniform escorted Hani over to one of the squad cars, Amador went inside, then came back out a couple of minutes later and motioned to me. I crossed the street and met Amador at the front of the bay. "He says he's just an employee, doesn't know anything," Amador said. "Looks like the right bike," he said at last. "But the VIN number is gone. Have to see if the techs can retrieve it."

Hani was trying to engage the officer watching him in conversation, but the officer was stone-faced. Amador and I walked over to him. "This is Detective Kanapa'aka," Amador said to the mechanic. "Let's talk about that bike in the back."

Hani looked at me. "You da police?" he asked. "I tought you wanna buy a bike."

"Where'd that bike come from?" Amador asked.

Hani shrugged. "Here when I come to work."

"Look, brah, the guy who owned that bike? He *wen maki*," I said. Hani's face blanched as he realized the bike's previous owner was dead. "We think whoever stole the bike is who killed him. You can tell us who brought it to you, or we can arrest you for murder."

"I didn't kill nobody," he said. "I got a wife and two keikis. I can't go to prison."

"Then tell us where the bike came from," Amador said.

"I'm telling you, brah, I don't know," he said. "I just work here. The bike was here when I come to work this morning."

Amador reached out to shake my hand. "Thanks for your help on this. I'll follow up with the garage owner, but I'm going to take Hani in just to be sure he doesn't tip the guy off."

I was about to protest that Ray and I could handle the follow up when I remembered that this was Amador's case. "Keep us in the loop," I said.

"Will do." We left him to the cleanup and drove back to Kapolei. By then it was almost the end of the day. We found Salinas in his office and briefed him.

"Good work," he said. "Any progress on the Haberman threats?"

"More and more evidence that the threats are connected to the crucifixion, and to other harassment around the island," Ray said, and I nodded. "We'll see what Amador comes up as he traces the bike."

"This case is very high profile," Salinas said. "Let's try and keep the heat on this Amador guy on the Windward Shore, rather than on the Bureau. And remember, any questions get referred to Randy Vernon." I already knew the Bureau's press liaison, and knew he was about as communicative as the Sphinx. "I don't want to see either of your names in the paper unless Vernon okays it."

Salinas looked at both of us. "There's a key that will unlock this investigation," he said. "Find it."

Ray and I both left for home soon after the meeting was over. As I turned onto Aiea Heights Drive, I saw Dakota climbing the hill from the stop where the Punahou bus dropped him. He'd begun the school year wearing the T-shirts and board shorts he already owned, but very quickly had asked us to buy him some chinos and collared shirts. He had a backpack slung over one shoulder, and his shoulder-length black hair was gathered into a ponytail.

I pulled over and rolled down my window. "Hey, kid, want some candy?"

"I can't get into cars with strange men." Then he opened the door. "But I'll make an exception in your case."

"How was your day?" I asked, as I put the Jeep back in gear.

"Okay."

"Did you see Dylan?"

He turned toward the window and I got a glimpse of how my parents must have felt when I was an uncommunicative teenager.

"Listen, kid, we can do this the easy way, or the hard way," I said, putting on my best cop voice. "Did you talk to Dylan about the card he gave you yesterday?"

He glared at me.

"So," I said, turning along a curve. "I'm going to use my deductive skills. If you hadn't seen him, you wouldn't be so closed up. So you did, and you talked to him."

Dakota didn't say anything.

"If you had a good conversation, you'd be all happy. Since you're not, I figure you said something you think was dumb, and you got embarrassed."

He barked out a short laugh. "As a detective, you suck," he said. "We had English in third period today and we talked after class. Then he told me to follow him, and we went into the boys' room. We were by ourselves, and he kissed me."

Dakota and I had never talked fully about what happened to him when he was living with his drug-addicted mom, and then on the streets, but I was pretty sure he was not a virgin. At sixteen, he was a good-looking kid, with dark eyes, clear skin and just the hint of a beard along his chin line.

"Kissing is fun," I said.

"Then this other kid came in to take a piss and we had to stop."

"Did he see you kissing?"

Dakota shook his head. "But it kind of harshed the mellow, you know?"

"Believe me, I know," I said. I'd never made out in the boys' room at Punahou, but I've gone around the bases a few times in places other than a ball park.

"He asked me if I wanted to come over to his house on Saturday and hang out," Dakota said, as I pulled into our driveway.

"What did you say?"

"At first I wanted to, but then I changed my mind and said I couldn't."

I heard Roby barking from inside the house, but I didn't get out of the Jeep. "Why?"

"He's a nice guy, and I'm fucked up. It'd never work out."

"From what I've seen of you over the last couple of years, I'd say you're a pretty nice guy yourself. You've had some tough times. Big deal. You're young, you can get over them."

"My mom's a crack whore and my dad was a sperm donor," he said. "I don't have a real family like Dylan does. I'm living on charity and I could be out on my ass any day."

How could he think that Mike and I would ever kick him out? I took a deep breath. "I think our family is very real," I said. "And I'm hurt if you think there's any chance that Mike or I would want to kick you out."

He opened the door to get out but I grabbed his arm. "It took me a long time to figure out who I am," I said. "And maybe I'm still feeling my way sometimes. But there's one thing I know. I don't walk away. It's not in my character."

When Dakota turned to me, he had tears in his eyes. "But what if I turn out like her? Get hooked on drugs? Steal from you. Turn tricks."

"From my experience, people who do those things have something broken inside, and the drugs dull the pain," I said. "The stealing and the hooking start because they need money, or the thrill, or the empty pleasure. I don't think you're like that. You started to break when everything crashed down with your mom and all, but I know how strong you are, and I've seen how you bounced back. You aren't so broken now, and as long as I'm around you're never going to be."

He began to sob, and I let him rest his head on my chest and cry while I kept my arm around him, and a warm breeze ruffled the palm trees and the damn dog kept on barking.

By the time Dakota and I returned from walking Roby, Mike's truck was in the driveway and the scent of a charcoal fire wafted past us from the back yard. "You go see what Mike's making for dinner," I said to him. "I'll take Roby in."

Dakota darted around the side of the house like a carefree kid, and I went inside with Roby, poured food in his bowl and gave him fresh water. We all sat out on the picnic table in the back yard as the sun set and the stars came out. Dakota gobbled three burgers and a pile of grilled green peppers and went inside to do his homework or text his friends or maybe call Dylan and make plans for the weekend.

"Interesting conversation with Dakota on the way home," I said to Mike, when we were stretched out on our lounge chairs in the back yard. The sun had gone down and the moon was full.

"About?" Mike asked.

I told him about Dakota's mini-breakdown, and the way I'd reassured him. "You're going to be a great dad, you know," Mike said.

"Back at you," I said, and we bumped fists. Then I filled him in on the progress Ray and I had made on the crucifixion case. "Any progress on the arson at the day care center?" I asked. "Salinas wants us to pull someone in before the press figures out that all these incidents are connected, and that the Bureau is investigating. I could use a viable suspect."

"Remember those flyers I put up around the hospital on Friday?" he asked. "Got a call today from a nurse on the night shift. She was off over the weekend and just saw the flyer last night."

"Did she see something?"

He nodded. "She's trying to quit smoking and when she gets the urge she goes outside and walks around. She was outside around five-thirty in the morning when she saw a pickup truck at the traffic light. A teenage girl was driving, and it seemed like she'd stalled the truck and was trying to get it started. A teenage boy was in the passenger seat, and he was yelling something that sounded to her like a foreign language. The kicker is that the truck smelled like smoke."

"Cigarettes?"

He shook his head. "Wood smoke. The girl got the truck going and they drove off. She didn't get a good look at it or at either of the two kids."

"You think two kids did all that damage at the day care center?"

He leaned forward. "I think it's possible. Not many other reasons why a pair of teenagers would be out at five thirty in the morning in a truck that smelled like wood smoke. I passed the information on to Amador this afternoon and he's going to nose around."

We sat together under the stars, and eventually we went in and watched the KVOL news again. Ralph Kim had another update on the crucifixion story, including a remote from the crime scene and an interview with Mary Makao about the discovery of Lina's cellphone.

"He's good," I said grudgingly, as Ralph led his cameraman up the hill. He couldn't get close to the trailers, but he did include a wide angle shot of the marijuana field.

"Was this a drug deal gone horribly wrong?" Ralph asked. "We're still on this story."

Mike turned off the TV after Ralph's report was over. "If he keeps pushing the drug angle, that should keep him from finding out the real story."

"It's just a matter of time," I said. "It might give us some relief from media pressure for a day or two, but if Ray and I don't get a break soon we'll be in trouble with more than just KVOL."

"I have good news and bad news," Rizaldo Amador said. He'd called us at about ten o'clock on Wednesday morning, as Ray and I were going back over the autopsy reports on Lina Casco and Rigoberto Flores, hoping to find a clue that had so far eluded us.

"I like good news," I said.

"I spent some time yesterday afternoon with the owner of the garage," he said. "He finally coughed up the name of the guy who sold him the bike."

"Haole?" I asked, hoping we might be able to make the connection to the other incidents.

"Nope. Hawaiian guy from up this way, in Laie. Went out to see him, and he insists he found the bike at the bottom of a ravine, when he was out hiking. Figured it was abandoned, so he dragged it up to the street, loaded it in his pickup, drove it down to Honolulu and sold it."

"You believe him?"

"For now. He took me to the place where he found the bike, and there were track marks along the side of the ravine. Looks like somebody pushed the bike down there."

"What about fingerprints?"

"We pulled a couple of partial prints off the bike. Once we eliminated the ones that matched the Hawaiian guy, we had a couple of others that might have come from whoever pushed the bike down the ravine, which may also be who killed Flores and Casco."

"And the bad news?"

"No match on any of the prints in the database. But if we come up with a suspect, we can try to match them."

I was surprised, because I expected someone who'd committed such murders to be in the system. Juvenile records were sealed, though, so if the two teenagers the nurse had spotted leaving the arson scene had been responsible there might not have been a match. The idea that two teenagers could wreak the havoc we'd seen at the crucifixion site didn't ring true for me, but I wanted to follow up on them with Amador anyway.

"Mike told me about the kids in the smoky truck," I said. "Any idea who they could be?"

"Lots of run-down pickups up here," he said.

"Didn't the nurse say she heard them speaking a foreign language?"

"I talked to her myself. Says it was more like gibberish than a real language. Probably just kids fooling around. My kids are big on Pig Latin right now. Or Igpay Atlinlay, as they call it. Course, neither of them are old enough to drive, thank God."

Something about a kid speaking gibberish rang a bell in my brain, but I couldn't place it. I thanked Amador, and Ray and I spent the rest of the morning searching for similar crimes on O'ahu. I was surprised at how many results came up, though most of them had to do with crosses being planted on someone's lawn, and none of the crosses had writing like we'd found at the crucifixion site.

Ray's phone rang shortly before we were ready to break for lunch. He talked for just a moment, then said, "We'll be right out," and hung up.

"That was Susan Haberman," he said. "She got another one of those letters today."

On the long drive from Kapolei across the bottom of the island to Wailupe, we rehashed every detail we could think of, but made no progress. We passed through a series of showers, and when we reached the Habermans' house it wasn't raining but the clouds were dark and heavy.

Susan Haberman met us at the door. There were dark circles under her eyes, and she moved nervously as she led us into the living room. Through the big windows, I saw the Pacific roiling in the wind, whitecaps smashing against the dock and rocking the sailboat moored there.

"Thank you for coming out so quickly," she said. "I've been so nervous and upset that I've had a hard time concentrating on anything."

"I can imagine you've been having a tough time," Ray said gently. "You said you got another letter?"

She nodded. "This morning, in the mail. After you were here, I decided we were going to put gloves on when we picked up and opened the mail. I'm glad I did."

She paused for a moment, and the maid came in. "Can I offer you anything?" Mrs. Haberman asked.

"We're good," I said, looking at Ray, who nodded. "Can we see the letter?"

"Of course." We sat down at her dining room table and she handed us a plastic sleeve similar to the ones she'd used for the other letter, with a standard number ten envelope inside.

"I went out to the mailbox myself around eleven," she said. "We got the usual pile of junk mail and magazines, but then I noticed this plain envelope in the middle with no stamp or postmark. I was so upset I nearly dropped it."

"You didn't get the new security camera installed yet, did you?" I asked.

She shook her head. "The company is supposed to come out next week."

"No one else here in the house has touched this?" Ray asked.

She shook her head, and we looked at the envelope. Like the one we already had in evidence, the Habermans' full names and address had been printed on a computer. Ray handled the sleeve gingerly, turning it over so we could look at the back. Nothing there.

Hoping to preserve any fingerprints that might be on the envelope, or whatever was inside, I put on a pair of plastic gloves. It was a lot harder to retrieve fingerprints than most people believed, and it was more likely to get a partial print than something usable. A whole constellation of factors had to be in place to get clear prints.

First, the envelope didn't look like it had been wet; water could wash away prints. Whoever handled the paper had to have enough sweat on his or her fingers to leave a print. Fortunately, in our hot, humid climate, that wasn't a big problem.

The paper was a smooth surface, which was more conducive to retaining prints; rough or textured surfaces like tree bark are bad. And even if there was sweat and a receptive surface, a light touch wouldn't leave a print, while touching and dragging would smear the impression.

I accepted a letter opener from Susan Haberman, then slit the envelope open. I let the single sheet of paper fall out, then unfolded it.

As with the other letters, there was no salutation, no date. Just a series of paragraphs. This one, though, was longer than the previous ones. The same Biblical phrases were repeated, including the one from the Book of Ezra that had been referenced on the cross beneath Rigoberto Flores's body. There was a new one, too:

The prophet Nephi tells us that the righteous are "white and delightsome." Our leaders tell us that people should marry those of the same racial, social, economic and educational background. To do otherwise is to defy the will of the LORD.

Below that, the person had typed:

Those who defy the will of the LORD will pay, either in fire or flood. In Genesis 19 it is written "Then the LORD rained upon Sodom and upon Gomorrah brimstone and fire from the LORD out of heaven. Thus He overthrew those cities and the entire plain, destroying all those living in the cities—and also the vegetation in the land."

Be afraid, you sinners, because your time is coming soon.

I didn't want to tell Susan Haberman that the same quote had been found at the crucifixion site, because that would only upset her. I did notice the mention of the word "fire," and wondered if the writer was referencing the arson at the day care center.

I looked at Ray. "You ever heard of a prophet Nephi?" I asked. "Doesn't sound like any of the familiar ones."

"Not that I recall from the King James version of the Bible," he said. "But I can't say I memorized every prophet from the old and the new testament."

While he looked at the letter again, I pulled out my iPad and searched online. "Listen to this," I said a moment later. "Nephi is regarded by The Church of Jesus Christ of Latter-day Saints as a major figure in the Book of Mormon, as a prophet, political leader, and record keeper."

"The Book of Mormon? But everything else was from the Bible," Ray said.

"According to this site, the Book of Mormon includes a lot of material from the King James Version," I said. "Including big chunks of the Book of Isaiah which show up in the Book of Nephi."

"Mormons?" Susan asked. "Why would they care about us?"

"Has your husband ever dealt with the Mormon church, or with Mormon plaintiffs or defendants?" I asked.

"Not that I know of. He believes in religious freedom, the separation of church and state, and all that."

"Religious fanatics come in all varieties," I said. "And they always have some justification for their actions from their scriptures. That's not to say that whoever sent this really is a Mormon. They could just be stealing bits and pieces from various doctrines."

"We'll take the letter and the envelope for fingerprint analysis," Ray said. "If we get lucky, we'll find a print that will lead us to whoever has been threatening you."

"I appreciate that, Ray," she said. "But I'm through counting on luck."

I looked up at her. For the first time since we'd arrived, she had stopped fidgeting. "What do you mean?"

"I'm taking my children out of school before things get any worse." She sat forward on the sofa. "We're flying to Washington to stay with my husband."

I didn't want to say anything in front of the senator's wife, but I thought that was a very good idea. We took the letter, said some reassuring things, and walked back outside. "I want to look more into this Mormon connection when we get back to Kapolei," I said. "This book of Nephi quote just reinforces what we've been seeing. A lot of these incidents have been happening on the Windward Shore, where there are a lot of Mormons."

"I never think of the Mormons as a particularly violent group," Ray said.

"I think like any other, they have their weird offshoots," I said. "Some of those survivalists in the Pacific Northwest are Mormons."

Ray nodded. "And a lot of Mormons are preppers. Apparently being prepared is part of their religion."

When I graduated from Punahou and went to UC Santa Cruz, one of the nicknames I was tagged with was preppy, because Punahou was a college preparatory school. But lately that term had been coopted to describe people preparing for a coming apocalypse.

"On the surface, stockpiling food, water and guns so they'll be ready for whatever comes is a reasonable idea," I said. "All you have to do is read the news to see what kind of mayhem is going on around the world. It's not a big jump to worry that somebody could start something here."

While we waited at a Zippy's drive-through, Ray said, "This cop I knew back in Philly was sure that terrorists were going to knock out the power grid, so he bought a house out in the country where he put in solar power and water filtration."

"That's one of the more rational responses," I said. "I've heard about people who think God is going to rain down fire and terror like Sodom and Gomorrah."

"Or that some virus like Ebola will become airborne and wipe out half the population," Ray said. "The cop I knew had all kinds of contingency plans."

"Sounds like he'd be good to know in case of a crisis," I said. "Too bad he's on the other side of the country."

When we got back to the FBI office, we went straight to the fingerprint lab.

We looked through the lab window and I saw Kit Carson there in a dark green business suit and matching heels, her sunglasses once again perched on her red hair.

A heavyset haole man in his fifties was showing Kit something in a microscope. We waited until they were finished to walk in.

"Eric is an evidence genius," Kit said, after introducing us. "He's matched six prints from the crucifixion victims' trailer to offenders in the database, some of whom we didn't realize had any connection to the drug trade. I have a lot of interesting conversations ahead of me."

She left and Eric asked how he could help us. Ray handed him the letter and envelope in their plastic folder. "You think you could see if there are any prints on this?" he asked.

"I can try. You might want to make copies of this before I get it all dirty."

I nodded and took the plastic folders over to a copy machine while Eric swiveled to another place at the long table and began assembling his materials.

I was glad to hear Kit's recommendation. Computers only send back possible matches from the database, and there was a real art to actually making the match to the sample. I didn't want to trust that Eric was good just because he worked for the Bureau.

I kept the originals in their plastic sleeves as I made the copies, then returned to Eric. Ray and I pulled up bar stools to watch as Eric dusted the letter and the envelope. It was pretty nice having a tech at our disposal who could drop what he was doing and look at our evidence—but a high-profile case like a crucifixion also pushes you to the front of the line.

While Eric brushed a combination of aluminum powder and volcanic dust on the pages, I looked around the lab. Up on the wall were big posters of fingerprints, showing arches, whorls, and loops. According to one poster, loops were the most common pattern, with approximately sixty percent of fingers showing them. Thirty percent had whorls, and only about five to ten percent showed arches. It was rare to have more than one pattern on any given finger, but a person's hand could contain different patterns on each finger.

There was nothing usable on the envelope, which wasn't surprising, as it had gone through the mail, and then Mrs. Haberman had used gloves to handle it. "You might be getting lucky," Eric said, pointing to an arched pattern appearing on the bottom right corner of the letter. "That looks like a pretty good specimen."

He fed the print into the system and we waited again. I knew from experience that it could take anywhere from twenty minutes to two hours to get a match, and Eric didn't need us hanging around.

"I have a quick project to finish for Agent Carson, but I can do that while the computer is working its magic," he said. "I'll try to have something for you by the end of the day."

We thanked him and left the lab. "I feel like we're adding pieces to the puzzle," Ray said, as we walked back to our office. "I just can't see the whole picture yet."

"Look at it this way," I said. "There are close to a million and a half people in Hawai'i, right? And only about seventy thousand of them are Mormon. We're narrowing our suspect pool all the time."

"Assuming our suspects are Mormon," Ray said. "That's still a big jump."

"Then it's time for us to do some homework," I said. "Prove that we have Mormons behind this case, and then prove which Mormons are responsible."

I read a couple of names of Mormon church groups to Ray. "The Church of the Firstborn of the Fullness of Times. True and Living Church of Jesus Christ of Saints of the Last Days. The Church of the Firstborn and the General Assembly of Heaven."

"That's a real mouthful if somebody asks you where you worship," Ray said. "Didn't you once say that your father's parents were Mormon?"

My granny, a severe Idaho-born woman who had not been mellowed much by spending nearly seventy years in the islands, had followed her first husband, a Mormon missionary, from Idaho to Laie, where there was a large Mormon stake. After his death, she had moved down to Honolulu and met my grandfather, and my dad and his siblings had been raised as Mormons.

"Yup. But my dad stopped going to the Mormon church when he met my mom. My brothers and I grew up in a mishmash of religions, going to Catholic churches for midnight mass, Shinto temples and a couple of others just for variety."

I'd never explored the Mormon part of my heritage, so the research Ray and I did Wednesday afternoon was fascinating. According to Wikipedia, the lazy researcher's best friend, The Church of Jesus Christ of Latter-day Saints had over fifteen million members, and over eighty-five thousand missionaries around the world.

At least two dozen sects had spun off the mainstream, some of them unsanctioned. Most were fundamentalist churches, often under the leadership of a charismatic preacher. One prophet claimed to be the Holy Ghost of the father of Jesus; many groups practiced plural marriage and disregarded the laws of the United States. Leaders of one sect had even been accused of murder.

One thing that jumped out at me was that quotes from the

Book of Mormon often referenced the LORD, all in capital letters, rather than just God. That matched the references in the letters Susan Haberman had received.

Though some had only a few hundred members, others numbered in the thousands—and one even had a quarter of a million believers. Most were located in Utah, Montana, or Arizona, though there were offshoots in the Midwest, in Mexico and Canada and England. Only two sects were listed in Hawai'i. One that had been founded in Lanai in the 1800s and was long since defunct, and another called the Children of Noah.

The entry read: "The Children of Noah was organized in 1982 by Robert Noah Kilgore, a charismatic preacher with a message of the coming apocalypse. Located in Laie, Hawai'i, the group has approximately 100 members, many of them members of Kilgore's extended family. Their practice is based on Mormon fundamentalism, racial purity and plural marriage."

"Holy crap," I said to Ray. "Did you see this? About a group called the Children of Noah? They're based up in Laie, right where all this stuff is happening."

We looked for more information online, but the church had no website and we found only the vaguest mentions of them in blogs and databases. "You seem to have old friends and distant cousins all over the place," Ray said. "Have any up in Laie who might be able to tell us more about this group?"

"Can't think of any off the top of my head," I said. "But I'll ask around." I sent out an email to my family and close friends, asking if they had any connections to the group. Then Eric called us back to the fingerprint lab.

We stood at his computer screen as he pointed to a print. "This one came from the letter you brought in." He brought another window up and positioned it beside the first. "And this one came from the rear fender of the motorcycle."

"It's a match?" I asked.

He pointed out a couple of the key points on both. "I can say with at least ninety-five percent certainty that these prints came from the same individual." He looked at us. "However, I still don't have a match to anything in the database."

Ray and I walked back to our office, talking over each other as we tried to figure out where the connections were. "Whoever sent this letter to the Habermans also had his hands on Rigoberto Flores's bike," I said.

"The three white guys who were harassing Flores and Casco at the bar could be the same ones who have been bothering people all over the Windward Shore."

"And the psychologist off the Pali," I said. "And maybe they're connected to whoever burned Haley Walsh's day care center."

We stopped at Salinas's office to let him know what we'd found. "We need to know more about this group called the Children of Noah," I said. "To see if their verbiage matches what we've seen on the letters to the Habermans, on the graffiti and on the cross."

"Does the FBI have anybody looking into religious cults?" Ray asked.

"Not per se," Salinas said. "If a religious group is involved in criminal activity, they'd be investigated by the task force looking into that particular activity. But we have to be very careful not to impede freedom of religion. Your best bet for information is probably a university professor, someone in a religion department who could give you some insight."

I made a note to look for someone like that, and then Ray and I left the office. It was one of those picture-perfect days that the tourist office likes to brag about and I was enjoying the cloudless skies and the light breeze that flew past my open Jeep. Then a large black bird zipped past my windshield and I braked instinctively, even though it was long gone. The encounter reminded me once again that even though our islands are beautiful, they can be deadly, too.

As I turned onto Aiea Heights Drive, my cell trilled with the tone I'd reserved for Terri Gonsalves, Bruce Springsteen's "Glory Days." I loved picking out the right ring tones for my family and closest friends, and the Springsteen song reminded me of how long Terri and I had known each other.

Because it's illegal in Hawai'i to speak on a cell phone without a hands free device, and because I'm a cop, I pulled into a drugstore parking lot so I could answer the call.

"I was up in Laie on Monday on some Trust business, and while I was waiting for my meeting I picked up a flyer from that group you emailed about, the Children of Noah," she said, after we'd exchanged greetings and family updates. "I was going to call you about it anyway, because I think their message of racial purity is very disturbing."

"Read me what you've got."

I listened carefully and caught mentions of the prophets Ezra and Nephi. The language sounded very similar to what we'd seen.

"Can you fax it to me?" I asked when she was finished. "Let me give you the number out in Kapolei." I didn't know the number by heart, so I had to wrangle my wallet out of my pocket and read her the number from my card.

"I'll fax it as soon as I get to the office tomorrow morning." Terri had taken over administration of her family's charitable foundation and spent her time looking for ways to improve life in the islands. "I'm glad you've made this move to the FBI, Kimo," she said. "I think you can do a lot of good there."

"Hope so," I said. As I pulled back out into traffic, I thought about what she'd said. Everyone else who had encouraged me or congratulated me on the move had focused on what working for the Bureau could do for me—rein in my impulses, get me out of the line of fire and so on. Terri was the first to believe that I could have an effect there, and I liked that idea better.

We had a quiet evening, dinner and then Mike and I both helped Dakota with different parts of his homework. After he went to bed, Mike and I watched the news again. Ralph Kim's story was about the animal shelter where the two German Shepherd mixes who belonged to Flores and Casco had been taken. He tried to make it a heart-tugging piece about the dogs, but the fact remained that they'd been used to guard marijuana fields.

Thursday morning, while I waited for Terri's fax, Ray and I went back over each of the mixed-race incidents we had recorded, looking for elements that might tie them together. We came up with three things: a focus on the Windward Shore, particularly around Laie; two or three haole males in their late twenties or early thirties; and a pickup truck which might have a busted taillight.

We pulled up a list of garages up and down the Windward Shore and called each one, hoping to find one that had repaired a pickup's taillight, but came up blank. When we finished I checked with Salinas's secretary and got the flyer Terri had faxed over. Ray and I looked at it. The headline was "Returning Racial Purity to Hawai'i."

> The LORD declares, in Genesis 6:9: "These are the generations of Noah: Noah was a just man and perfect in his generations, and Noah walked with God." The phrase "perfect in his generations" means that all of Noah's ancestors were the same race, making him a "perfect" human being and worthy of being saved, chosen to build the Ark and repeople the earth after the Flood.
>
> The Prophet Ezra said, in Ezra 10:10-11: "Ye have transgressed, and have taken strange wives, to increase the trespass of Israel." Deuteronomy 7:1-4 bans mixed marriages: "Neither shalt thou make marriages with them; thy daughter thou shalt not give unto his son, nor his daughter shalt thou take unto thy son."
>
> The prophet Nephi tell us that the righteous are 'white and delightsome.' Our leaders tell us that people should marry those of the same racial, social, economic and educational background. To

do otherwise is to defy the will of the LORD."

The rhetoric continued to trace almost every ill of modern society, with the possible exception of global warming, to God's displeasure that we had forsaken these words, spoken by his prophets.

According to the flyer, the Children of Noah had begun their quest for racial purity in Hawai'i because God had already demonstrated his anger with humanity in the islands with volcanoes, hurricanes, and tsunamis. Worse disasters were in store unless the islanders repented and ceased bastardizing the white race by intermarrying.

"I'll put together a profile on Robert Noah Kilgore," I said. Ray said he would do some more research on the group, see if they had been involved in any demonstrations or police actions.

I began with property records and found that Kilgore had purchased a four-acre tract of land in 1980, on the outskirts of Laie. Over the next decade he had accumulated additional parcels, some adjacent, some not. Then he had sold it all to a company called Ark Ventures, LLC. Further checking established that he was the owner of that company, which now controlled over five hundred acres of land. Building permits had been issued over the decades for construction on Kilgore's property—a house, barn, and numerous outbuildings.

I found a marriage license between Robert Noah Kilgore and a woman named Glorilynn Michelle Snow, issued in Laie in 1980. Birth certificates for five children between them: Ardell, Brogan, Cord, Dinah, and Emerette.

Kilgore was also listed as the father on the birth certificate for Orris Kilgore, whose mother was a woman named Hilma Packer. And he was the father of twins, Marie and Donald Kilgore, by a woman named LaDonna Harmon.

Harmon was my grandmother's first husband. Had he had other siblings, or cousins, who had moved to Hawai'i with him, or followed him there? Wouldn't it be weird if I was somehow tangentially related to the Children of Noah?

I pushed that away and looked at death certificates and divorce decrees. Since I couldn't find anything for Glorilynn, I assumed that Kilgore had begun practicing plural marriage. All the children were born at home, attended by a midwife. Glorilynn Kilgore had filed a Form 4140, an exception to compulsory school attendance, for each of the eight children, indicating that she would be home-schooling them.

It looked like Kilgore was careful to adhere to legal requirements—registering marriages and births, accounting for his kids' educations, getting the right building permits. He wasn't giving law enforcement any opportunity to meddle in his business.

Kilgore had a pickup truck registered to his name. The first three letters of the plate were KTE, which was close to what Sarah Byrne had written down from the truck belonging to the guys who'd harassed her and her boyfriend.

I kept on searching. Though the oldest six children were already adults, I found no evidence they had received high school diplomas or attended college. The work was mind-numbing, but I found marriage licenses for five of the six, as well as records of their children's birth and home schooling. They all had drivers' licenses as well, which required a single fingerprint with the application.

The prints we had found didn't match anyone in the database, but that didn't eliminate the Kilgores, as, I presumed, each of them had nine other fingers we didn't have prints for.

I captured the driver's license photos for each person who lived at the address for Ark Ventures, LLC, and filed them away on my iPad, then synched the photos to my phone as well. I didn't always have the iPad with me so I wanted the photos available if I didn't.

The only one of the six who wasn't married was the oldest girl, Dinah, and she was the only one who didn't list the property as her legal address. Had she escaped? Her license listed an address in Pearl City, an urban area clustered around Pearl Harbor. When I ran a check on the address it came up as one of the franchises that rented out mailboxes.

Dinah didn't own any property and when I called my friend Karen Gold at the Social Security office, Karen said she had no work records. Like Rigoberto Flores and Lina Casco, she appeared to be living off the grid.

Dinah was an uncommon name, so on a whim I did a general search for "Dinah" and "Hawaii." I scrolled through a few pages of links until I found one for a blog by a lesbian activist named Kelsey Lampart. I didn't know her, but her name was familiar, because she often organized protests and demonstrations, and was frequently quoted in the media.

I clicked through to the blog. "Giving women names from the Bible is a way of reinforcing the patrimony," she wrote. "Dinah, daughter of Jacob and Leah, was raped by Shechem, the son of Hamor the Hivite. My friend Dinah lives with the burden of that name, though it's most likely she was given it just because she was the fourth child of her religious parents who needed a girl's name that began with D."

Dinah Kilgore was the fourth child of religious parents. Was she the one who Kelsey Lampart called a friend? Did that mean that Dinah Kilgore was a lesbian? If anyone knew, it would be the mother of my children, who had a Rolodex of almost every lesbian on the island.

Before I could say anything, Sandra said, "I hate you and Mike with a white-hot passion."

"And aloha to you, too," I said.

"Really. If you hadn't been willing to donate I wouldn't have gained all this extra weight from carrying the babies that I can't seem to lose."

I restrained myself from saying that Sandra had never been that slender. "Do you know Dinah Kilgore or Kelsey Lampart?"

"I don't know Dinah, but Kelsey is the personal trainer Cathy and I use. She comes to our house now, but we first met her at the Olakino Gym in Aiea."

I choked back a comment about Sandra and exercise. "Mahalo," I said. "You are the mother of my children and I owe you everything."

"Hah," she said, and hung up.

Almost as soon as I hung up with Sandra, my phone buzzed with a text from Judy Evangelista, our tough girl informant. "Need to c u asap," she wrote. "Call me."

I obeyed. "Howzit, Judy," I said, when she answered. "What's so urgent?"

"You gotta get out here to Waikiki, D," she said, with the initial she used for all the detectives she knew. "There's some shit gonna happen on Saturday you guys gotta know about. But I don't know the whole story so you gotta come out here. Can you meet me at Kalakaua and Lewers in about an hour?"

"What's the shit that's gonna happen?" I asked.

"Can't go into it now. I gotta go. But be there in an hour, okay? And you can bring me the cash you owe me for that tip on the hot bike when you come."

She hung up.

"That's odd," I said. "Judy's not usually the type to get excited."

"She keeps all the excitement for clients," Ray said. "Ooh, baby!"

It was close to lunchtime, so Ray and I decided to head to Waikiki and grab something to eat on the way. Before we left, I called the Olakino Gym and learned that Kelsey Lampart would be in late that day, teaching a class that ended at five-thirty.

We got to Waikiki about fifteen minutes before we needed to meet Judy and strolled down Kalakaua Avenue to the corner of Lewers Street. As usual, the sidewalks were crowded with tourist couples, the men in hibiscus patterned aloha shirts in bright reds and blues, their wives in matching blouses or muumuus as well as beachgoers in bikinis, shorts and puka shell necklaces. Interspersed were young men and women in the kind of sanitized aloha shirts that identified them as the staff at hotels and restaurants—muted patterns, with oval name tags over the breast.

Judy was waiting outside an art gallery with stylized glass sculptures of dolphins and whales in the window. She wore her standard outfit of low-riding jeans, midriff-baring white T-shirt, and multiple heavy stainless steel chains around her neck. She dropped a cigarette to the ground and stamped it out, then approached us.

Ray and I had picked up Judy on an assault charge a couple of years before, and discovered she was the kind of girl who knew the Honolulu underworld and worked it to her advantage.

"You got my cash?" she asked.

"Hello to you, too," I said. I opened my wallet and pulled out five crispy twenty-dollar bills. I handed them to her.

"Sweet," she said. "I read about that crucifixion deal in the paper. That's harsh."

I was surprised that Judy read the newspaper, but I didn't let it show.

"You think the same guy sold that bike who killed those people?" she asked.

"We're still investigating. You know anything about it?"

She shuddered. "I know some creeps, but I hope I don't know nobody that bad."

"So what was so urgent, Judy?" Ray asked.

She pulled a cigarette out of a crumpled pack of Marlboros. "You know Sneaky Pete?"

"The dealer?" he asked.

"No, the vacuum cleaner salesman." She rubbed her fingers together in the universal gesture for cash.

I wasn't about to give her anything more without getting something new. "I gotta tell you, Judy, both of us switched over to work for the FBI for a while. So if you've got information on drugs, you need to talk to somebody at HPD."

"I know where you work," she said. "You think I'm stupid or something?"

I didn't return with the obvious answer. "How'd you know?"

She shrugged. "Word on the street. Coconut telegraph." She took a drag on her cigarette. "So you want to hear or what?"

I opened my wallet and dug in the back for the reserve fifty-dollar bill I kept there for paying informants. I held the bill between two fingers. "So? What do you know?"

"One day Sneaky Pete asks me if I'm a hundred percent haole. I tell him I may have a Portagee name, but I'm more Hawaiian than most people on this island. He tells me that's too bad, he's got this freaky Mormon dude, only wants to fuck white girls. I say I can pass, but he says that's not good enough. Says the guy's always quoting shit from the Mormon bible about not letting the races mix."

I looked at Ray and could tell he was thinking the same thing. A Mormon who didn't like racial mixing. Could he be connected with the Children of Noah?

"You know anything more about this guy? Name, age? Where he's from?"

"I think maybe Laie. I was talking to Sneaky Pete, and he asked me if I ever went up that way and I said hell to the no, what am I gonna do up there? So then he says that's good, because the freaky Mormon dude said something bad is going to happen up there this weekend. It sounded scary and I thought you guys ought to know."

"You're a smart girl, Judy," I said. "You know where we can find Sneaky Pete?" He didn't have the kind of regular habits or hangouts that Judy did.

"I just gave him a skully," she said. "That's why I had to rush when I called you. I know he likes to take a little nap afterwards. He's in the back room of the T-shirt shop at the Aloha Marketplace."

"I'm sure it was a hella good one," Ray said, as I handed her the fifty.

"You ever look for a little variety, D, you come to me, all right?" she said to Ray. Then she looked over at me. "I know I get no business from you, D-squared. But I know a boy with a sweet mouth and a sweeter ass, you ever get interested."

She turned and sauntered away. I wondered if Sneaky Pete had paid her for the blow job or if she'd just traded for some weed. Either way, he was about to have his little nap disturbed.

Sneaky Pete, aka Peter Petrocelli, was a pimp and drug dealer who had worked his way up from being a lookout for bigger kids on the mean streets of Portland, Oregon. Once he had gotten too old for that job, he'd graduated to snatch-and-grabs and turning out high school girls. He had come to Honolulu in search of warmer weather and a cooler scene. We'd rousted him a few times but the charges never stuck.

When we walked into Shorty's Shirts, I recognized the busty wahine behind the T-shirt counter. Her name was Monica, and she turned tricks for Sneaky Pete on the side. We walked inside, skirting a tourist family arguing over whether the ten-year-old son could get a vampire T-shirt that read "I'd rather be drinking blood." We powered past Monica toward the back room, despite her efforts to stop us, and banged the door open, startling Pete from his slumber.

"What the fuck?" he said, jumping up from a faded couch along one wall.

Unfortunately for him, he'd never zipped up after Judy's tender ministrations, and his board shorts flopped to the floor. His half-hard dick pressed against the pouch of a pair of tattered cotton briefs only a straight man would continue to wear.

"Yo, Petey," Ray said, assuming the South Philly Italian accent his parents had forced him to abandon as a kid. "You developing a new clientele? Mormons who only like white girls?"

I closed the door behind us and leaned against it.

Petey scrambled to pick up his garishly patterned yellow-and-black shorts. "Just the one dude," he said, as he zipped up.

"Freaky Mormon type. You know those dudes? White shirt, tie, always talking about God and shit? Can't have extra wives any more so they got to get their variety on the street."

"You know this freaky Mormon type's name?" Ray asked.

"Bob. Least that's what he calls himself."

Bob. Didn't mean he was Robert Kilgore, but didn't mean he wasn't.

Ray pulled a chair over and sat down backwards on it, and motioned Pete back to the couch.

Pete sat. "What do you want with Bob?"

"He ever say anything about a group called The Children of Noah?" Ray asked.

Pete shrugged. "Sometimes he gets started preaching on me, talk about how whites should only stay with whites, that I shouldn't let white girls go with black dudes, that kind of thing. He told me that even a dirty bastard like me had to follow the Lord's words." He snorted. "Look who's calling who a dirty bastard. Dude wears lace panties, likes to have the girl piss on him."

"You know anything that might connect this guy Bob with a bunch of assaults on mixed-race couples and families?" Ray asked. "Or that crucifixion up on the Windward Shore?"

Pete looked from Ray up to me, guarding the door. "What's in it for me?"

"You know we work for the Feds now," I say. "Can't make any promises, but you get in trouble, we could put in a good word for you."

"I'm a citizen," he said. "I pay my taxes. You may not believe me but I love the fucking US of A. So I'm gonna give you this out of the goodness of my heart, because nobody should get killed like that. Bob was here a couple of days ago, and he asked me if I ever went up to that theme park by Laie, Islands of History. I told him what do I look like?" Sneaky Pete laughed.

"And?" Ray asked.

"And he said that I ought to stay away from it this weekend, because there's this big event going on full of sinners on Saturday, and I might get hurt if I was there."

I knew the park he was talking about; we'd been taken up there on school field trips. It was a collection of pavilions, each featuring a different island in the Pacific, focusing on the music, dance and culture.

"This weekend?" I asked. "Anything more than that?"

He shook his head and then looked at his watch. "We done here? 'Cause my nap time is over and I gotta get to work."

"One last thing," I said. I pulled up the photo from Robert Kilgore's license and showed it to Pete. "Is this Bob?"

He peered at the screen. "Yup. I recognize that hairy mole on his chin."

Sneaky Pete scurried out like the little rat he was. Now we had to act on what we'd learned.

"So what do we do with this information?" Ray asked, as we walked back to my Jeep. "Tell Salinas? Tell Amador up in Kahuku?"

"Tell them both," I said. "But first we need our own action plan."

We walked beside the Alawai Canal on our way back to where I'd parked the Jeep. The water shimmered in the high sunshine and a line of palm trees swayed in the trade wind. An outrigger canoe team stroked past us, working in harmony, and I pictured Kilgore as the steerer, skippering the canoe and directing the rowers.

"You think we should pay Mr. Robert Kilgore a visit?" I asked. "Ask him about his taste in sexual activity?"

"No, I think we should go back to the office and do some research first," Ray said. "Like real cops would do."

Ray and I had originally been paired together as HPD detectives because our boss knew that I had a tendency to rush into things, while Ray was a detailed, by the book cop. Years later, we were still working the same dynamic.

"Fine," I huffed as we reached the Jeep. "We'll do it your way."

We had to wait at a stop sign as a parade of elementary school kids, holding hands two by two, crossed the street on their way to or from a field trip. Would there be school trips to the Islands of History this weekend? Or just families trying to enjoy the sights and teach their kids about island culture? What would happen if Bob's plans were carried out?

As we drove, Ray looked up Islands of History on his phone. "They've got a big multi-cultural festival going on this weekend," he said.

The last time I'd been to the Islands of History was when I

was in high school, and I helped my brothers manage their keikis on a family trip. At the time I'd thought the place was small and cheesy, but now I realized it was pretty big and there were lots of opportunities to cause mayhem there.

"We have no way of figuring out what Freaky Bob and his family are planning for this weekend," I said. "And the chances that we'd be in the right place at the right time to catch somebody would be slim. I hope Salinas agrees that we have enough to justify some kind of a team."

When we got back to Kapolei we went directly to Salinas's office. He was on a phone call, and he motioned us to sit. When he hung up, he said, "I hope you have some progress to report."

Ray and I went over what we had, beginning with the letters to the Habermans and the miscellaneous other threats, up to the crucifixions. "We have two points of connection," I said. "At least one print from the latest letter to the Habermans matches a print on Rigoberto Flores's motorcycle."

Ray picked up the thread. "And the language on this flyer from the Children of Noah is a pretty close match to the content of the latest letter to Susan Haberman. Kilgore's oldest sons fit the profile we've been assembling. Several of the people who were harassed in person reported two or three adult Caucasian males. One gave us the first three letters of a pickup's license plate, which matches one registered to Kilgore."

"People at the bar in Hauula said a similar group of men were arguing with Flores and Casco shortly before they were murdered," Ray added.

"This afternoon we talked to a couple of our sources," I said. "A pimp named Peter Petrocelli told us that he often finds girls—only all-white girls—for what he calls a freaky Mormon dude named Bob. He identified a driver's license photo of Robert Noah Kilgore, the leader of the Children of Noah."

"The last time Bob talked to Pete, he told Pete to stay away from the Islands of History theme park in Laie this weekend," Ray said. "Because something is happening there and Pete could get hurt. We checked, and the park is celebrating multi-culturalism at a festival on Saturday. It's just the kind of thing that would set off Kilgore and his church."

"This is all solid work," Salinas said. "But if we're going to mount an operation at this private property, we're going to need a lot more. What else can you get?"

I looked at my watch. "I'm meeting later today with a woman I hope can lead me to Kilgore's oldest daughter," I said. "She seems to be the only one of her siblings who has left the fold. I hope she can give me something more substantial."

Salinas nodded. "Keep me in the loop. If we're going to move on Saturday we'll have to make a decision tomorrow."

As we walked back to our office, Ray said, "I'm going to keep searching online. If Kilgore is planning something there may be some more clues out there. I'm also curious about this compound where they live."

"I'll let you know if I get hold of Dinah Kilgore, and what she says," I said, and I left to drive back to Aiea. There was an accident on the H-1 just before Pearl City, and I was lucky to be able to get off the highway and onto the Kam. In the distance I could see the high conning tower of a Navy ship, and it was strange for me to realize that I was working for the Feds now, not the Honolulu PD.

The gym where Kelsey Lampart worked was in a free-standing building just off Moanalua Road, and a wall of glass faced the street, with a long row of exercise bikes facing outward. Behind them, about a dozen young men and women lifted weights and ran on treadmills.

At the front desk, I showed my badge and asked for Kelsey. "She's not in trouble, is she?" the blonde receptionist asked.

"Not at all," I said. "I just want to ask her a couple of questions."

She looked down at a schedule in front of her. "She's teaching a spin class now, but she'll be finished in fifteen minutes, and then she has a break."

"That's fine. I'll wait."

While I waited, I wondered what had happened to Dinah. Had she escaped from the Children of Noah? Or was she really in hiding at the compound, using the mail drop for illicit activities? I had a gut feeling that she was a clue somehow.

I was lost in thought when a petite haole woman came up to me. "I'm Kelsey," she said. "Are you looking for me?"

Her dark blonde hair was pulled back into a ponytail, and she wore electric yellow compression shorts and a blue microfiber top. I introduced myself and she said, "Oh, right. Sandy called and told me to expect you. You're one of the dads, aren't you?"

"I am. Sandra said you might be able to help me get hold of a woman I'd like to talk to. Dinah Kilgore."

Her eyes narrowed. "What do you want with Dinah?"

So I was right. The Dinah Kelsey had mentioned on her blog was Robert Kilgore's oldest daughter. "Just to talk to her."

"It's not about her father, is it? Because she walked away from him and all that stuff years ago."

"Look, Dinah's not in trouble. But I do need to talk to her about her father. I need whatever inside information she has."

"Are you going to put him away? He's crazy, you know."

"Right now, I'm just looking for information on a case I'm investigating," I said.

"I'll call her," Kelsey said. "If she'll talk to you, I'll give you the phone."

I wondered why Kelsey was so protective of Dinah. Were they just friends? Or something more?

Kelsey turned and walked away from me, and I waited in the lobby. Kelsey came back a couple of minutes later with a piece of paper. "Here's her address," she said. "She's there now, but she has a yoga group coming over at seven. She can't work anywhere or her father will find her, so the best she can do is teach classes at home for cash."

I didn't recognize the address, but I knew I could put it into my phone and get directions. "Thanks," I said.

"If you hurt her, you'll answer to me," she said, and then turned sharply and walked away.

The address Kelsey Lampart gave me was a two-story apartment building with staircases at each end and a crumbling concrete railing along the second floor, on a tiny side street in Waimalu, close to the Pearl Harbor shore. As I got out of the Jeep the sound of a plane landing on the reef runway shook the air. I climbed the stairs and found the shades pulled down on the single window of apartment 2C, and there was no doormat or name plate. All part of Dinah's effort to stay anonymous, I thought.

I knocked hard on the door. When I heard footsteps inside, I held my badge up to the peephole. "FBI," I said. "I'm looking for Dinah Kilgore."

"Why?" she asked, without opening the door.

"I'd just like to ask you questions," I said. "Nothing criminal. And nothing I find out will ever get back to your father."

I heard the sound of chains ratcheting back, and the door opened. I half expected bats to come flying out, but instead a slim, petite woman in her mid-twenties said, "You'd better come in."

Because of her size and unimposing manner, I could see how Kelsey might feel protective of Dinah. I'd taken yoga off and on for years, and I could tell that Dinah was probably quite strong and flexible. She could take care of herself physically. But there was an emotional fragility that enveloped her like an aura.

While she closed the door and set the chain behind me, I looked around. The apartment was not gloomy, as I'd expected, but light and airy, painted a sunny yellow. Impressionistic paintings of snow-capped mountains were hung on the walls, and the furniture was rattan with floral prints.

I introduced myself, as a detective with HPD working with the FBI on an assignment that had brought her father to our attention.

"You should know that my father is crazy," she said, as she sat down. "I figured that eventually the police would get after him. What's he done now?"

"I'm just gathering background," I said. "It looks like you're the only person who's ever broken away from that compound. I was hoping you could give me some insight into what goes on there, and your father's beliefs."

"It's a crazy mishmash of the Bible, the Book of Mormon, and stuff he came up with himself. He thinks that the Apocalypse is coming closer because of all the mixed-race people diluting the white gene pool. He won't hire anyone to work for him who's not what he calls racially pure."

"White, you mean," I said.

She shook her head. "No, he'll hire anyone as long as they're not mixed. He has a couple of Japanese workers and a Chinese man. He even used to have a black man from Africa for a while. He won't hire Hawaiians or Filipinos or any other people he thinks are mongrels."

There was that word again, mongrels.

"He follows the old Mormon tradition of plural wives, right?"

"He never calls them wives," she said. "My mother wouldn't stand for that. But he does sleep with each of them occasionally. After Emerette was born, he said he was going to sleep with Hilma so my mother wouldn't have to have more children. Hilma stopped with Orris, and then he started up with LaDonna. But she's not quite all there, and my father wasn't happy that both twins took after their mother. That's when he decided he was done."

"What do you mean by not all there?" I asked.

"LaDonna's just dumb, in my opinion. But the twins? They're strange. If Donnie ever saw a doctor, his diagnosis would be somewhere on the autism spectrum. Marie? She's smart enough, but there's something misfiring in her brain. I don't know if she's psychotic or schizophrenic or whatever, but she's a strange little girl. Of course, when I left the twins were only eleven, and I haven't them in five years, so maybe they've improved."

She leaned forward. "Or maybe they've gotten worse. My father's cult is a whole lot crazier than you can imagine."

"That's The Children of Noah?"

"When I was about fifteen, he had a vision that God was going to destroy the Earth in another flood, and that he had been chosen to lead his family to safety. He started designing an ark and he began buying breeding pairs of animals. But like I said, that was years ago. I don't know what he's been up to since."

She stood up. "I've been rude. I haven't even asked if you wanted something to drink."

I asked for a glass of water, and she walked over to the galley kitchen. The room was only about ten by ten, and I figured the adjacent bedroom was about the same. For some reason I was reminded of the opening lines of one of my favorite books as a teenager, "In a hole in the ground there lived a hobbit."

Dinah's apartment had the same coziness of a hobbit hole, and I could see she'd worked hard to make it safe and comfortable. I didn't see any personal photographs—not of her family, or her with friends.

She brought me the water in a plastic glass decorated with palm trees. "Did you always know you were gay, Detective?" she asked, as she sat down again.

It took me a moment to process that leap. Either Kelsey had told her I was gay, or she'd recognized my name. I'd had a very public coming out a few years before, and I still volunteered for the occasional GLBT event.

"No, I didn't," I said. "I was about thirty-two."

"I was way ahead of you, then," she said. "When I turned eighteen, my father began pressuring me to marry and give him grandchildren. He brought nice Mormon boys home for dinner, but I didn't connect with any of them. I knew that if I stayed there, he'd force me. There was no question of telling him that I preferred women. So I left."

"That couldn't have been easy," I said.

"It wasn't. My father tracked me down and dragged me home. I ran away again, and then again. The last time I did I met Kelsey, and she helped me stay underground for a while. I learned yoga from her, and I started to teach private clients. I use a different name for that, I never let anyone take my picture, and I'm very careful who I talk to about my past. I do my best to stay off the grid so there's no way he can trace me."

"Is your father a violent man?"

She nodded. "He wants his way. He beat all of us with his belt when we were kids. Emerette and I were easier to manage, I guess. But he knocked the boys around a lot."

"And yet they all stayed."

"It's all they know. The first time I ran away I knew nothing about the outside world. They don't have television or Internet. My mother taught all the kids herself, and the textbooks she used were from the 1950s. My father beat us if we brought in any outside materials."

I told her a bit about the different threats that had been arising against mixed-race couples and families, and the connections we'd made to the Children of Noah. "We're afraid that he might be planning something bigger," I said. "Do you know if he keeps a stockpile of weapons?"

"We always had guns around when I was growing up," she said. "My father collected all kinds. He and the boys used to go out in the hills and practice target shooting."

I remembered how Rigoberto Flores and Lina Casco had been killed. "How about knives?" I asked.

"Of course. We started raising goats when I was little, and my brothers all had to learn how to kill them and skin them."

That meant that her brothers had the skill to have dispatched Flores and Casco so expertly. "Sounds like there's a lot of possibility for mayhem," I said. "We have some intelligence that indicates he may be planning a larger action at the Islands of History theme park this weekend. There's a multicultural festival going on and he warned a couple of people to stay away from it."

"He's always hated that place," she said. "I remember when we were kids my mother wanted to take us there, and he got so angry he hit her and knocked her down. A festival like the one you mentioned is the kind of thing that would really set him off."

"Anything else you can think of I should know about? Any other weapons?"

"When he was a teenager Orris started to play with chemicals, and he loved blowing things up. At first my father got angry but then he let Orris start experimenting, let him order stuff by mail and read books about science." She paused. "And Marie has a taste for fire."

"What do you mean by that?"

"She was always starting little fires when she was a girl. My father built a big stone fireplace at the back of the yard, and she used to cremate any animals that died. Right before I left the last time, she set one of the storage sheds on fire."

She shuddered. "It was awful. A couple of the goats got too close and were incinerated and the smell was atrocious. My father started beating Marie and Donnie tried to protect her, and it took Ardell, Brogan and Cord to get everyone separated. Orris, Emerette and I just huddled in the corner, scared out of our wits." She looked at her watch. "I'm sorry, Detective, but I have a group in a half hour and I have to get ready."

I stood up. "Thank you very much for your time, and for your insight. If you don't mind, I'd like your phone number, in case I have any more questions."

"I don't—" she began.

"I know you have a phone, because Kelsey called you before I came over. I promise you I won't give it to your father or anyone involved with him."

She frowned, but she picked up a photocopied flyer for her yoga classes from the table beside her and handed it to me as we walked to the door. Just before she opened it, though, she asked, "My mother…is she still alive?"

"As far as we know," I said. "We haven't been up to the compound yet."

"My father is a force of nature," she said. "But my mother did her best for us."

"Sometimes that's all we can hope for," I said.

On my way home, I called Ray and told him what I'd learned from Dinah Kilgore. We arranged to meet the next morning for a brainstorming session and I drove home thinking about what Dinah had said. Her father sounded like many of the cult leaders I'd read about, mixing fear, discipline and religion into a murky stew of obedience. I could easily see him pushing his children into a violent campaign.

I was about to get off the H-1 at Aiea when my cell phone rang. I pushed the Bluetooth button and answered. "Howzit, Mom?"

"It's your father," she said, her voice shaking. "He was having trouble breathing so I had to call the paramedics. We're at the hospital now. Queen's. I'm waiting to hear what the doctor says."

"I'm on my way." I hung up the phone, made a complicated series of turns, and found myself right back on the H-1. I called Mike's cell but he didn't pick up, so I left him a message.

I remembered a scare we'd had a few years before, when my father had similar trouble breathing. Since then, my mother had put him on a diet and begun watching his sodium and calorie intake. Mike's father had recommended Dr. Rivera, a cardiologist who was a friend of his, and my father had been seeing the man regularly.

When I got to the hospital, my mother and both my brothers were standing outside a curtain in the emergency room. "How's Dad?" I asked.

"They have him on oxygen," Lui said. "There might be something wrong with his heart."

"The same thing he had before?" I asked.

"It's been getting worse," Haoa said. He blinked a couple of times, as if he was holding back tears, and I felt a zing of fear run through my body.

A petite Indian woman in a doctor's coat approached us. "You are Mr. Kanapa's family?" she asked.

My brothers and I spoke at the same time. "Kanapa'aka."

"Sorry," she said. "I am still learning to pronounce Hawaiian names. I understand he has had a history of mitral valve prolapse? And been treated with beta blockers and diuretics?"

"That's correct," Lui said. "The last time he had an echocardiogram his mitral valve was about fifty percent occluded, and his cardiologist said that he might need a valve replacement at some point in the future."

I looked at my eldest brother. He'd always had a good memory for details, and as the oldest son he was accustomed to bossing the rest of us around. "His cardiologist should be on his way," Lui continued. "I called him as soon as I heard from my mother."

"Very good," the doctor said. "Your father is stable now, and we have him hooked up to oxygen to help him breathe. He should wait here until his cardiologist arrives, and he can be admitted then."

She went on to the next patient, and I stepped around the curtain to see my father propped up in a bed with an oxygen mask over his face. He looked weaker than when I'd seen him at the apartment. His eyes were closed, but his chest moved up and down with a regular rhythm.

He opened his eyes and started tugging the mask off his face. "Dad! No!" I said, putting my hand over his. His eyes blazed and he wrestled feebly with me. Both my brothers came behind the curtain, followed by a petite Filipina nurse.

She walked up to my father and pulled his hand away. "You can't take this off, sir. You need it to breathe." She reached into her pocket for a roll of medical tape and began to tape his hand to the bed.

"Do you have to do that?" Haoa asked.

"Unless you want him to pull the mask off," the nurse said, and she ripped the tape with an abrupt sound that shook me.

Or maybe it was my cell, vibrating in my pocket. I pulled it out and saw that it was Mike calling, and I stepped outside to talk in the hallway. "How's your dad?" Mike asked.

"Hard to say. They have him on oxygen and he's not happy. I'm going to stay here for a while," I said. "You all right with Dakota and Roby?"

"Sure. You don't want me to come down? Or send my dad? Sometimes a doctor can be a better advocate for a patient than a layman."

"Maybe he could just call down here and talk to the ER doctor, or my dad's cardiologist when he gets here," I said. "And then translate for my mom and me."

"I'll talk to him. You stay strong, K-man, all right? We've known this was going to happen for long time."

"He's going to get better," I said. "He's tough."

"And he's what? Eighty?"

"No." I had to do the math for a minute. "Seventy-four."

"Still, that's pretty old. He worked hard all his life, he has high blood pressure, heart problems, breathing problems. I'm just saying, be prepared."

"Call your dad, all right? I'll be here."

I hung up. I knew Mike was trying to be kind but I didn't want to consider bad news.

By the time I got back to my father's bedside, Haoa was gone, and Lui put his arm around my shoulder and steered me away. I was worried he was going to say the same thing that Mike had, that we needed to be prepared to say goodbye to our father, but he didn't.

"Any news on those crucifixions on the Windward Shore?" he asked. "I understand the FBI has a big interest in them and I heard your name come up."

"The investigation belongs to HPD," I said. "I can give you the name of the detective in District 2 who's handling it."

"Ralph already has that," Lui said. "But the story is dying out without any new developments. Can't you give me something I can run on the eleven o'clock news? Just a hint, a direction where Ralph can look."

"Ralph can look up his own ass," I said pleasantly. "Maybe he can find his brain there."

"Kimo," my brother said. "I changed your diapers, you know."

"You were ten years old when I was born," I said. "You probably had just been potty trained yourself by then." I pushed away from him. "I'm going back to check on Dad."

He snorted and walked away, his car keys jangling in his hand.

"I'll stay with your father until they put him in a room," my mother said, when I found her by my dad's bedside. "You should go home."

"How did you get here?" I asked.

"In the ambulance."

I held up my hand. "I'll stay and take you home."

My mother protested; she could take a cab, it might be hours, I had to go to work the next day. I brushed all that aside and sat down beside my father.

My mom and I talked for a while as my dad slept. Then I heard Dom's voice out at the nurse's station and I stepped out to see him. "You didn't have to come all the way down here," I said.

"Are you kidding? Al's like my brother." I realized that in addition to Dom and Soon-O being ohana through my relationship with Mike, now they shared grandchildren with my parents. I felt overwhelmed by emotion. I could never have imagined, years before when I was dragged out of the closet, that my life, and my heart, could have opened up so much.

Dom walked behind the curtain to my father's bed, and though my mother stood, Dom still had to bend down to hug her. "Lokelani," he said. "How are you holding up?"

"I'm fine," she said. "I'm just worried about Al."

"He's a tough old bird. And he'll get the best care possible. I'll make sure of it."

Dr. Rivera arrived a few minutes later. He was a solid-looking man in his late fifties, and I liked the way he greeted my mother and then went right to my dad. While Dr. Rivera examined him, Dom pulled my mother away, and I followed.

"I'm pretty sure Dr. Rivera is going to recommend the mitral valve replacement that Al and I have been talking about. He's only going to get worse until he has that done."

Dr. Rivera joined us. "I see Dr. Riccardi has already briefed you," he said. "I can schedule your husband for surgery tomorrow afternoon."

"So soon?" my mother asked.

"It's serious," Dom said. "The quicker we get it resolved, the better Al will be."

The surgeon went through the operation, with Dom helping us understand some of the medical terms. "You have a choice between a bioprosthetic or a mechanical valve," Dr. Rivera said. "Each has its pluses and minuses."

"What are they?" I asked.

"If we give him a mechanical valve, he'll be on blood thinners for the rest of his life, which can cause their own complications. But the bioprosthetic valves last only ten to fifteen years before they have to be replaced."

"What does that mean, bioprosthetic?" my mother asked.

"The raw materials are either taken from a pig or a cow."

"Dad loves kalua pig," I said, referring to our practice of burying a pig in the ground to roast over coals. "That's probably what he'd want. He could be one with the pig."

"Kimo," my mother scolded. She turned to the surgeon. "Are you sure he can survive the operation?"

"We can never be a hundred percent sure," Dr. Rivera said. "But I can tell you that your husband won't last much longer without intervention. We're giving him heavy doses of Lasix to reduce the fluid buildup, but if we don't go forward it'll just come back."

"Al and I have already talked about the possibility of the surgery. And my son is right, my husband said he preferred the valve made from a pig. It's his 'aumakua."

The cardiologist was Hawaiian, so he knew what my mother meant. In the Hawaiian religion, the 'aumakua is a spirit animal who acts as a healer and advisor. "Then his 'aumakua will protect him," he said.

Dr. Rivera turned us over to the Filipina nurse, and we woke up my dad. Dom explained to him about the operation, and my father nodded and signed all the forms. Then Dom left, and soon an orderly came down to take my father up to the CICU.

We followed him up to the unit, me holding my mother's hand. When we got there, the nurse said, "You probably want to go home now. It's going to take us a while to get him set up on the monitors, and then he's just going to sleep."

My mother leaned down and kissed my father on the forehead, and I did the same. He opened his eyes for a moment, but then closed them again.

It was close to eleven by the time I got home. Dakota was already asleep, and Mike was sitting up in bed with *Firehouse* magazine, wearing the reading glasses I thought gave him a sexy, scholarly look. "How's your dad?" he asked.

I shrugged. "Dom helped interpret for us with that friend of his, my dad's cardiologist. He's scheduled for surgery tomorrow." I started taking my clothes off.

"If he's a friend of my dad's, he's a good guy," Mike said. When I'd stripped down, he patted the side of the bed. "Come here."

I snuggled up against him.

"If Ray were here, he'd probably be singing that song from *The Lion King*," Mike said. "The Circle of Life and all."

"It would be really creepy if Ray were here now," I said.

"You going to take tomorrow off?"

"I can't. This case is heating up, and there may be some kind of an incident on Saturday. I need to be at work to prepare for it."

"The FBI can manage without you for a day, and I know how close you are to your family."

"Our family." I told him how good it felt to see Dom in the ER. "I'll see how my dad is in the morning." I knew that I ought to be there with my mother, but I also knew I had responsibilities at work. How was I going to balance them?

I woke up early Friday morning, fed and walked Roby, then called my mother. She was going to the hospital to sit with my dad until the surgery, which was scheduled for four o'clock in the afternoon.

"Why so late?" I asked. "Don't they do these first thing in the morning?"

"Dr. Rivera has other operations. He squeezed us in as a favor to Dominic."

Good to have a doctor in the family, I thought. "I'll come down and sit with you while he's in surgery," I said. With the phone at my ear, I dug out a deck of cards. When I was a teenager, my mother and I had often played cards for an hour or so at the end of the day, when we waited for my father to come home for dinner.

"Don't you have to be at work?"

"I'll be there most of the day," I said. "And Ray can cover anything that happens after I leave."

As I drove to work, I worried about how I'd manage. Was I going to be able to concentrate on the Children of Noah, knowing that my dad was going into surgery? Would I be able to get away to be with my mother, or would the job take over? I was still conflicted when I got to the Bureau office. I told Ray about my dad.

"My uncle had one of those valve jobs a couple of years ago, and he bounced right back," he said. "I'm sure your dad will be fine."

"Your mouth to God's ear," I said. "I need to tell Salinas. We might as well fit a briefing in, too."

We found Salinas in his office, and Ray jumped in with what he'd learned the day before. "I got hold of some aerial photos of the property and then compared them to building permits.

Kilgore has only pulled permits for the major work—the houses and the greenhouses for their aquaculture business. And there's an electrified fence around their entire property."

He sat back in his chair. "I also tracked legitimate weapons purchases. From what I can see, they own way more weapons than they ought to. There's no way to tell if they've constructed any underground bunkers or safe rooms, but there are a number of outbuildings, also without permits. Could be legitimate farm buildings or could be weapons storage."

Salinas frowned. "This is starting to get very ugly. What else?"

"There's an oblong field that's almost at the edge of the nature preserve with what looks like rifle targets at the far end," Ray continued. "Next to the field where the goats graze, there's a very large building about as long as a football field and three stories tall. No plans on file for it."

"That may be where they're building the ark," I said.

Salinas and Ray both looked at me. "An actual ark?" Salinas asked.

I nodded, and told him about my visit with Dinah Kilgore the day before. "Dinah said they had started work on it when she left."

"But she's been gone from that compound for five years," Salinas said when I finished. "A lot could have happened in that time."

"I agree. But it's the closest we'll get to an insider view."

"He's been buying breeding pairs of various animals." Ray looked down at the papers in front of him. "Last purchase was a pair of greater kudu, antelopes with wicked curving horns. He's got a pretty decent zoo up there by now."

"Anything else?" Salinas asked.

"I also spoke to a guy at the IRS," Ray said. "All he would tell me is that there's an open investigation into one or more of the people registered at that address for possible tax evasion." He looked at Salinas. "Any way you can get more information, Fed to Fed?"

"I can try," Salinas said. "Email me what you need." He sat back in his chair. "How does this all relate to that information you provided yesterday? About a possible incident at that theme park?"

"It's still all conjecture," I admitted. "Dinah Kilgore said that her father has always hated that park, and that an event like the one tomorrow would really set him off."

"It's Friday morning, and you believe that there may be some kind of incident at a public location tomorrow," Salinas said. "We need an action plan. You have to do something to confirm the problem from some other source, and then identify and marshal the resources necessary to counteract it."

"We're on it," Ray said, and looked at me.

"There's one more thing," I said. "Personal. My dad is having some surgery this afternoon and I'd like to cut out early so I can be at the hospital with my mom."

"Bad timing," Salinas said. "But health problems usually come that way. I hope it's nothing major."

"We won't know until it's done," I said.

"Just keep in touch with Donne and make sure you're in the loop on everything that happens."

I agreed, and Ray and I walked back to our office. "I wish we had a way to know how close Kilgore is to finishing that ark," I said. "That might indicate that they're getting ready for something big. I'm going to call Amador, see what he knows."

I also had to make sure that Amador didn't move in on the Kilgores for the murder charge before we knew everything that the family was up to. It was the kind of conversation that I hated having with someone from the Bureau when I was working for HPD, and I was determined to do it the way I thought it should be done.

But first, I wanted to get as much information as I could. "Yesterday afternoon we came across a preacher named Robert

Noah Kilgore," I said, when Amador answered. "You ever run into him or his family?"

"How much time do you have? I've got a whole dossier on him and his kooky family. He says it's his duty to repopulate the world with white people," Amador said. "They live on a compound outside Laie where they raise goats, and they also have a big greenhouse with a thriving aquaculture business that pays the bills."

He agreed to email the dossier to me, and to recite the high points over the phone. "Bob's one of these messianic types," he said. "He believes in self-sufficiency, and his family grows their own food, makes their own energy. They even purify their own water. His wife runs a school for the kids. Seems like the only times they ever leave the compound is to get into trouble."

"What kind of trouble?"

"His boys have a tendency to drink too much," Amador said. "There's three of them that work on the goat farm—Ardell, Brogan and Cord. Every couple of months, they go down to a bar in town and get drunk, start yelling and breaking shit and generally going wild. Mormons aren't supposed to drink, you know, but somehow those boys get a pass and Daddy Bob always pays the damages."

"How bad have they gotten?"

"Usually it's just a broken chair or table, but the worst was when they broke some guy's arm. Guy got paid a lot not to press charges."

"Do you think they could be the ones who killed Flores and Casco?" I asked.

"They've never been that violent, but anything's possible," Amador said. "They're all built like linebackers, but they got barely one brain between the three of them. I'll put together a photo array and go back down to that bar."

"Hold off on that for a bit," I said. I told him about our suspicions that Kilgore and his family could be planning something for the Islands of History theme park the next day.

"That's my turf," he said. "When were you going to tell me that?"

"We don't have anything more than a suspicion right now," I said. "You can be sure that once we know more I will tell you and get your department to join in. Anything else I should know?"

"Keep an eye out for Daddy Bob's other kids. I have my suspicions about his one girl, Marie. I haven't got any proof yet, but there's something off about that girl, and there have been a couple of small, unexplained arsons around her daddy's property. She and her brother could be the teens in that pickup the nurse saw."

"The ones speaking gibberish," I said. "I think I met them both once. Anything else?"

"There's also one boy who's supposedly a brainiac," Amador said. "Orris. He's the one who put together the plans for the goat farm and all the solar energy that powers everything."

That connected with what Dinah Kilgore had told me, that her father had been taking advantage of Orris's intelligence. I thanked Amador and hung up.

"We need some way into that compound," I said. "How?"

"The only person we know who might have access is Dinah Kilgore," Ray said. "But I doubt she'd be willing to go back there."

"But maybe I could convince her to call her mother," I said.

"How are you going to do that?"

A plan was starting to form in my head. I told Ray what I hoped to do, and headed to one of the electronics superstores, where I bought one of those pay-as-you-go cell phones that can't be tracked. I got it activated and loaded with a hundred dollars' worth of minutes. After I showed my police ID to one of the clerks, he helped me install a software program that would record conversations to the phone's memory.

It was only a few minutes from the store to Dinah's building. I was hoping that she'd be home because I had the sense that she didn't get out much. I knocked on her door and waited.

I was about ready to give up when the door opened. "I have an idea," I said.

Dinah looked me up and down. "About what?"

"About how you can set yourself free from this prison you've built."

She didn't say anything, but she stepped back and let me come inside. "I brought you a gift," I said, and handed the phone to her.

"I already have one of these," she said.

"This one's special. It's going to let you connect to your mother again."

She shook her head. "That's never going to happen as long as my father is alive." Then she looked at me. "You're not going to kill him, are you?"

"I don't want to see him killed. I want to see him locked up, so he can't hurt you anymore, or anyone else." I took a deep breath. "I need more proof that your father could be planning an attack of some kind tomorrow at the Islands of History," I said. "I want you to call your mother and see if she can confirm that."

"She won't say anything against him."

"If we work it right, she doesn't have to." I explained my plan to her.

"You think that will make her say something?" she asked.

"I sure hope so."

She sat back on her sofa and didn't speak for a while. I saw her look around her tiny apartment, and wondered if she saw it as I did, as little bigger than a jail cell, though with invisible bars.

"When I was a kid, we helped out with farm chores first thing in the morning. Then around the middle of the day, when it was too hot to work outside, we went up into the attic for schoolwork. My mom had my dad put big fans up there, and a phone line so she didn't have to run downstairs. She might be there now."

She nodded once, then reached for the phone. I showed her how to start up the software, and then she dialed a number she must have known by heart. I heard the phone on the other end ring a couple of times, then someone answered.

"Mama? It's Dinah."

Her voice broke, and suddenly she was crying, and it sounded like the woman on the other end was, too. "I know, Mama, I've missed you, too. I want to see you again." She wiped her eyes with the back of her hand and continued. "I was hoping maybe you could meet me this weekend, at that Islands of History park. There's a big festival going on and we'll blend right into the crowd."

She listened for a moment. "Well, then we sure don't want to go there. But if all the boys are going with Daddy then you and I could still meet."

She talked to her mother for another moment or two, then hung up. "She's still too much under his thumb," Dinah said, shaking her head. "She wants to see me and she understands why I don't want to live up there anymore—but she won't do anything to disobey my father."

She handed the phone to me. "But this should give you the evidence you need. Now if you don't mind, I'd like to be by myself."

"Thank you," I said. "You've probably saved a lot of peoples' lives today. I hope it leads to good things for you, too."

I got up and let myself out. Back in my Jeep, I figured out how to listen to the recording of Dinah's call to her mother. "Oh, no, sweetheart, that's a terrible place. It's full of those mongrel people your father is always complaining about." She lowered her voice and I had to strain to hear. "And Saturday would be just the worst day. He and the boys are going over there to make some trouble. Orrin has been working in his shop and I think he might be making a bomb."

Well, I thought. Kilgore might be in for more trouble than he was expecting.

By the time I got back to Kapolei it was early afternoon. I played the recording for Ray, and then we went to Salinas's office together.

"I know we can't use it as evidence," I said before I played the message. "But I was there for Dinah's part of the conversation."

"It's not enough to get a search warrant," Salinas said. "I wish it was, so we could just swoop down on that compound and take the lot of them into custody. And even if we could get a judge to sign off, I think it's too dangerous to approach that compound when they may be heavily armed. I'm not going to be the one to authorize another Waco."

I understood the parallels to David Koresh's compound in Waco, and the carnage that resulted when the FBI laid siege to his property. "So instead we put innocent citizens at risk?" I asked.

Salinas glared at me. "Our job is to make sure that this property is so well protected that no one is at risk," he said. "I want you two to go up to this park, liaise with local law enforcement and the property's security team. I'll get things moving down here."

Before we left, we printed up copies of the driver's license photos of each of the Kilgores to distribute to the theme park staff.

Ray and I left in our own cars so that I could head directly to the hospital once we were finished with our meetings. I plugged in my Bluetooth and called Amador. I explained what we had learned. "Ray and I are on our way to Islands of History right now. Can you meet us there?"

"Will do. And I'll call the director of security there. She'll need to be in the loop."

Going from Kapolei to Laie was probably the most awkward route on the island, because the Ko'olau Mountains got in the way. I had to take the H-2 through the heart of O'ahu to the

North Shore, then follow the Kam around the top of the island to Laie. It was over an hour's drive at the best of the times, and I worried that I might not be finished at the theme park in time to get to the hospital.

After I hung up with Amador I called my mother's cell. "Howzit, Mom? How's Dad doing?"

"We're waiting for them to take him downstairs for the operation," she said. "He hasn't been able to eat anything all day and he's in a terrible mood."

I knew what a bear my father could be when he was unhappy; my brothers and I had borne the brunt of his temper when we misbehaved as kids. "I feel your pain," I said.

"He's still got that oxygen mask on but he hates it. The nurse was going to strap his hands down again unless he promised not to move it. Oh, good grief. Hold on." It sounded like she turned away from the phone. "Alexander Kanapa'aka," she said, in her sternest voice. "If you touch that mask one more time I will personally tape your hands to the bed. And if something itches you can bet I will not scratch it for you."

My dad grumbled loudly in the background.

"Honestly," my mother said to me. "Your father."

"Why doesn't Dad have a middle name?" I asked.

"What a silly question."

"Whenever you're mad at us, you call us by all our names. But dad is only Alexander. What's the matter, his parents couldn't afford extra names when he was born?"

I was trying to jolly her along but she wasn't having any of it. "I have no idea why your father has no middle name, Kimo. But if he had one, you can bet I would be using it right now. Al!"

"All right, I'll let you go, Mom," I said. "I'll call you later."

Though my mom was petite, and my dad, my brothers and I all towered over her, she had always ruled our house with an iron fist inside a velvet glove. She and my dad had squabbled often, especially when he let his temper take hold, and I could just imagine the fights that were looming ahead of them.

Would Mike and I maintain the same strength in our relationship, I wondered, as I turned inland on the H-2. When we were tired, or stressed, we often snapped at each other, though there was no menace in it on either of our parts. I often said that there was a lot of free-floating testosterone in our household, which had only increased with the addition of Dakota going through puberty. Oh, and you could throw in Roby, a male dog who had never been neutered.

The highway ended at Wahiawa, and I merged onto the Kam for the climb over the spine of the island. After a couple of miles of commercial sprawl, the countryside took over. Once I passed the typical tourist crush at the Dole Plantation, miles of farmland stretched on both sides of the road, tractors creeping along the shoulder and crops ready for harvest.

The view of the North Shore, as I crested the rise, never failed to make my heart leap, and I longed for the days when I could grab a board and head for the waves, without having to worry about or care for anyone else. The last couple of weeks had been tough, closing out cases at HPD, preparing for the move to the Bureau, then learning to navigate an unfamiliar environment. Then, to top it off, my father, my rock, was in failing health.

But I was an adult, I reminded myself, a father, and I had responsibilities. Even so, it was torture to drive along the Kam with the Pacific crashing just outside my window and know that I couldn't stop to surf. Through Haleiwa, past Pipeline, Sunset Beach, and a dozen other surf spots already crowded with guys and gals in wetsuits. The Kam turned inland after Kawela Bay, hugging the cliffs of the Ko'olau. Every turn provided a new breathtaking view of rocky cliffs, craggy islands and blue water.

The surfers I passed were a mix of colors and other racial indicators, and as I drove through Laie, where Kilgore and his family lived, I wondered what could cause someone to resent the mix we had in Hawai'i. There had to be some trauma, I thought, some inciting cause that sent Robert Kilgore off on this dangerous tangent.

But more important, what could they be planning that would disrupt the festival? Amador had said that the three goat-farming brothers weren't very smart, but I had a feeling from everything I had learned about Kilgore himself that he was sharp and manipulative.

Both Amador and Dinah Kilgore had said that Orris was very bright, and that he was the brains behind the technology used at the compound. Dinah's mother had mentioned that she thought Orris was making bombs. What kind of trouble could he be cooking up?

The youngest daughter, Marie, had a taste for fire. Would there be arson involved as well?

The signs for Islands of History were large and colorful, and tall palms lined the entrance to a big parking lot called the Coconut Grove that held about a hundred cars. I noted two other lots on the opposite side of the street which were closed at present; I figured they were used for overflow on busy days.

I parked beside a light stanchion with a banner hanging from it that read *Elima*, the Hawaiian word for five, with a big number five beneath it. The lot seemed to be about two-thirds full. A series of school buses were parked along one side, and three women I assumed were the drivers stood beside one bus, talking and smoking cigarettes.

The property was surrounded by a chain-link fence, painted dark green, with a line of areca palms camouflaging the fence from the inside. Arecas were clustering palms, meaning that several trunks grew from one root, with fluffy fronds that created a dense foliage barrier. I followed the fence line for a few hundred feet until I found a gate, locked from the inside. I peered through the trees and saw a path that led toward one of the pavilions.

I walked back around to the ticket booth, a low-slung building with a traditional thatched-palm roof. I stood in the shade and watched a big family group buy tickets and then walk through the turnstiles. When Ray arrived, he asked, "Have you ever been up here before?"

"A bunch of times as a kid, either on school or family trips. But I haven't been here in years."

"I did some research on this place while you were with Dinah," he said. "Been here since the 1950s, about twenty acres in size. There's a canal that winds through the property, and six pavilions, each representing a different island group in the Pacific."

He motioned to a two-story structure to the right of the gates into the park. "That's the back wall of an outdoor amphitheater," he said. "Built in the 1970s. They put on a show there every hour, about how people from the South Pacific arrived here. The online reviews say that it's kind of cheesy."

"Based on what I remember, I'd agree," I said.

We turned in the other direction and I could see the thatched roofs of some of the pavilions Ray had mentioned. "I remember some kind of parade on the canal," I said.

He nodded. "Yeah, three times a day a parade of outrigger canoes starts at Tahiti. They wind their way along the canal, stopping in front of each island to put on a show."

We saw Rizaldo Amador approaching and met him at the ticket office. "I called the director of security for the park," Amador said. "She's going to take us around and hear what's going on."

While we waited for the families ahead of us to buy their tickets, I looked around at the security of the entrance. Once you had your ticket, you walked over to a series of five turnstiles, only one of which was operational that afternoon. A deeply tanned young woman in a hibiscus-print pareu, a Tahitian wrap-around dress, took the tickets and let visitors through the turnstiles. At one end was a handicapped entrance where the attendant could open a swinging door to let in wheelchairs.

No metal detectors or security scans. I spotted a couple of cameras high up on poles and wondered what they were used for.

We moved up in the line and Amador showed his badge to the clerk and asked her to call security. A slack-key guitar melody floated out from tall speakers.

The ticket clerk made a call, then stepped outside to push open the handicapped entrance and usher us through. Amador led us down a trail made of crushed rock, under the shelter of palm trees. The tropical foliage everywhere was damp and lush, interspersed with waterfalls and red, yellow and purple hibiscus, anthurium and plumeria.

Most of the buildings looked to be made of wood, and I hoped that the lumber used in them had been treated against fire, but the age of the property made me doubt that.

We stopped at a single-story flat-roofed building just beyond the amphitheater. A sign painted on rough-hewn wood read "Park Administration."

Marilyn Tuafono was a very large Samoan woman with dark hair wound into a French braid. Her khaki military-style uniform was crisply pressed, with a name badge over the right breast.

"What's this all about?" she asked, as we sat down across from her desk. "Rizaldo said you believe someone's planning an attack here?"

Ray and I alternated explaining what we had learned about Bob Kilgore and the Children of Noah. "I've seen the signs for their compound," she said. "But I had no idea they were such troublemakers. What makes you think they'll be here tomorrow?"

I explained what we'd learned, ending with a confirmation from Dinah Kilgore's mother. "But you don't know what kind of trouble?" Marilyn asked. "They going to say mean things to people, or blow something up?"

"That's what we don't know," I said. "We'd like to look around the property for points of vulnerability. Since the Kilgores live close by, it's reasonable to assume that they've been here before and scoped the place out."

We gave her a stack of photos of the Kilgores from their drivers licenses. "Not great likenesses," I said. "But if you could pass them out to your security and ask them to keep an eye out for any of them, it would help."

"What kind of staff do you have on board for tomorrow?"

Amador asked.

"Because of the crowds we're expecting, I already have my full complement in place," she said. "That's a security guard at each of the six pavilions and two at the amphitheater. I'm the rover. We're all connected by walkie-talkies. In addition I have a bunch of local teenagers directing traffic in the parking lots, and a couple of big Samoans by the front gate to catch anyone trying to sneak in without a ticket, or bringing in their own food or beverages."

"How many of your security staff have police training?" Amador asked.

"I was an MP in the Army. One of my security guards was a cop for a while on the mainland, and another went through the police academy and quit after a year on patrol."

"Any of them armed?" Ray asked.

She lifted the tail of her uniform shirt to show us the holstered gun underneath. "I'm the only one licensed to carry weapons on the premises. I don't want anybody going crazy. We haven't had any incidents more serious than a couple of drunks in the past few years."

"There's no chance you could cancel this festival tomorrow, is there?" I asked.

She looked at me like I was crazy. "This is one of our major events during the year. We've spent a lot of money on promotions all over the island. We're hoping for record crowds. To cancel now would be a disaster."

Not as big a disaster as what might happen if they didn't cancel, I thought, but I kept my mouth shut.

When we stepped out of the administration building, the sun was high and hot, and Marilyn Tuafono, Rizaldo Amador, Ray and I moved into the shade. "What time do you open tomorrow?" Ray asked Marilyn.

"At noon. I have additional staff at the parking lots to direct traffic and run people up to the front gate, from the farthest lot, in golf carts."

She stood up. "Let me walk you around."

A muscular bare-chested Māori guy with full face paint passed us, wearing a big shell necklace and the traditional piu-piu skirt, followed by a group of female dancers in grass skirts and coconut-shell bras. We started with a tour of the amphitheater because it was in between shows.

I estimated there were about two hundred hard plastic seats resting on long metal bars, ten rows divided by a central aisle, ten seats to each side. A canvas tent with a tall central pole covered the area, protecting the patrons from sun and rain but allowing cool breezes to come through.

The stage was elevated a few feet, garlanded with maile leaf and plumeria leis that looked plastic even from far away. There were three steps down on each side so the performers could walk out into the audience. A heavy curtain hung from the proscenium arch so we couldn't see what was on the stage.

"We have ushers stationed on each aisle to make sure that people fill in all the seats," she said. "And two downstage guards, one at each set of steps, to make sure patrons don't exit that way or interfere with the performers during the show. We don't allow photography or video recording, and the ushers stay in the audience during the show to enforce that policy."

We checked each of the emergency exits, and then walked behind the curtain. A giant map of the South Pacific covered the entire back wall, with tiny lights highlighting each island group. Two big outrigger canoes rested on the wooden floor, and there were cheesy wooden waves painted blue in front of them.

The backstage area was crowded with props and costumes for later parts of the program. Performers and technicians were conducting light and sound checks.

To one side was a large open cabinet stacked with the materials used in the fire dances—tubes, hoops, fans, torches and so on. "Where do you keep the fuel for the fire dances?" I asked.

"I'll show you," Marilyn said. She led us out through a fire exit to the area behind the theater. "We use standard liquid petroleum gas, the kind for barbecue grills, and we keep it in big canisters in that shed over there." She pointed to a small metal outbuilding with a padlock on the door. "Only the lead dancer can open the lock and dispense the gas."

I remembered that one of Bob Kilgore's daughters was a firebug. If she lit a fire nearby, could it spread to the gas storage? "Is there anyone stationed back here?" I asked.

Marilyn shook her head. "There's a lot of activity going on during and between shows. And there's a locked gate that keeps patrons from getting in."

Amador asked a couple of questions, and then we went back past the admission gate. There were a lot of places along the way where someone could lurk unnoticed, which I didn't like.

A bunch of families waited in line, carrying diaper bags, pushing strollers, applying sunblock to each other. That reminded me that the stakes were high—if something happened, a lot of innocent people could get hurt.

"No metal detector at the gate?" Ray asked.

"We've never had a problem," Marilyn said.

There's always a first time.

"Though several of the major theme parks already have metal detectors, we don't want to give customers the sense that things might be unsafe inside," she continued. "We are small enough that we want people to feel at home with us. Visitors are very sensitive to the experience of entering a theme park, and we want to make sure our security measures aren't invasive."

"I saw a sign out front that says weapons aren't allowed on the premises," Ray said. "Do you do anything to enforce that?"

"The guards at the gate will ask to look into big bags if they feel it's necessary. And there's little reason why anyone would bring a gun to a family park."

Once again, I was surprised by Marilyn Tuafono's naiveté, but I let it slide. If something bad happened, she'd change that attitude herself.

I looked at staff members around us as we walked toward the first pavilion. The men wore faded aloha shirts and kukui nut leis, and the women wore matching hibiscus-print pareus. I wondered how easily they could move in those in an emergency.

We passed a big lagoon, with two outrigger canoes and a half-dozen small ferry-style boats docked at a landing. "People who want to experience paddling an outrigger canoe can do so here, for an extra fee," Marilyn said. "Our staffers will take them out through the lagoon and let them ride back in on the surf. The other boats take visitors around the lagoon and the canal when the parade isn't running."

On the far side of the lagoon I saw a big boathouse with open doors, and through them I could see a series of outrigger canoes lashed together in twos, with flat platforms joining them. "Who has access to the outriggers over there?" I asked.

"Only staff members," Marilyn said. "There's a gate that leads to a path around the lagoon. During operating hours we have someone stationed there to keep patrons out, and when we close the gate is locked."

From the lagoon we walked to the Tahiti pavilion. It was a complex of small open-air buildings with thatched roofs around a paved circular area in the center. A group of kids sat on a rubber mat and colored in one area, while in another a buff, shirtless man explained his tattoos and the history of tattooing in the

South Pacific. Across from him, a half-dozen men in loincloths clacked sticks together in a ritual dance.

"Each of our pavilions has its own set of activities, entertainment and gift shops," Marilyn said, as we watched. The last building, the only one with walls and a door, stocked merchandise that ranged from authentic grass skirts to postcards of Gauguin nudes to hula-dancer swizzle sticks.

I kept my eyes out for anyone acting suspicious, but for the most part everyone looked like they were at the park to have fun. The younger men wore ball caps, rock concert T-shirts, board shorts and rubber slippers. They held small children in their arms. For the most part, the young women looked tired, pushing strollers and carrying bags of diapers and snacks and bottled water.

When the four of us passed the Tongan pavilion, a woman was demonstrating how to make tapa, a bark cloth. At Samoa, a big guy in a plus-sized red skirt entertained a crowd by dragging men up to the stage to mimic his movements and then play drums. At the final pavilion, Hawai'i, a woman in an elaborate feathered cloak blew a conch shell and led a parade of island elders in a ceremony.

As the procession ended, the sound of men blowing conch shells resonated through the park from loudspeakers hidden among the trees. "That's the signal that the canoe parade is about to start," Marilyn said. "To minimize crowds, we schedule the presentation in the theater and the canal parade at the same time."

She led us to a place along the canal where we had views in both directions. There were six double-hulled outrigger canoes in the procession, each of them with a central platform between the two hulls. Each had the name of the island it represented outlined in plastic flowers. The Hawaiian canoe stopped in front of us, and the three men and three women on the platform did a very stylized hula, the women swishing their hips, the men on their knees miming warrior movements. All the performers looked so happy—I guessed a paycheck could do that for you.

Tourists and the occasional local families clustered on the

wooden benches or the stone wall along the canal. Everyone had a camera or a cell phone to take pictures, and I wondered how many of those shots would ever be seen again. Even on a weekday, the place was crowded. How bad would it be on a special-event Saturday? Bob Kilgore and his family would be able to blend easily into the crowds, making whatever mischief was on their minds.

What could it be? The fire dances were a clear point of vulnerability. The Kilgores could turn a knife dance bloody, or they could start fights with other patrons. They could knock down or ignite some of the flimsier decorations. There were too many possibilities.

When the canoe parade was over, we walked back to the entrance. "What's special about tomorrow?" I asked Marilyn. "What makes this a multicultural festival?"

"Not much, I'm afraid," she said. "It's more a marketing gimmick than anything else. We have some portable displays about contributions that different cultures have made to Hawai'i, including some of the ones we don't focus on here…Japanese, Korean, and so on. Our staff will be putting those displays up this evening after the park closes."

It was going to be a logistical challenge to keep an eye on so many different venues without a clear idea of what the Children of Noah might try. As a parade of school kids in matching orange T-shirts passed us, holding hands two by two, I remembered the ark that that the Children of Noah were building. How far would Kilgore go in his pursuit of racial purity? Would he kill innocent children?

By the time we were finished our tour, I was more worried than I'd been at the start.

"I'm on my way, Mom. Dad in surgery yet?"

"They took him down for preparation an hour ago," she said. "I'm waiting in the family lounge outside the operating rooms."

"I should be there in about half an hour," I said. "He's going to be fine, you know. Remember what Haoa used to say when Dad threatened him?"

My brother had been a bit of a rebel as a teenager, stretching the limits of our father's patience sometimes. "Dad used to say, 'I'm going to kill you!' and Haoa would say 'Only the good die young.'"

She laughed. "He was such a troublemaker then," she said. "But your father isn't so young anymore."

"He's still got a few good years left in him," I said. "Who else will keep you in line? None of us could manage that."

I hung up and tried to focus on the road, because that section of the Kam hugs the side of the mountain, with a steep drop down toward the ocean. But I couldn't stop worrying about my father. He was seventy-four, and he had a lot of health issues: he weighed too much, which caused too much strain on his back and his feet; his doctor was monitoring him for diabetes; and he'd had heart problems for a while.

How long would he be around? I wanted him to know his newest grandchildren, to be around to mentor them, play with them, and tease him the way he had done with Lui's and Haoa's kids.

My father had always been my role model. Though he wasn't perfect, he was a good man, and he cared about his family, his work, and his culture. I liked to believe that my interest in being a cop began with his attitudes toward the less fortunate. Back when he ran his construction firm, he hired men and women who needed a second or third chance. Sometimes they succeeded, at other times they disappointed him. But he persevered. My parents made charitable donations, and for years, when he was able, my father had volunteered with groups that built or renovated properties for the disadvantaged.

When I got to the Queen's Medical Center, I found my mother in the waiting room, a paperback romance novel closed on her lap. She was a dedicated reader, and I inherited my love of books from her. She always had one of those paperbacks in her purse, and since their move to Waikiki she had taken to spending afternoons on the balcony overlooking Diamond Head, lost in a story.

I kissed her cheek and sat beside her, then pulled out the deck of cards. "You want to plan gin rummy?"

She nodded, and as I dealt the first hand, I could tell that she was remembering those nights we'd played together when I was a teenager. "I haven't played cards in years," she said.

"I'm sure you still remember."

Lui had to be at work that afternoon, though he promised to keep his cell with him. Haoa was bidding on an important landscaping job at a big hotel, and he was going to join us as soon as he finished. So it was just my mom and me.

Sitting with her reminded me of being a teenager, the way she and I had spent time together after my brothers had left home. I was the baby of the family, ten years younger than Lui and eight years younger than Haoa, and once they had both left for college I had loved being the only one at home, not having to fight with my brothers for attention.

We played for an hour or so, until she said that she wanted to close her eyes for a few minutes. While she did, I opened my iPad. I had been meaning to read up on the surgery my father was undergoing but I hadn't had the time. It was hard to concentrate, so I jumped around to a bunch of different sites. The surgery was minimally invasive, which was a good thing—just a couple of small cuts to his chest. But he might have to go on a heart-lung machine during the procedure, and that made me nervous.

Around five-thirty I gave up and stepped outside to call Ray. "How are things going?"

"Lots of hustle and bustle," he said. "We had a big meeting that finished about a half-hour ago. We're going to meet up at the park tomorrow morning at eight so we can do more recon and get people in place before the crowds arrive. The park will open at ten, and we'll have agents stationed at each pavilion, at the entrance and the amphitheater."

"Where are you and I stationed?"

"We'll be at the Tahiti pavilion," he said. "That's the one closest to the entrance. We're supposed to wear casual clothes so we can blend in, with our weapons out of sight but easily accessible. Any word on your dad yet?"

"Still in surgery."

"He's tough," Ray said. "You have to be strong, too."

"I know," I said. I thanked him and went back inside, where I found Haoa pacing around, full of nervous energy.

"How long is this operation supposed to take?" he asked.

"Dr. Rivera said it would be two to four hours," my mother said.

"Then why isn't he finished yet?" Haoa asked.

"We're not sure what time the surgery started," I said.

"I'm going to ask," Haoa said.

My mother and I watched as Haoa stalked over to the nurse's station. "I hope he's polite," my mother said. "Those people have very difficult jobs."

And there, in a nutshell, was the lesson I had learned from both my parents as I was growing up. To have compassion for others, to treat them the way I would want to be treated.

From across the room I watched Haoa's body language. He leaned against the counter, he smiled, and the nurse laughed. That was my brother, I thought. If I wanted to consider the gifts that each of us had, I'd say that Lui was the most businesslike, the most organized and thorough. Haoa was the one with the charm and the intuitive connection to people and to the earth. I got the bull-headed determination to see things through. The three of us made a good team, and I was glad to have both of them as my brothers.

Haoa returned a couple of minutes later. "She looked at the schedule and said he's still in surgery," he said. "But it's not uncommon to have these operations go on longer than expected. They're pretty routine, but each patient is different. She said Rivera is one of the best doctors they have here."

Lui called after the evening news was over. I told him that we had no idea what was going on. "I'm on my way," he said, and I was glad. I wanted all of us to be together in case anything went wrong.

I took another break to go outside and call Mike. I told him there was no news, that I'd call when I had some. Then I dialed his father. "It seems like the surgery is taking a long time," I asked Dom. "Is that a bad sign?"

"You can't worry like that," he said. "All kinds of things could be delaying that have nothing to do with Al. A nurse who needs to step out. A piece of equipment that's not working correctly."

"But there could be bad things, too, right?" I asked, remembering what I'd just read. "Blood clots, breathing problems, even a heart attack or a stroke?"

"You know what I always say, Kimo. You can get hit by a bus walking across the street. I'm not going to lie to you; anything can happen in that operating room. But I trust Rivera and I know he'll do everything he can to get Al a solid outcome."

I went back to the waiting room, where Haoa kept pacing. "You're making me nervous," I said to him. "Why don't you go outside and pull some weeds for a while?"

"Tatiana says I'm too stressed lately," he said. "She's been trying to get me to meditate."

I had to suppress a laugh. My brothers and I were all type-A achievers, and I couldn't imagine any of us calm enough to meditate. The closest I got was out on the waves, when I could let all my land-based cares wash away. Lui arrived a half-hour later, and he and Haoa stepped outside to talk.

That's the way it had always been when I was a kid. Lui and Haoa were a joint task force, and I was the outsider. As we got older, things had changed a lot, and we got along very well. But at times of stress I could see us reverting to our older patterns.

Finally, around eight o'clock, Dr. Rivera emerged from a pair of swinging doors. He didn't smile, and my heart did a big flip-flop.

"He's in the recovery room now," he said. "I'm afraid the surgery didn't go as smoothly as I had hoped. As I mentioned, since a mitral valve replacement is an open heart surgical procedure, we had to put Al on cardiopulmonary bypass. His heart stopped twice, but we were able to revive him, and the valve is in place. Now we wait."

"For what?" Haoa asked.

"We're giving him drugs to prevent his rejection of the valve, but there's always a chance of complications. He'll be on a respirator for at least a few hours, and since there's a risk of atrial fibrillation we'll have him on a heart monitor. If all goes well, he'll be in the CICU for two days or so, then moved to a regular room. After that you'll want him to spend a couple of weeks in rehab."

"When can I see him?" my mother asked.

"He's going to be knocked out for the rest of the night, but if you want to peek your head into recovery and see that he's sleeping, you can do that."

We went in one by one, just a minute apiece. When it was my turn, I stood by his bed and watched him breathe. His face was pale, and he'd lost weight over the last few months. I saw the lines in his hair where my mother must have combed it for him.

He still had that oxygen mask on, but his chest rose and fell slightly. "You hang on, Dad," I whispered, and I leaned down and kissed his forehead. "We still need you too much to let you go."

My mother, my brothers and I walked out to the parking garage together. "He's going to be fine," Lui said, as if, being first boy, whatever he said had to be true. I hoped he was right.

I called Mike from the hospital parking lot and told him what Doctor Rivera had said. "His heart stopped twice?" he asked.

"Yeah, but they were able to start it again."

"I hope this new valve will fix him for a while, K-man," Mike said. "But you know he's going to take a while to recuperate, and even then he might not have much time left."

"He's going to be all right," I said. "He's going to be around to play with Alpha and Omega."

"I hope so, too," Mike said. "Drive carefully. Love you."

I told him I loved him too. It was already way beyond dinnertime, and my stomach was grumbling, so I stopped at a drive through and grabbed a big Caesar salad with grilled chicken, and a cheeseburger. I ate the burger as I drove up Aiea Heights drive.

I sat with Mike at the kitchen table, Roby at my feet, and I ate my salad. I fed the dog a couple of bits of chicken, and Mike and I talked about my dad, and about the plan to stake out Islands of History the next day. "I thought you were going to be riding a desk at the Bureau," he said. "Wasn't that the whole plan for you switching over from HPD? So you wouldn't be in danger?"

"I'm not the kind to sit around and fill out paperwork. You know that about me."

"I still don't like it," he said. "Why couldn't you get into some kind of money laundering case? White-collar criminals who don't kill people?"

"Nobody's going to get killed," I said.

"Besides the two who already have been? Forgotten about those crucifixions? Whoever is behind them is inhuman. I hate you going up against people like that."

This was an old argument. Mike wanted to protect me, keep me from putting myself in danger chasing criminals. And I hated thinking of him walking around fires, searching for evidence where there could be hotspots that could flare up at any moment and incinerate him. But we were who we were, and no amount of wishing was going to change that.

"Ray will look out for me," I said. "We'll have a whole SWAT team on standby in case of trouble. We'll be wearing Kevlar vests under our shirts. I promise you, we will take every precaution."

He grumbled, but he knew as well as I did that I was going to that theme park the next day, and that I would do whatever I could to keep people safe. He stood up and started noisily loading the dishwasher. "I'm going next door," I said, and he grunted.

Dom answered the door, and I followed him to the living room. Dom and Soon-O's house was the opposite of ours, and it was always a little disorienting to see the kitchen door on the other side of the room, the staircase flipped, and so on.

Mike's parents' house was also more adult, I guess, than ours. Real art work on the walls, landscape paintings of the Korean countryside, where we had some framed posters from places we'd visited. Matching furniture, bought new, while ours was hand-me-down.

"How's Al?" Dom asked, as I sat on the sofa, Dom across from me in his recliner. I told him about the surgery, the fact that my dad's heart had stopped twice, and then about all the complications Dr. Rivera had warned us about.

"There are always things that can go wrong," Dom said. "Medicine is still an art, Kimo. We're always learning and discovering new procedures and materials. And doctors, good doctors, try not to pretend that we're God and we know everything. That's why Rivera told you about those complications, so you can be prepared for whatever happens."

"I just want him to be okay," I said, and my voice cracked.

Dom got up and joined me on the sofa, and put his arm around my shoulders. "I think your dad still has some spark left in him," he said. "And your mom takes excellent care of him. I'd say the chances are good for a full recovery. But it never hurts to send a couple of messages to the big man upstairs. Soon-O and I have been saying prayers for his health, and we'll keep on doing that."

All of Mike's family were practicing Roman Catholics. I wished I had Dom's certainty; I believed in a higher power of some kind, but I rarely prayed.

"And whatever happens, you know you'll have us to fall back on," he said. "I'll never replace your dad, but Soon-O and I both think of you as our second son. I hope you believe that, despite the rocky start we had."

Once Dom had come to realize that Mike and I had both been complicit in our troubles, and that we loved each other and were committed for the long haul, he had been nothing but warm and generous to me. It felt good to have that reassurance from him.

When I left him at his doorstep, instead of walking right into our half of the duplex I went around to the backyard. I sat in one of the big Adirondack chairs and looked up at the stars. They were the same ones that had guided my ancestors to this speck of rock in the middle of the Pacific. Some had come in a spirit of adventure, others in search of better lives, still others in pursuit of souls to save. But it was their courage and their willingness to face adversity that linked them all together.

I stared upward and asked them to guide my father on his journey through this danger, and back to health.

And then I prayed. I asked my granny's God and all those Mormon prophets to take care of her son and allow him to stay with us a while longer. I asked the same of the God that Mike and his parents worshipped; those tiny babies shared blood with them, and I hoped that would be enough for His intercession.

I prayed to Amaterasu, the Shinto goddess of the universe, who had guarded my Ojisan's family from generations in Japan, and to every one of the Hawaiian gods I could remember. I began with Wakea, the sky father, because I hoped he would hear the prayer of a son who loved his father. I asked Kāne, the god of procreation, ancestor of the Hawaiian people, to allow my father to stay among us so that my children could learn the life lessons he had to teach. I reminded Lono, the goddess of fertility, that she had blessed us with these babies, and asked her for the same help.

I asked Ku, the god of war, to help my father in his fight to return to health. And finally, I asked Kanaloa, the god of the underworld, to delay bringing my father to his side.

I finished my prayers and stayed out in the yard for a while, until Mike came out to sit in the chair beside me. He took my hand and squeezed. I knew that I would lose my father one day; as Robert Frost once wrote, nothing gold can stay. But I would have Mike by my side, and together we would face whatever life, or any of those gods, presented us with.

Saturday morning I woke to the feel of Roby's breath as he sniffed my face, and when I opened my eyes his big head was right in front of me. "Thank you for the wake-up call," I said to him, as Mike stirred beside me.

I climbed out of bed, and Roby pranced around, eager to get outside. "I'll take him," I said to Mike, as I pulled on a T-shirt, a pair of shorts, and rubber slippers.

With Roby's leash hooked up, we walked out the door and I called the CICU at Queen's. My father's nurse told me that he'd woken up in the night and tried to pull the oxygen mask off again. "He kept calling for one of those Norse gods," she said. "It was very strange."

It took me a minute to make the connection. "Loki?" I asked. "My mom's name is Lokelani."

"Oh, that explains it, then. We're checking his vitals regularly, but he's probably going to be knocked out most of the day." I thanked her and hung up as Roby tugged me down the street in pursuit of something, eventually stopping to grab a tennis ball someone had left on the grass. He grabbed it in his mouth and presented it to me.

"Sorry, don't have time to play this morning," I said. "Daddy Mike will play with you later."

He kept the ball in his mouth as he toured his preferred urination locations, and then we went back home. Roby galloped into the bedroom and jumped up onto the bed, where he dropped the ball right beside Mike's head.

Roby sat up on his haunches grinning, and I tossed the ball out into the hallway for him. "What's on your schedule for today?" I asked Mike.

"I want to trim the big kiawe in the backyard," he said. "I'll chop up the branches and put them aside for the next time we have a luau and need wood for the pit. Dakota's going over to somebody's house for the day. He says they're just going to hang out, and the boy's parents will be there."

"Dylan," I said. "The boy who gave him the card, and kissed him in the boys' room. I'm glad he decided to accept the invitation."

Mike sat up and yawned. "You have your vest?" he asked.

I nodded. "I promise I'll put it on as soon as I get up to the park," I said. "And that I'll be careful." I leaned down and kissed his bristly cheek, and Roby galloped back in with the tennis ball in his mouth.

I left the two of them to play. I grabbed a couple of breakfast bars from the kitchen and got into my Jeep. To comply with the directions I'd gotten from Ray, I'd worn an extra-large aloha shirt that had once belonged to Haoa so that it would hang loosely over the thumb holster on my belt, with my HPD-issued gun. I had my personal gun in a shoulder holster as a backup. Board shorts and deck shoes without socks would give me extra mobility.

It was a bright, sunny day with a cool breeze, and I drove up to the Windward Shore with the windows open, even though the chilly wind as I crested the Ko'olau raised goose bumps on my upper arms. I was buzzing with nervous energy. In the best case scenario, Robert Kilgore and his family would try something at the park and be immediately thwarted, giving us grounds for search warrants and subpoenas and the opportunity to put them all out of commission for a long time.

But it's an axiomatic law of police work that the best case scenario rarely happens, so I hoped that whatever went down, it would be with a minimum of chaos and casualties.

The farthest parking lot from the park entrance was open, with an HPD officer at the gate. I showed him my ID and he let me drive in. I parked at the first available spot, beside a series of big dark unmarked SUVs that I knew from experience belonged to the Bureau. I stepped out of the Jeep and pulled off my aloha shirt and my shoulder holster. I put on the Kevlar vest, and before I put the holster back over my shoulder I popped the magazine one more time to make sure it was loaded. After I put Haoa's shirt back on I checked myself in the side mirror. I looked like I'd put on about ten pounds.

I saw Ray up ahead with Salinas, Kit Carson, and Ryan Tomlinson, a lanky African-American agent with a Southern California drawl. Ray wore an oversized Philadelphia Eagles T-shirt hanging loose over a pair of khaki shorts, white socks and white sneakers with stripes in the same shade of dark green as the T-shirt.

It was the first time I'd seen Salinas in anything other than his Bureau drag. He wore what looked like a microfiber fishing shirt, with epaulets on the shoulders and vents under the arms, hanging loose over a pair of navy dress shorts.

Kit Carson had gone for the preppy mom look, with Ralph Lauren-logo polo shirt, madras skirt and sandals. Tomlinson wore a too-bright aloha shirt of impressionistic palm trees against a neon orange sunset. To my eye, we all looked like FBI agents no matter how we dressed—it was something about the posture and the sense of awareness. But I doubted civilians would notice us.

Salinas distributed tiny radio earpieces that would allow us to communicate with each other. A teenager in an open-air bus the size of a Hummer limousine pulled up, and the five of us clambered in.

Marilyn Tuafono and her staff were waiting with Rizaldo Amador and about a dozen agents, most of whom I recognized, at the entrance to the property. "The bomb dog is doing a run," Amador said.

The HPD officer with the bomb dog appeared and told us the park was clear, and Marilyn led us all inside. We went over our assignments, and through the screen of trees I saw the parking lot behind us begin to fill up with cars. Amador distributed a one-page sheet with photos of the Kilgores. "There are two more kids, the sixteen-year-old twins, but they don't have drivers licenses yet so we don't have photos of them," he said.

Dinah Kilgore's photo was there, along with the rest of her family, though I doubted she'd be making an appearance at the theme park that day.

The conch shells blasted, and Marilyn told us that was the signal to open the gates.

Ray and I walked to the Tahiti pavilion, finding ourselves a place in the shade to stand as the crowds poured in. We hovered in the background through a fishing demonstration and a program on coconut bread-making.

The crowds around us grew, and there were times when it was nearly impossible to thread your way through the masses of people. It was hot, and the smell of sweat and spilled food rose around us. "If there's an emergency, this place is going to be a bear to evacuate," Ray said.

"Yesterday when I walked around outside I saw what look like emergency exits," I said. "Though I'm not sure where they are on the inside."

We both scanned the area, looking for the tell-tale exit signs, and Ray found one first. "Look over there, beneath those paddles on that stand. There's an exit light just below it. Can you see?"

I squinted and saw it. "I hope they have better lighting for it when something happens," I said. "Or at least some staff there to shepherd people."

The conch shells blew, and people began to move around the property, some heading back toward the amphitheater, others toward the next pavilion. Ray and I kept scanning the crowds, looking for anyone who resembled the men in the photos, or anyone looking suspicious. Even though we stuck to the shade, it was still damned hot with that Kevlar vest under my shirt.

My cell phone buzzed and I saw the call was from Mike. I stepped into a quieter area to take the call. "Dakota's up there," he said.

"Up where?"

"At the Islands of History. He just posted a photo of himself and Dylan on Instagram. I signed up to follow his stream, and get an alert every time he posts."

"I should have done that," I said. "Can you tell where at the park he is?"

"I couldn't from the picture. But I'm worried about him, K-man. Dylan is half-Japanese and he and Dakota are holding hands in the picture. Either of those things could set off your crazy guy, right?"

"The mixed-race thing, sure," I said. "Did you call him?"

"He's not answering his phone. I know you're too busy to go looking for him, so I'm on my way up there right now."

I hung up and turned to Ray, and explained that Dakota was somewhere at the park. "You'll never find him in this crowd," Ray said. "Best thing to do is just stay in one place and wait until he comes by."

I was about to argue when I realized he was right. There was no way I could find Dakota without at least a clue as to where he was. I pulled out my phone and texted him that I was at the Tahiti pavilion and wanted to see him.

I didn't want to frighten him, but there was no way I wanted him at that park if something dangerous happened. But how could I find him?

I paced back and forth at the Tahiti pavilion, glancing at my phone every minute or two to see if Dakota had answered my text. Nothing. Each time I saw a guy with Dakota's build and dark hair I went on alert, but it was always someone else.

"Kimo," Ray said. "You've got to get your head back in the game here. The most important thing we can do right now is keep our eyes out for the Kilgores."

I took a deep breath as another conch shell blast rang through the air. "You're right," I said after it was over. Families began to assemble by the side of the canal for the parade, little kids up front or on their fathers' shoulders, and Ray and I stepped back to get out of the way and make sure we could move if we had to.

The first outrigger canoe, representing Tonga, came around a bend in the canal. A group of men in tall straw hats and grass skirts performed the *kailao*, a war dance, to the accompaniment of drums. With so much noise in front of us, it was hard to hear our radios and to keep our attention on the crowds, and I worried we might miss something crucial.

It was a relief when the parade continued and the Tongan canoes moved on. Canoes from each of the island groups represented at the park stopped in front of us, each performance something native to that group. It would have been fun to watch if I wasn't so keyed up, scanning the crowd for signs of danger.

As the morning wore on, we went through another cycle of blasts, more demonstrations at the Tahiti pavilion and the beginning of another canoe parade. I kept looking for Dakota but couldn't see him.

Then our radios crackled with Tomlinson's voice, all his Southern California affect gone. "I've got one of the Kilgores in Samoa," he said. "Pretty sure it's the oldest one of the goat farmers. Ardell. At first I thought he was with a family, but then he split off and I realized he's on his own."

Salinas said, "Keep a visual on him. Anyone else see any of the Kilgores?"

"I've got Brogan in the Solomon Islands," Kit Carson said. "He's watching the warrior games demonstration with his hands in his pockets. Couldn't be more casual."

Ray elbowed me. "Look over there."

A haole man in a plaid shirt, cargo shorts and faded running shoes stood by the entrance to the Tahiti pavilion, with his back to the wall of the kiddie play area, out of the way of people going past. He was in his late twenties, but he was balding prematurely. He had a weak chin and wore wire-rimmed glasses

"That's Orris Kilgore, isn't it?" I asked Ray. When he nodded I added our ID to the radio chatter. As I listened to other IDs come in, I figured that Kilgore himself, his four oldest sons and his daughter Emerette were on the property. Donnie and Marie could be around us, too, and I wondered if I would recognize them again from that brief time Mike and I had seen them at that convenience store.

"Any of the Kilgores doing anything?" Salinas asked.

The result was a chorus of negatives. In each case, it seemed, the Kilgore family member was alone, simply observing the situation around him or her.

"What do you think they're planning?" I whispered to Ray.

"Orris is checking his watch. That may mean he's part of some synchronized action."

It was a few minutes before one o'clock. Would something begin to happen as the clocked ticked to the hour?

I looked back at Orris Kilgore, who had turned slightly sideways. The pockets of his shorts bulged as if he had nodes growing out of his sides. "Look at Kilgore's shorts," I said to Ray. "Doesn't it look like he's got tennis balls in there?"

As we watched, he pulled a ball wrapped in duct tape out and hefted it in his hand. I got on the radio. "Are any of the other Kilgores carrying tennis balls?" I asked. "Because Orris has pockets full of them."

Ray and I began moving around the periphery of the exhibit, closing in on Orris's position. A bunch of agents were trying to talk over the radio at the same time until Salinas came on. "Sound off one at a time!"

We were still a couple of hundred yards from Orris, and we had to move around a crowd watching the tattoo demonstration. As we did, each of the agent teams replied. Five of them had positive reports. The last was Tomlinson, who said, "Those could be small bombs. You put about a hundred strike-anywhere match heads in a tennis ball, then cover it with duct tape, and you've got something that can cause trouble."

"The ball Orris's carrying is wrapped like that," I said.

"That's enough for a stop and search," Salinas announced. "Teams, move in and apprehend, with extreme caution."

Ray and I made it around the tattoo crowd and had a clear run toward Orris Kilgore. As we moved quickly ahead, he checked his watch one more time, then began hefting tennis balls toward each of the different areas under the Tahiti pavilion.

"Orris has started tossing his balls," I shouted into the radio as chaos erupted around us. The balls exploded in bright flashes, starting small fires. The crowd went wild, dashing in front of us and blocking our path to Kilgore. People were screaming and children were crying in the mad stampede to exit the area.

Orris was still in the same place beside the play area, tossing tennis balls, oblivious to the people rushing past him. The fire sprinklers came on, drenching people from high posts, and the exit signs illuminated and began flashing.

Ray and I pushed and shoved but it was like fighting against a big wave. I pulled my badge from where I'd clipped it to my belt and held it up. I was about to say "Police!" and remembered to shout "FBI! Everybody out of the way."

It made little difference. Crowds jammed the aisles, pushing and shoving, little kids crying and people screaming in terror. A couple of staffers tried to direct the crowd but the herd mentality had taken over and it didn't look like anyone was listening.

Ray pressed forward, holding his badge up like Moses with his staff. I clipped my badge to my belt and followed, keeping my eyes on Orris. I remembered the location of the emergency exit, and I grabbed Ray's arm and directed him so that we were between Orris and the way out.

Orris ran out of tennis balls and turned toward us. It was obvious that he knew exactly where the exit was and he was on his way there. He hadn't counted on Ray tackling him halfway there. The two of them fell to the ground, and I pulled my handcuffs from my belt and bent down.

Orris was a skinny nerd, and Ray was a hundred-eighty pounds of gym-trained pissed-off cop, so there wasn't much contest. Orris went face down on the ground, and his glasses flew off and were crushed by the crowd.

Ray was on top of him, and he pulled Orris's hands behind his back so I could snap the cuffs on. "Good work, partner," I said, as Ray stood up.

Together, we hauled Orris to his feet. Most of the crowd was gone by then. Ray and I began moving Orris toward the main entrance, where we hoped to meet up with members of Rizaldo Amador's department who could take him into custody.

We'd only gone a few feet, though, before my cell phone buzzed with a text message. "Man got D, need help fast!" I read. "Behind theater."

It was Dakota's phone, but I didn't know if he was the sender, or Dylan had taken it from him. Either way, Dakota was in trouble. "You okay with this dirtbag?" I asked Ray. "Somebody's got hold of Dakota behind the theater."

"Go," Ray said, and I took off at a run.

I left the Tahiti pavilion at a run, heading toward the main entrance in the midst of a the tide of people. Several agents from the SWAT team in full gear stood along the path, shepherding people toward the exit. As we approached the ticketing pavilion, I swung around the back of the crowd, and an officer held up his baton toward me. "Everyone must exit," he said.

I lifted the edge of my shirt to show my badge, and the Kevlar vest underneath it. "FBI," I said, and he stepped aside.

I plunged into the crowd trying to exit from the other direction. I had my phone in my left hand, my gun in my right, and I used my left thumb to press the speed dial for Dakota's cell.

It went right to voice mail. I didn't want to stop long enough to text him; unlike teenaged boys I couldn't run through a crowd and text at the same time. I slipped the phone back into my pocket.

I didn't have to look far for Dakota. Ahead of me the crowd cleared, and a man I recognized as Bob Kilgore was pushing ahead, holding a gun to the head of a teenaged boy who I assumed was Dakota's friend Dylan. Dakota was right behind him, hopping from foot to foot. It was obvious he wanted to do something to save his friend but didn't know what to do.

Because Kilgore held Dylan so close it was hard to get a clear shot. I stepped aside and let the crowd surge past me. In my peripheral vision I saw Dakota stop and bend down to the ground, but I couldn't see if he had picked something up. All I saw was him stand up straight, and then lunge forward at Bob Kilgore's back.

Kilgore howled in pain and loosed his grip on Dylan, who reached back and grabbed at Kilgore's groin. I saw his hand flex, and Bob howled in pain. Dylan slipped from Kilgore's grasp and Dakota took his hand. They both began to run toward the exit, following the crowd.

I barely had time to catch Dakota's eye and give him a thumbs up before I saw Bob take off in the opposite direction, still hunched over in pain. I keyed my radio, and yelled, "I have eyes on Robert Kilgore, in front of the theater. Need backup!" It was already a lot quieter there, because the bulk of the crowd had passed, though I still heard shouting from behind me.

As I released the radio button, my phone rang with Mike's ring tone. As I fumbled for it in my pocket, I stumbled over a Styrofoam cooler someone had dropped. "What the hell is going on in there?" I heard Mike say as I regained my balance.

"It's crazy, but Dakota's all right," I said, as I ran after Bob Kilgore. "He and Dylan are on their way to the exit."

Mike started to say something more but I had to drop the phone back in my pocket because Bob disappeared around the back wall of the amphitheater and I wanted to use a two-handed grip on my gun.

By the time I reached the theater, the park was eerily quiet and my footsteps were loud as they crashed over plastic cups and discarded food wrappers.

I heard bits and pieces of radio transmissions through my earpiece. Tomlinson and his partner announced that they had the third goat-farmer, Cord, in custody. Kit Carson and the agent with her had cuffs on Brogan. I couldn't tell from the rest of the voices if anyone was coming to help me.

The theater was built to look like a mountain, with vines creeping up the sides and tall king and queen palms around it. The backstage area was blocked by a wooden fence with a padlock, but someone had already kicked in the gate. I pushed through and began to run down a beaten dirt trail that curved around the side of the theater.

I heard the sound of arguing, a man's voice and another, higher, that could have been a woman's or a child's. I crept around the side of the building, both hands on my gun. A teenage girl in a pink T-shirt and torn jeans crouched beside the back wall with a cigarette lighter in one hand and the end of a thin white rope in the other. I looked down the rope to where a big length of it was coiled on the ground, then a few feet across the dirt to a big ball of fabric leaning against the back wall of the theater.

As her father spoke to her, I recognized the girl as the one Mike and I had met at the convenience store.

"You've got to do it, Marie," Kilgore said. He was standing a hundred feet from her.

"I don't want to, Daddy," she said. "If I do, I'm gonna blow up with everything."

"We all have to make sacrifices, baby girl," he said, in a soothing voice. "We've talked about this, remember? Sometimes a sacrifice is required for a larger goal, and this one is all yours. You love the fire, after all. You've been setting fires since you were old enough to strike a match."

I stepped back and spoke into my radio. "I have Robert and Marie Kilgore behind the amphitheater," I said. "Marie's got a bomb rigged to blow."

Then I shut my radio off, because I wanted to get as close as possible to Bob Kilgore, and I didn't want radio chatter to give away my position.

"You're crazy, Daddy," Marie said, as I edged my way back toward them. "I know what that is because I'm crazy too. And there ain't no way that blowing up this dumb building is gonna get me to Heaven, or make things better for people on Earth." She tossed the cigarette lighter behind her, over the fence, and stared defiantly at her father.

"You aren't the only one who's got a lighter, baby girl," Kilgore said.

I heard a rustling in the underbrush and then a new voice shout, "No!"

A boy of about Dakota's age stepped out of the foliage separating the theater from the canoe landing. It was Marie's twin, Donnie.

"Go away, Donnie," Marie said.

"You can't kill yourself, Marie," he said. "What would I do without you?"

"What are you doing here, boy?" Bob demanded. "You shut up and let your sister do what God intends her to do." He walked up to the coil of rope between Marie and the theater. He pulled a couple of pieces of paper from his pocket, crumpled them, then lit them on fire. He dropped the lighter and the paper on the coil of rope and sprinted away.

Donnie began shouting in that gibberish he used with his sister. It sounded like there were actual words, but I couldn't tell what language it was. His voice grew higher, like a keening wail. He fell to the ground, flailing around like he was having some kind of seizure.

It was too much for Marie. She dropped her end of the rope fuse and ran toward him, answering him in the same weird language.

The burning paper had ignited the thin nylon rope by then. Black smoke rose, with the smell of burnt plastic and celery. I pulled my radio from my pocket and keyed it in. "Need help behind the theater stat," I said. "Three suspects, at least one of them armed, and an explosive device with a lit fuse."

Marie was kneeling beside her brother, cooing to him, tears streaming down her face. I hesitated for a moment. Should I stay behind and try to extinguish the fire, save the twins? Or go after Bob Kilgore?

The choice was easy. I had to save lives, if I could.

I grabbed Marie's arm and she shook me off. "I'm the only one who can talk to him when he gets like this," she said.

He was still keening in that weird language.

I looked over at the rope. The coil was completely engulfed in flames, and the fire had begun racing along the rope toward the theater. "You both have to get away," I said. "Before that bomb goes off!"

I heard the theater's back door bang open, and Mike appeared

with a fire extinguisher, which he began spray
fabric and rope. I didn't have time to ask him h
to show up there; I was too busy trying to get M
to move. All three of us began choking from th
around us.

In another minute, the rest of the cavalry arrive
to get Marie to stand up, and Tomlinson handed m
cuffs for her. Beside me, Ray was lifting Donnie up,
him as soothingly as you would to a baby.

Mike was still spraying the fire on the rope, though it
like he'd managed to extinguish it. What was he doing
I thought wildly. He needed to get away. What if that
exploded? Let somebody else handle it. This wasn't even his

Ray began moving Donnie toward the main entrance, an
had no choice but to follow with Marie. The twins stayed clo
to each other, their shoulders touching, as we walked forward
Donnie had stopped screaming but Marie kept talking to him in
their secret language.

Where was their father? Had he managed to escape from the
property in the chaos? Or was he somewhere else inside, perhaps
with other hostages? And where was Mike? Was he still back
behind the theater? What if that fire reignited and Marie's bomb
went off?

Marie stopped talking to Donnie for a moment to look around
us, and almost immediately Donnie began screaming again and
kicking at Ray. Marie tried to squirm away from me, despite the
fact that her hands were cuffed, and it took a couple of HPD
cops to help us subdue them.

Ray and I relinquished our hold on the twins and let the
uniforms take them away. We stopped just inside the entrance
and I struggled to catch my breath. Where was Mike? Where was
Dakota? Were they safe? Did I need to go back into the park to
find them?

Donnie and Marie both screamed bloody murder as they were bundled into the back of separate cruisers for the ride to the Wahiawa station. "I need to find Mike," I said to Ray. I turned to go back into the park.

Ray grabbed my arm. "Call him," he said. "He could be on his way back."

I looked around. "I can't take that chance," I said. "He could still be back there fighting that fire."

"Let him do what he does," Ray said, maintaining a grip on my arm. "You can't save everybody, Kimo. Call him."

My hand shook as I pulled my phone out of my pocket and pressed the speed-dial button for Mike. While I waited for the call to connect I looked ahead of us to a scene that could have come from a disaster movie. In the front area of the parking lot, paramedics were treating people with minor wounds, police officers struggled to maintain order, and patrons were desperate to find their families and friends and then get the hell out of there.

Beyond them, I could see swirls of colored lights from what looked like every police cruiser on the island, and a row of TV news vans setting up their antennas.

When Mike, Dakota and I got our latest cell phones, Dakota had programmed ring tones for all three of us. He'd chosen "This Time it's for Real" by the Jersey band Southside Johnny and the Asbury Jukes as his tone, while Mike's was the opening bars of "Disco Inferno" by the Trammps. Mine, of course, was the *Hawaii Five-O* theme song—the original version by The Ventures.

As I scanned the area, I heard, softly but in growing volume, the rapid drum beat that introduced McGarrett and Danny to the world. And there Mike was, coming back through the gate from the parking lot. Ray let go of my arm and I rushed toward Mike.

I was sweaty and dirty and so was he, but neither of us minded as we crashed together.

When we finally released each other, I stepped back and said, "You're crazy! What were you doing! You should never have been here. You could have gotten killed."

"When I got here I saw Ray, and he told me where you were, that there was an explosive back there. I took off for the theater and found that extinguisher."

"I'm so glad you're all right," I said. A couple of paramedics hurried past us, pushing a stretcher with a woman in an oxygen mask on it.

"Right back at you, K-Man," Mike said, and he grinned. Then we both had the same thought.

"Where's Dakota?"

Mike got to his phone first and punched in the speed dial. He pressed the speaker button and held up the phone so we could both hear it ringing. Then Dakota said, "Dad?" in a voice that nearly broke my heart.

"We're both here, we're both okay," Mike said. "Where are you?"

"By the Gordons' car with Dylan and his parents," Dakota said.

"You're okay?" I asked.

"Yeah, we're good," he said.

"What did you do to the guy who was holding Dylan?" I asked. Mike raised his eyebrows and I mouthed, "Tell you later."

"I saw this plastic sword on the ground and I grabbed it," he said. "It had this thick handle, and I jabbed that into that fucker's asshole."

I heard nervous laughter in the background.

"Then Dylan grabbed the guy's balls and he let go, and we took off. Did you arrest him?"

"Not yet," I said. "But he can't hide from us now."

"I want to see that you're okay," Mike said. "You stay right where you are. What section of the parking lot are you in?"

I saw Francisco Salinas standing beside a pool of water that had run off the roof of the Tahiti pavilion. It looked like he'd been soaked by the fire sprinklers; his hair was plastered down on his head and his microfiber shirt and shorts were wet. He was talking to Agent Tomlinson, who looked just as wet.

Salinas caught my eye and waved me over. I said, "I've got to go. Make sure Dakota gets home. I love you."

I leaned up and kissed Mike's cheek. He grabbed my hand and squeezed, then began walking toward the parking lot. He and Ray high-fived each other, and then Ray and I walked over to Salinas.

"It looks like Bob Kilgore slipped away," Salinas said. "I have a warrant on the way. We're heading to his family's compound now, while we have some of the family in custody. I want everyone we can muster in the vans. I have the MRAP on the way to meet us."

The MRAP, I knew, was the Mine-Resistant Armored Personnel Carrier, a kind of Humvee on steroids, that was used in only the most serious raids. "Agent Tomlinson's going to brief us all before we leave. We can use the park administration office."

Ray and I listened to the radio chatter as we followed Salinas and Tomlinson back into the park. Ardell, Brogan, Cord, Emerette, Donnie and Marie had all been taken to District 2 headquarters in Wahiawa for booking and interrogation.

We walked into a large meeting room beside Marilyn Tuafono's office, used for park training, with a computer and a projector. While Bryce Tomlinson got set up, the rest of the agents arrived, about a dozen more, most looking worse for wear. Those who had black dust on their faces and arms cleaned up, while those who were soaking wet used paper towels to dry off.

Tomlinson pulled up the aerial photos of the compound and we looked at them with him in groups of two and three. From what I overheard before it was time for Ray and me to meet with him, he had done some study of the raid on the Branch Davidian compound in Waco, Texas, and the lessons that could be learned from it. That made me feel a bit more confident about the operation ahead of us.

Tomlinson dashed that confidence almost immediately. "My recommendation was to abort this raid until we can gain further intel about the Children of Noah and their compound," he said. "That was one of the key mistakes the ATF made in attacking the Branch Davidians. They had no idea what to expect."

"So why are we going forward then?" I asked.

"Because the decision rests with me," Salinas said. "I want to take advantage of the reduction in defensive ability at the compound, with all four of Kilgore's sons and two of his daughters in custody."

"What were the other mistakes the ATF made in Waco?" Ray asked. "And how are we going to avoid them?"

Tomlinson held up his hand, the lighter-colored palm outward, and began to tick off on his fingers. "Lack of intel is number one. We can't do much about that at this point. We have the information from Kilgore's daughter and Detective Amador, the building permits Detective Donne found, and aerial photographs. That will have to do."

He bent down his thumb. "Second mistake was not enough firepower. We have that covered. We have an agent bringing additional weapons from the gun vault, and you'll each be issued M-4s."

Ray and I had both had qualified at HPD with the M-4 carbine, an assault rifle used by the military. It was a hell of a weapon. I'd never fired the M4-A, which could go fully automatic, but the semi-automatic capability of the M-4, along with the three-round burst option, was enough for me.

Tomlinson bent down his index finger. "Third mistake was a lack of sniper teams. We've got that covered. There will be a SWAT sniper positioned by the main entrance, and another aimed at the front door of the main house." He pointed at the building on the aerial photo. "Both of them will be able to relocate as necessary."

So far the plans were looking pretty good, I thought.

"Fourth mistake was lack of field medical help for wounded agents. We've got that covered as well. And we have a plan for strategic retreat in place in case there are threats there we haven't planned for. Which brings me to the last mistake in Waco—overconfidence in planning based on lack of intel. I'm trying to be the voice of reason here to avoid that."

He turned his attention back to the aerial photos and pointed. "To give you an orientation, the ocean on this side, the mountains over here. There are six separate barns and a big chicken coop. These are windmills, and these rectangles on top of some of the buildings are solar cells. And this is the big shed where they're building the ark."

There was a murmur among a couple of the agents who hadn't realized quite how elaborate Kilgore's operation was.

Kit Carson raised her hand. "If I remember my Bible correctly, Noah assembled a breeding pair of every creature on earth. Has Kilgore done the same thing?"

"He's trying," Ray said. "The good news is that he hasn't acquired any major predators yet—no lions or tigers or bears."

"Oh, my," Kit Carson said, and we all laughed nervously.

"There are some animals to watch out for, though," Ray said. "We need to be careful approaching any of those barns."

I pointed up at about a half-dozen small buildings clustered around the main house. "What are all those?" I asked.

"That one looks like a garage for their vehicles," Tomlinson said, pointing. "These others are houses."

"From what Dinah Kilgore told me, all the kids still live on the property," I said. "I expect that each of the adult sons has his own house by now."

"Good point, because that reminds me that there are likely to be many women and children on this property, and we need to exercise extreme caution to minimize civilian engagement and casualties. The plan is that SWAT will go in first in the MRAP, because we don't know what to expect. Once they have secured the property, the rest of us will begin a building to building search for Kilgore."

Tomlinson shut down the computer and we began filing out of the building to head back to the parking lot. I looked at Ray. "So much for us riding a desk," I said.

"Best laid plans of mice and men, and all that," he said, and we followed the rest of the personnel out.

"Kimo! Over here!" Ralph Kim's voice rang out over the crush of reporters and cameramen at the front entrance to the park.

He yelled questions at me as I faced straight ahead and ignored him. A couple of HPD officers formed a cordon for us and Ray and I jumped on a golf cart which sped us to where the vans had been parked.

The armorer who managed the weapons cache at the FBI field office was waiting there for us, and Ray and I were issued M-4s. We examined the rifles carefully, making sure that we remembered how to use them. The reporters and cameramen had followed us out to the remote parking lot, and I could see them filming us behind a cordon of HPD vehicles.

"Listen up," Salinas called, and Ray and I joined about a dozen agents to gather around him. "I have the arrest warrant for Robert Noah Kilgore and the search warrant for his premises. We're ready to move out."

Ray and I jumped into one of the Bureau SUVs with Bryce Tomlinson driving, and followed the MRAP in a procession down the Kam, with an HPD cruiser leading the way, lights flashing and sirens going.

"People probably think Obama is here," Ray said, looking out the window at the cars stopped by the side of the road. A couple of people were taking pictures with their cell phones, and I figured our parade would be on the Internet in seconds.

It wasn't far from the Islands of History to Bob Kilgore's compound. The HPD cruiser stopped at the entrance and blocked traffic, and an agent in full gear jumped out of the MRAP and fiddled with the lock on the entrance gate. When he had it swung open, he jumped back in the MRAP and our procession moved slowly onto the property.

Fields ran on both sides of the road, fenced in with chain-link. Several different breeds of goats grazed to our right, including the pair Ray had mentioned, with those wickedly curving horns. In other fields I saw cows and sheep, some with black heads and legs, others in mixes of brown and white. Horses raced around a far paddock.

None of the animals paid attention to us as we continued up the curving road toward the main house, a two-story wood-frame that looked like it had been added on to several times. A number of smaller houses clustered around it, in the shade of several spreading kiawe trees.

The clutch of vehicles, including ours, waited as the MRAP pulled up in front of the main house. SWAT agents swarmed out and hurried inside, and around to the different houses surrounding it.

We peered out the windows of the SUV as the team began assembling women and children, down to infants in arms. Finally a message came over the radio that the property was secure, but Kilgore had not been found.

Our SUVs pulled up behind the MRAP and we got out. I looked over at the group of women and children and recognized Dinah Kilgore, standing beside an older woman who resembled her—same height, same flyaway hair. "That's Dinah over there," I said to Ray. "I want to talk to her."

"What's going on, detective?" she asked as I approached. "These men won't tell us anything."

"Your father and your brothers attacked the Islands of History park earlier today," I said. "Throwing tennis ball bombs, setting fires, and causing chaos. Ardell, Brogan, Cord and Orris are in custody, along with Emerette, Donnie and Marie."

Several of the women started to talk all at once, and I held up my hand. "First things first. Is Robert Kilgore here?"

No one spoke, though one of the babies began to cry. I looked at the woman holding him, and thought of my own children. I fervently hoped they would never find themselves in a situation like this.

My radio crackled in the silence. "A vehicle has been found in the garage that's still warm," one of the agents said. "May be an indication that Kilgore is somewhere on the premises."

The sun was blisteringly hot and I was sweating under my Kevlar vest and my aloha shirt. Some of the women and children were beginning to look uncomfortable, too. "Is he here?" I asked.

Still no response.

I looked directly at Dinah. "If he's here, and we can arrest him, then you're free. All of you."

"We have nothing to be free of," one of the young women said. "Father Noah protects us from the evils of the outside world."

There was a murmur of assent. "Is there somewhere he could be hiding?" I asked. "Are there any underground bunkers, or spaces between walls?"

Dinah turned to her mother. "You know he has problems," she said. "If the police don't take him, then he's only going to get crazier and put everyone here in danger." She took her mother's hand. "Please, Mama?"

"There's a cellar beneath Hilma's house," Glorilynn Kilgore said. "The one with the green shutters. He may be in there."

"God will punish you for your transgressions, Glorilynn," a somewhat younger woman said. She turned to us. "That's my house, and you have no right to enter it."

"We have a search warrant for the premises, and an arrest warrant for Mr. Kilgore," I said. Ray got on the radio to Salinas, and then Ray and I stood with the women and children and watched as the SWAT team surrounded the house with the green shutters.

They swarmed into the house, and the sun beat down on us, and a couple of children quarreled and that baby cried again. Hilma had her arms crossed over her chest, glaring at Glorilynn. Dinah held her mother's hand, looking confident.

It was probably only a couple of minutes but it seemed longer before Robert Kilgore emerged from the house's front door, with his hands cuffed behind him, and several agents with weapons pointed at him.

The warrant Salinas had received covered the entire property, and once Kilgore had been taken away by HPD, we began a house to house search for materials related to the firebombing incident.

Kit Carson approached us. "I want to see what they've been raising in those greenhouses," she said. "I could use some company."

"You think there are drugs there?" I asked.

"It's pretty damned expensive to run a property like this, even with rain barrels and solar panels. I wouldn't be surprised if the Kilgores had some illegal crops growing to raise extra money."

We walked down to the first greenhouse. The door was locked, with an electronic keypad. While Kit and Ray walked around the perimeter, peering inside, I did a quick online search on my phone, then punched four digits into the keypad.

The red light turned green, and I opened the door. "I'm in," I called to them.

"How did you crack that?" Ray asked as he walked back.

"Lucky guess. I figured that since Kilgore was obsessed with Noah and the flood, he might have used a date related to that. I found a site online that said the flood occurred 1,656 years after God created the world. So I tried 1656 and it worked."

We walked inside. The air was cool and damp, the walls lined with standard shelving units. Each unit had a fish tank on top, with garden trays full of plants beneath.

"Aquaponics," Kit said. "The fish fertilize the water, which gets sent down to the plants, providing them with nutrients to grow. The roots of the plants provide a bio filter for the water and then the clean water is circulated back up to the tank for the fish."

The first couple of shelving sets contained tomatoes, radishes, and a couple of other vegetables I couldn't recognize. But the rest of the room was used to grow marijuana.

"Impressive operation," Kit said. "Looks like I've got my work cut out for me."

"Do you think they knew the two crucifixion victims?" I asked. "If both groups were growing pakalolo, then the incident at the bar could have been the climax of a long battle."

"I think they might have known each other," she said. "We found the body of a dead goat beside one of the fields. They must be able to do goat DNA, right? Maybe it belonged to the Kilgores. We aren't far from where Lina Casco and Rigoberto Flores lived."

"Probably just over a couple of hills," I said. "A goat from here could have slipped away and ended up foraging over there."

Ray and I left Kit at the greenhouse and walked back up to the main house. We saw Dinah Kilgore and her mother standing in the shade cast by the house, and Dinah waved us over. "Thank you very much for what you did," Dinah said. "I feel like you've given me my life back."

"Don't be too quick to thank me," I said. "Did you know that your father was growing marijuana in those greenhouses?"

She looked at her mother, who wouldn't meet her gaze. "I didn't," Dinah said to me. She took her mother's hand. "But I'm here now, and I'll do my best to take care of my family."

She had a tough road ahead of her. If her mother and the rest of the family knew about and participated in the marijuana farm, the adults could face prison and confiscation of assets, and the children might end up as wards of the state.

"Kelsey knows a friend of mine," I said to Dinah. "Sandra Guarino. She's a great attorney. She just had a set of twins that my partner and I fathered, so she may not be able to help you, but she can certainly point you toward an attorney who can represent you and your mother if you need."

"Thank you," Dinah said. "I'll give her a call."

Ray and I continued toward the house, where Salinas stood on the front porch, talking on his cell phone. I felt bad for all those whom Robert Kilgore had conned—his wife, his other women, his children and in-laws and grandchildren. The lives they had known had been taken from them in a matter of minutes, and some of them might never recover from the loss.

I remembered the cold way Kilgore had treated Marie, expecting her to give up her life because he said so. No matter what happened, the rest of his family had to be better off without him.

My cell rang and I recognized my mother's number. "Howzit, Mom," I said. "How's Dad doing?"

Her voice was shaky. "His machines started beeping and the nurses rushed in. They put him on a gurney and rushed him away and no one will tell me what's going on."

"I'm on my way, Mom." I looked around. My Jeep was back at the Islands of History. How was I going to get to the hospital? What was wrong with my father? Why hadn't I recognized what was really important to me, and stayed by his bedside instead of risking my life at the theme park?

Ray seemed to know exactly what the problem was. "Tomlinson has the key to one of the SUVs," he said. "I'll get them from him and drive you back to the park." He spotted the agent near one of the outbuildings and took off at a run.

While I waited for him to return I called Dominic Riccardi. "It sounds like my dad coded at the hospital," I said. "Can you see what you can find out?"

"I'll call Rivera, and head down there," he said. "Are you there?"

"On my way, but I'm way up in Laie. At least an hour out."

"Don't worry," he said. "Rivera's a great doctor, and the staff at Queen's is excellent. Your dad is in good hands."

Ray returned with the keys to one of the Bureau's SUVs, and we jumped in. "How old is your dad?" I asked Ray, as he drove back down to the Kam.

"Sixty-five. Just retired last year. My mom made a big party for him, but Julie and I couldn't make it back there—it was just too much, with Vinnie still so young. But we're hoping to get back there this summer. My brother has a house at the Jersey shore, and my folks will be there most of July and August. I want Vinnie to get to know his grandparents."

My throat constricted. I wanted the same thing for Alpha and Omega.

"I know it's tough," Ray said. "But you've already learned a lot from your dad, and you're going to be awesome with your own kids."

"I hope so," I said. But I still wanted my dad around.

"I'll call Susan Haberman tonight and let her know that we've got the Kilgores in custody," he said. "I'm sure she's eager to get her kids back in school."

Ray pulled up beside my Jeep. "Julie and I will say prayers for your dad," he said. "Call me if you need anything."

I thanked him and got into the Jeep, where I turned the air conditioning on blast and stuck my head in front of the vent as I plugged in my Bluetooth and called Mike. I spent the next half hour on the phone with him, my brothers, and my mom. We were all on our way to the hospital, and I was scared that this was going to be a death watch, all of us around my dad's bedside as he breathed his last.

Cell service was spotty through the mountains and the Wilson Tunnel, and I gave up on calls. I had to make my peace with losing my dad, I thought. I would still have my mom, my brothers and their families. I'd have Mike, and his parents, Dakota, Sandra and Cathy and the twins. My life was much more fortunate than many, and I had to be grateful I'd had my dad's presence in my life for so long.

Even so, the thought of losing him hurt. My stomach ached and I had a headache building behind my forehead.

A few minutes after I turned onto the H-1, my phone rang again. Dom said, "Al's heart stopped briefly. That's why the monitors went crazy, and why they rushed him out of there so fast. He's in the OR right now. Rivera's putting in a pacemaker to regulate his cardiac rhythm."

"Another operation?"

"Very routine," Dom said. "The technology of those pacemakers is amazing these days. You'll see. Al will be right as rain now."

I parked near the hospital's front door and propped my police decal on the dashboard. I rushed into the hospital, fidgeting while I waited for the guard to swipe my driver's license and issue me a stick-on badge. Then I hurried back up to that second-floor waiting room, where I found my mother, my brothers, and Dominic Riccardi.

"He's still in surgery," my mother said, after I had leaned down to kiss her cheek.

"Perfectly routine," Dom said. "Not even open heart. Rivera has done a thousand of these."

"But not on my father," Haoa muttered.

My mother sat back down in one of the plastic chairs, next to Dominic. Haoa paced back and forth, and Lui was in the other corner of the room on his cell phone. As soon as he saw me, Lui ended his call and came over to me. "What happened today?" he asked.

I shrugged. "Beats me. It's Saturday. My day off."

"I saw you on the footage, Kimo," Lui said.

"Then you know what happened." I looked at my oldest brother. "Are you that much of a jerk, Lui? Our father is having surgery, and all you care about is your TV station?"

I realized that the rest of the room had gone quiet.

Lui exhaled a deep breath. "It's what I have to do," he said. "I can't operate on him myself. So I have to keep my mind on something else or I'll start screaming."

Haoa had stopped pacing, but he was looking at both of us wild-eyed. I realized that the three of us were so much alike; we all had to be in charge, and if we couldn't be we went nuts. I put my arm around Lui's shoulder. "Let's sit down, brah," I said. "I'll tell you what I can."

Almost all of what I told him was already public knowledge; I just helped him see how it all fit together. Haoa joined us, and for a few minutes we all forgot that our father was in perilous health. We were just three brothers, hanging out together.

When Mike and Dakota arrived, Dakota hovered by the door uncertainly as Mike walked right over to his father to talk.

"Come here, Dakota," my mother said. She stood up and opened her arms. "You're the only one of my keiki to come. Thank you." She kissed his cheek and he smiled. And then, without warning, she burst into tears.

Dakota had already been through a lot that day, but he seemed to know just what to do. "Come sit down, Tutu," he said, using the Hawaiian word for a grandparent of either gender. He put his arm around her and guided her to a pair of chairs, and she grasped his waist and cried as everyone else in the room watched her.

He talked to her in a low voice for a minute, and then she laughed and wiped her eyes. "You are just as bad as Kimo!" she said to him.

My brothers and I looked over at her. "What!" I said.

Then Doctor Rivera walked in. "Everything went smoothly, and Al is resting now. I think with this device he'll be out of the woods for quite a while."

Everyone had questions or thanks for the doctor and he answered a few, then had to leave. It was Saturday evening, after all, and I appreciated that he'd come in on such short notice to take care of my dad.

When it was my turn, I went in to see my father in the recovery room. He was groggy but conscious, and his color was better than it had been in a while, and he was breathing on his own. He needed a shave and his graying hair was tousled, but I thought he was still the handsomest guy I knew. I leaned down and kissed his grizzled cheek, and he opened his eyes.

"Keechee," he said, using my childhood nickname. His voice was raw. He smiled, and then he closed his eyes again.

I was frightened for a second until I saw his chest rising and falling with the rhythm of his breathing. Against the white pillow, in the fluorescent light, he looked more haole than Hawaiian, the lasting legacy of his mother and her Idaho Mormon heritage. The ancient Hawaiians used to touch nose-to-nose and inhale each other's *ha*, or breath. When the Caucasians arrived in the islands, they did not follow this custom, so the islanders began to call them ha'ole, literally, no breath. I couldn't avoid the irony— that my father, part Hawaiian and part haole, had been in danger of not breathing any longer.

Maybe all those gods I had prayed to for his return to health had listened. Or maybe my father was just a tough old bird, as

Dom had called him. Either way, I was grateful, and I squeezed my father's hand, then walked back outside to join the rest of my ohana.

About the Author

NEIL PLAKCY is the author of *Mahu*, *Mahu Surfer*, *Mahu Fire*, *Mahu Vice*, *Mahu Men*, *Mahu Blood*, and *Zero Break* about openly gay Honolulu homicide detective Kimo Kanapa'aka. His other books include the *Have Body, Will Guard* series, the *Golden Retriever Mysteries*, and numerous stand-alone works of romance and mystery. His website is www.mahubooks.com.

The author acknowledges the trademark status and trademark owners of the following wordmarks mentioned in this work of fiction:

Kevlar: E. I. du Pont de Nemours and Company

Jeep: DaimlerChrysler

Google: Google, Inc.

iPad/iPhone: Apple, Inc.

Kamehameha Schools: Kamehameha Schools

Foodland: Foodland Super Market, Ltd.

Fire Rock Pale Ale: : Kona Brewery LLC

Instagram: Instagram

Crocs: Crocs, Inc.

Jell-O: Kraft Food Brands

Facebook: Facebook, Inc.

Chanel: Chanel, Inc.

Star-Advertiser: Honolulu Star-Advertiser

James Bond: Danjaq LLC and United Artists Corporation

Wi-Fi: Wi-Fi Alliance

Kawasaki EL250B 88-95: Kawasaki Motors Corp., U.S.A.

Airstream: Airstream, Inc.

Toyota: Toyota Motor Company

The Church of Jesus Christ of Latter-day Saints: The Church of Jesus Christ of Latter-day Saints

UC Santa Cruz: UC Regents

Zippy's: Zippy's

Wikipedia: Wikimedia Foundation, Inc.

Rolodex: Berol Corporation

Marlboros: Philip Morris Incorporated

Bluetooth: Bluetooth Sig Inc.

Queen's: The Queen's Medical Center

Firehouse: Cygnus Business Media, Inc.

The Lion King: Disney Enterprises, Inc.

Dole Plantation: Dole Food Company, Inc.
Philadelphia Eagles: Philadelphia Eagles
Ralph Lauren: PRL USA Holdings, Inc.
Hummer: AM General
Styrofoam: The Dow Chemical Company
Hawaii Five-O: CBS Productions and Leonard Freeman Productions